D.B. SIEDERS

HELL

JINX MCGEE | BOOK TWO

BENT

HELL BENT

D. B. SIEDERS

CITY OWL
PRESS

HELL BENT
Jinx McGee, Book 2

CITY OWL PRESS
www.cityowlpress.com

Cover Design by MiblArt. All stock photos licensed appropriately.
Chapter Headings by SiederTree Studios.

Edited by Tee Tate.

For information on subsidiary rights, please contact the publisher at info@cityowlpress.com.

Print Edition ISBN: 978-1-64898-264-4

Digital Edition ISBN: 978-1-64898-265-1

Printed in the United States of America

ALSO BY D. B. SIEDERS

PRAISE FOR THE WORKS OF D. B. SIEDERS

"I was immediately drawn into *Catching Hell*, and the book never really let me go. Jinx is a snarky but lovable main character who really doesn't have much faith in her own abilities. Dominic is a great love interest, and I'm looking forward to finding out more about the both of them. Highly recommend." – *PenKay, Vine Voice Reviewer*

"A unique cast of characters drives this beautifully crafted tale that demands you keep a box of tissue on hand. *Waking the Dead* is a soul-wrenching look into the decisions one must make about life and death, not only for one's self, but for a loved one. Ms. Sieders knows how to put words on paper that touch the heart, and invigorate the mind." — *4.5 Stars from InD'Tale Magazine*

"Revolution brews in the spirit world of *The Quick and the Dead*. Vivian and Lazarus encounter a vibrant cast of allies—among them mambo woman Bijoux Briggs and Vivian's sister Mae, who was disabled in life but is powerful in the afterlife—and develop a love connection despite their complicated past." — *Publisher's Weekly*

"D.B. Sieders is a unique storyteller. *Crosscurrents* is a mix of science fiction and fantasy that is woven together perfectly. Ms. Sieders's characters are distinctive and the story is imaginative and fun." — *4.5 Stars from InD'Tale Magazine*

"For paranormal romance readers who are looking for something a little different, *Lorelei's Lyric* could be your first step into a whole new world." — *Romantic Reads and Such*

For my birth mom Mary Etta,
one of the most beautiful souls I've ever known.

CHAPTER ONE

Hell is empty and all the devils are here. — William Shakespeare, The Tempest, quoted on a T-shirt worn by Jinx McGee, Demon Hunter

I ran five blocks from HQ and straight into a fire of Biblical proportions. Specifically, the book of Revelations, complete with billowing smoke, weeping and gnashing of teeth, and monsters straight out of hell.

The apocalypse had started without me.

Chaos reigned.

People fled the flaming building in a blur of suits, heels, and head-phones. Many dragged passed-out co-workers and tourists missing their cowboy hats. No blood or obvious injuries, but demons could do a lot of internal damage. So could debris and falling bricks. I grabbed a man who held a fallen co-worker in a fireman's carry, flashing my PI badge. It was legit. He didn't need to know I was a PI of the paranormal demon-hunting variety. My organization was keeping a low profile, but if more buildings went up in flames, our cover might be blown.

Then the mundanes would know how close they were to annihilation.

The guy was panicked, barely glancing at my credentials.

"What happened in there?" I barked. I wasn't in the loop at HQ. Technically, I was excluded from field work, but I happened to be the only hunter in the office when the explosion hit downtown Nashville. This part of the city had already taken a beating thanks to a whackadoo human with a death wish, an RV, and a bomb. Unlike that disaster, this one had demon written all over it. Mundanes were out of their depth for this mess. The demon hunting team I worked for needed someone in the field to answer the distress call. I needed information. It was my way back in.

And I needed back in.

Not for my ego, but because I was supposed to save the world from a demon realm war.

Yeah, no pressure or anything.

The guy I'd grabbed tried to break free of my hold. I gripped him harder to get his attention. "Sir, we're here to help. What did you see? How many more people are in the building?" I caught his deer-in-the-headlights gaze and tried to exude calm and competence. "Please. We need to get the rest of your officemates out."

"Don't know," he said, still tugging. "I was at my desk crunching numbers for tomorrow's sales meeting when something hit...I don't know, it sounded like an explosion and then, like, some sort of aftershock went through like a wave. People started passing out and more booms like bombs going off. And then this...*thing* came out...some kind of giant monster, but monsters aren't real..."

Monsters were real, but most kept a low profile in the modern era. No, we were dealing with a different, more dangerous threat.

Demons. Ones who weren't supposed to be on earth ever again.

He stopped, caught his breath after a coughing fit, took a good look at me and frowned. "You shouldn't go in there. Wait for the cops, or SWAT, or someone qualified to handle the situation."

I squared my shoulders and tried to look menacing. All five-foot-one of me. I was getting sick of being underestimated based on height. And gender. "I'm a trained professional. Believe me, I stand a better chance than the cops."

Good grief, I was decked out in combat leather—demon variety, not cowhide, which would totally suck in the muggy heat of a Nashville summer—had a coms unit in my ear, my dark hair was pulled back into a tight bun, weapons strapped to various parts of my body, and I was wearing combat boots. I normally favored Doc Martens with custom embroidery for routine demon patrol missions, but civilians were involved in this one, so I had to look the part of mundane military/mercenary badass.

"We're a specialized unit," a familiar voice said as a large hand snaked around and checked the pulse of the guy's buddy. Turning his dark, mesmerizing gaze on me, he said, "He's alive. No obvious injuries."

Fucking. Hell.

Demoriel.

I hadn't seen him since I almost died closing the gates to the hell and celestial realms. He and my demon-associated human colleagues saved me—at great cost. Cost to me. Thanks to the life-saving demon grafts I'd received, I was less normal, less human now than I'd ever been.

And Demoriel, who would always be "D" to me, my long-lost best friend and almost-lover who came back into my life to help with the mission, had lied to me in an act of betrayal of gargantuan proportions. Lies of omission counted. His father was the head demon in charge, the one we were fighting, and D hadn't disclosed that juicy little tidbit until his father forced him to confess during the battle.

Then he'd given me part of his demon essence to save my life, and promptly ghosted me for over two months.

I locked gazes with D and glared. He arched a brow and slapped the civilian, with his buddy in tow, on the back. "We've got this. Get yourself and your friend out of the area. There are paramedics less than a block away."

The man nodded and took off running, or rather shuffling. His buddy was at least as big as he was. I could carry a heavier load while running, which made his dismissal of yours truly total bullshit. He'd questioned my abilities because I'm a short woman, but obeyed the big, burly demon who showed up out of nowhere? Not the man's fault. He didn't know D like I did.

I tried to think of something clever or impressive to say, but what came out of my mouth was, "What the hell are *you* doing here?"

He flinched. Good. He should feel bad about lying to and ghosting me, and then showing up out of the blue—again—to move in on my case.

"I'm here to help," he said, raising his gloved hands. I could see the blades strapped to his sides as his leather jacket rose. The harness holding the sheaths fit his defined torso like a glove. He looked good. Better than good. He had sharp, defined features rivaling anything Michelangelo carved out of marble. Full, sensual lips, raven hair, dark skin, and a body that didn't quit. He was beautifully made and knew what to do with his body.

I should know. I did know, and my body remembered. It wanted more. So did my heart. But he'd broken it twice. So why was part of me glad to see him?

More civilians poured out of the flaming building, along with an unearthly roar. It set my demon-hunter senses on high alert. By contrast, a sizeable number of people in the vicinity stood glued to their phones, oblivious to the danger and destruction around them.

That wasn't strange or suspicious at all.

D's voice brought me back from distraction.

"I owe you a conversation. I owe you more, but right now, you need to get these people to safety. I'll take care of whatever demonic entity caused this."

"The hell you will." I squared my shoulders and got in his face, or rather his chest. Like most everyone else on the planet and other realms, he was taller than me. The bastard loomed, but I wasn't backing down. "I—"

A high-pitched male voice interrupted me. "I'm going in."

I spun around to find a pudgy young man sporting the beginnings of a mustache and decked out in camo from head to toe, black streaks painted across his face. High on testosterone, ego, and probably speed. Ugh. Just what we needed. An idiot wannabe soldier with a hero complex and, judging from the way he fidgeted and nearly dropped his gun, no skills to back it up.

The only things missing were a tiki torch and one of those yellow snake don't-tread-on-me flags the nutball "militiamen" carried.

Great.

The crazy kid gripped his AR-15 and squared his shoulders. "The only thing that stops a bad guy with a gun is a good guy with a gun."

Oh, for the love of lollipops. I stepped in front of him, bringing the beginning of his sprint to a screeching halt. The way the fool carried his weapon told me he was untrained or poorly trained, and his fevered gaze and aura of excitement proved he'd never been in an actual combat situation. It wasn't fun, glorious, or ego-boosting. It was terrifying, traumatizing, and if you didn't keep bring your wits, training, and good sense, it was deadly.

And that was just human combat. Battling demons was next level.

The fool was out of his league.

I faced off with the witless zealot, hoping to talk him down. "First of all, no, you're not a good guy and you aren't going to stop anyone with your gun. Second, there's a whole ass demon in there. You know, fire, brimstone, destruction from a beast slithering from the bowels of hell? That," I said, pointing to his weapon of mass human destruction, "isn't going to do anything except piss it off."

Boice's voice burst from the com device in my ear. "That's so racist. I'm starting a new hashtag—not all demons."

"And you're more likely to take out civilians," D said, glowering at him. "Why don't you sit this one out, Gravy Seal."

I grinned before I caught myself. I was mad at him, but I appreciated the perfect snarky comeback. Was I jealous I hadn't thought of it? Totally.

"Trinity says you're on evacuation detail. That's an order." Damn Boice. He was officially my least favorite roommate. One of the twin demons of technology, he and his brother Roice took care of all things tech and strategic as well as overseeing communications, which included issuing orders from our boss, Trinity Jones. Master strategist and the brains of our operation, she'd been a colleague until I promoted her when our former boss disappeared.

Lately, I questioned the wisdom of that decision. Mostly because she'd taken me out of the field for my "safety."

"Sorry, I didn't catch the last part," I said, making crackling sounds with my voice. "Something's jamming the frequency."

D rolled his eyes.

Boice snorted and said, "You are such a bad liar. And you're not signed off for field work yet. Rescue the humans and let your backup neutralize the threat."

"Jane," D said. He always called me Jane, never Jinx. It always turned my insides to mush. "Your turn will come. Get the humans to safety—especially the fools glued to their phones. I'll take this battle. You'll take the war." With one last longing look, he pulled out his knives and ran toward the burning building.

Damn it, he was right, and I hated him for it.

Fortunately, I had a target for my rage. The Gravy Seal sneered at me and took a step, intending to bulldoze his way over me. The guy wasn't in shape. If he'd ever been military, which I had reason to doubt, he'd gone soft. But he was bigger than me. He most likely thought I was helpless because I was small.

His mistake.

I punched him in the gut. Hard. The look of shock on his stupid face was priceless, and the way he doubled over caused the seam of his ill-fitting camo pants to rip. It filled me with more satisfaction than I'd experienced in a while. I took his weapon and clocked him in the noggin with it. He'd live, but he'd have one hell of a headache. Maybe I'd knocked some sense into him.

Unsheathing my demon steel knife, I used it to julienne the gun, rendering it useless, then I picked up the nearest unconscious and bleeding body. I'd start with any human who'd passed out, carrying him or her to safety, move on to the conscious and injured, then I'd work on herding those who could walk or run to safety. My demon grafts gave me demon strength and stamina, which I could safely use in this situation. The injured humans and frazzled paramedics were too panicked to pay much attention to the odd sight of a tiny woman carrying people away from the burning building.

Yeah, yeah, I'd go back for the Gravy Seal, but I'd save his dumb ass for last.

I propped the unconscious human against the wall of a building near one of the ambulances and ran back into the fray, grabbing a few of the cell phone zombies along the way and yelling at them to get the hell out of the danger zone. It took some effort, but once I got their attention they stumbled off in an apparent daze.

One woman cried out as if in pain when her phone crashed to the ground. She doubled over and started muttering something about lights and colors. Weird. Maybe she'd been hit in the head by debris? I didn't see any injuries. There was no apparent damage to her clothing, no smudges of smoke on her face or in her perfectly coifed blond locks. Nope. The only thing wrong with her appeared to be an unnatural obsession with her phone.

I put a pin in that observation for later and got busy hauling more injured.

My lungs burned and I had an impressive series of scrapes and bruises by my tenth rescue. I managed five more, along with directing those who could still walk or run to safety, before the police and fire department arrived and started cordoning off the area. I hoped everyone got out of the building, but I was afraid there would be casualties.

They wouldn't be the first humans killed by demons, but they were the first in the new war sweeping the world.

Seven powerful demons had escaped before I could secure the portal to the hell realm, and allegedly seven celestials had gotten loose, too, itching for a rematch against demon kind. Lord Belial had once led legions against celestials on earth, nearly wiping out the fragile human population. He was at it again, and I was supposed to stop it.

Too bad I couldn't even get permission to fight the demon who'd wreaked havoc on downtown Nashville.

The scene was heartbreaking. This part of downtown Nashville had barely recovered from a bombing—this one by a human—a few years back. Now, flames licked the steel skeleton of a multistory building, smoke billowing out and debris littering the streets. A tiny cowgirl hat and toy horse smeared with soot had fallen on a crumbling sidewalk. I hoped the child they belonged to had escaped to safety.

Shouts of alarm and terror competed with sobbing and orders barked by first responders. At least the fire hadn't spread to other buildings. A group of bachelorettes in matching T-shirts held icepacks to various body parts, their hair messy and mascara running. They'd come to Music City to have a good time. Instead, some asshole demon had tried to roast them.

Not on my watch.

This was my city. I had to protect it.

Energy bubbled within me, my celestial heritage manifesting as it did when I got really pissed off. I couldn't call it to me any better than I could control my borrowed demon powers, but when it came to me, I was an otherworldly force. Shame to let it go to waste.

Ignoring shouts from firefighters, I ran toward the building and leapt through the flames that burned like the devil but didn't mark my skin or clothing—perks of demon grafts and demon leather. Thick black smoke blocked my vision, so I used my other senses to navigate through wreckage. Climbing through rubble and hoisted my body over metal beams, I made my way to what was left of the third floor.

A pair of wraiths flew toward me. Thugs of the demon world and not particularly powerful in the hierarchy, they were used as guards for other more powerful demons. The immaterial demons didn't appear to be on the attack but fleeing the destruction. I threw my demon steel knife and pierced both sinuous, smoky forms, nailing them to an exposed wall stud. They shrieked with pain and rage as I approached, their unearthly screeches guaranteed to give me a migraine.

"Shut up!" I yelled, twisting the knife and trapping their immaterial essences in place. "Who are you working for? What are you guarding?"

"Release us, demon huntress," they hissed. "And we'll tell you."

"Nope. Tell me or I'll keep twisting my blade until there's nothing left of you."

Their phantom eyes widened. These two must've had a run in with my kind before and were used to catch, warn, and release or catch and toss back to the hell realm through a secure portal. We normally didn't get rough with demons in the field outside of combat.

That was before the great and powerful demon escape.

I didn't do torture, but I had no qualms about dispatching these two. If they'd been captured before and warned, they knew the consequences of unauthorized activities on earth. Whatever had caused the explosion that set this building on fire was most definitely unauthorized.

I twisted the knife again and the wraiths began to fade. Before I could dispatch them out of existence, a roar of a bigger, more deadly demon echoed through what was left of the halls of this inferno. Had to be the demon D was fighting, and he'd been fighting it for a while. I might be angry with D, but I had his back. With a groan of frustration, I pulled my knife out of the wood and released the wraiths and ran in the direction of the battling demons.

Rounding the corner and narrowly avoiding a flaming bit of ceiling as it fell, I spotted D locked in a blade battle with a monstrosity of a demon. Red and scaly, it looked like a humanoid dragon complete with huge wings, deadly fangs, and wicked claws it used like knives. I'd never seen anything like it. Before the seven powerful demons escaped, I'd chased and captured lesser demons. Some tempters were power hungry and looked for easy pickings on earth. Others were refugees seeking a safe haven away from the hell realm. Now I understood why.

This was what they were running from.

And the demon leaving bloody claw marks over D was only one of many we'd have to defeat before we could banish the big, bad seven.

If I stood and stared at the terrifying creature for much longer, I'd chicken out. The power I held washed over me, and I didn't fight it or attempt to control it. Instead, it was my partner in a deadly dance designed to destroy the enemy demon. It led me to approach the battling demons, knife drawn and glowing brilliant red in the presence of raw demon power before flashing purple. The purple came from my celestial heritage as celestial blue mixed with the red demon signal. Then, blue overtook the glow of my knife, a signal for the raw celestial power coursing through me.

My power was ready. I was ready.

I saw an opening and took it. I leapt, my compact body designed for gymnastics combined with a decade of training and power coursing through me. My knife slashed across the demon's left wing, tearing a wide gash. Hopefully the wound would keep it from ever flying again.

The dragon demon roared and spun, slashing at me with deadly claws. I ducked and rolled, stabbing my knife into its side while D struck at its neck.

The demon twisted, dislodging my knife and dodging D's blow. He kicked and sent me sliding across the floor. D spun and got in a shoulder hit. Dark blood poured out of the demon's wound, and he roared with pain and rage. I rolled and jumped back to my feet. Distracted by its injury, the demon failed to block my next strike to the side. I followed D's lead and slashed instead of stabbing.

If we bled the beast, we could slow it down and together, we could destroy it.

D punched it in the jaw, and I dropped to the ground, slicing through the demon's Achille's tendon on one leg, then the other. The demon collapsed. Before D or I could deliver a killing strike, the demon disappeared in a burst of red light and smoke.

"Damn it! He got away!" I screamed in frustration, my celestial energy crying out for blood and death.

D stared at me, jaw gaping.

I looked at my knife. It now glowed so brightly blue it was almost blinding. My skin glowed, too, as the sigils that made up a series of tattoos, the physical embodiment of my demon grafts, crawled along my skin. I had no idea what D saw when he looked at me in this state, but it scared him.

To his credit, he rushed over to me in spite of his fear and gripped my shoulders, looking me over for injuries. I pulled out his grasp and swatted his hands away. "Don't touch me."

He yanked back his hands and stepped back. "I won't hurt you if you promise to show me the same courtesy."

Metal groaned above us. I had a split-second warning before a chunk of the floor above us crashed down, just enough time to rush at D and push him out of the way.

Unfortunately, the maneuver left us in a tangle on the floor of a burning building. We had to get out of there. I let D help me to my feet. He held on to my hand and pulled me as we ran through flames, jumped over burning hunks of furniture, and slid down the remnants of stairs until at last, we made it out of the building. We kept running past the first responders, injured humans, and those who'd come to gawk at the flaming building. No more phone zombies stood around like sitting ducks, thank goodness. Glad something activated their situational awareness.

I wasn't sure how many blocks we'd traveled, but at last, we ducked into an empty alley.

D let go of my hand and we both took a moment to catch our breath. All the while, I was getting an earful from Boice.

"Jinx, I don't know what the fuck you're doing, but you'd better get out of there ASAP. Trinity is sending in the calvary and you're on her shit list."

"I'm...out," I said between coughing fits and gulps of air. "Demon... looked like a dragon...had a one-night stand...with a goblin. It disappeared. One minute there...next, poof...gone."

I'd only ever seen D and a couple of his buddies dematerialize, so the dragon demon was at the very least on his level. As I'd found out recently, D was more powerful than I realized and probably had other powers he'd been keeping secret.

Speaking of... "Why didn't...you just zap yourself...out?" I asked D.

"I used all my magic fighting the demon, and something in the area was draining me. Didn't you feel it?"

Now that he mentioned it, I felt as worn out as my favorite old sweater, more so than I would have expected given my demon graft-enhanced stamina and the rush of celestial power. D looked as weary as I felt.

"Yeah," I said. "Not sure what it means, but it can't be good."

He looked away and muttered, "And even if I could have mustered enough energy to teleport myself, I wasn't going to leave you behind."

Boice had gone silent. I wondered if we'd lost contact before he spoke again. "The demon you described sounds like a Maak. They were known to humans as Zmeu, Machai, sometimes just as dragons when they were last seen on earth. The one you fought won't be the only one. They'll be working for Belial or for one of the seven escaped high-ranking demons. Not good."

"There were wraiths, too," I said. "Haven't seen those in a while. Definitely not good."

I wiped sweat and soot from my brow and rolled my shoulders. Looked like channeling my celestial powers didn't make me immune to the aftermath of battle. I'd be freaking sore tomorrow. Someday, these powers would protect me from pesky human aches and pains, not to mention fatigue. But it seemed today was not that day.

"Are we talking legions of dragon demons?" I asked. I couldn't imagine fighting an army of those things.

"No reports yet. This is the first open act of aggression since the demons escaped. You'll need to give me a report, including more details on the demon you fought."

Crap. I hated paperwork. "D did most of the fighting. I just showed up and—"

"Saved my ass," D said, sliding down the brick wall against his back. He was still bleeding.

"Nice." Boice yelled so D could hear him, and so he could blow out my eardrum. "You two going to kiss and make up?"

I wasn't going to dignify the question. Changing the subject, I said, "You going to cover for me?"

The question was meant for Boice, but D gave me wicked grin and said, "Sure."

I cast my gaze skyward and shouted. "It would be nice if these celestial powers worked on command!"

Naturally, no one answered. Celestials sucked. They were haughty, uncommunicative jackasses who never showed up to help unless the big, bad demons came out to flex. And one dragon demon apparently didn't merit an appearance.

Boice giggled. He hated celestials and it tickled him that my demon grafts were more reliable—which wasn't saying much—than the celestial powers I was born with.

"Get your ass home and do your paperwork. I'll say D filed it and I won't tell Trinity you did anything except rescue innocent bystanders." Boice would make me pay for it. Blackmail was his favorite pastime, along with insider trading, NFTs, and fanfic. I'd be cleaning toilets for the next decade.

"Speaking of rescue," D said. "I found this in the building. Want to take it Cooper?"

D reached into his inside jacket pocket and pulled out a tiny black ball of fur. It sat in the palm of his hand, completely still except for an occasional shudder. I reached for it and a small head popped up, hissed at me, and then disappeared back into the ball of fur, but not before I glimpsed two sets of pointed ears, a button nose, needle sharp teeth, and bright green eyes.

Oh. My. God.

I poked at it and a tiny tail emerged, puffy and flicking back and forth. One tiny murder mitten with wickedly sharp claws swatted at me.

The feral, scared, and a tiny ball of fuzzy cuteness was untamed and fierce, half-starved as it was. Fortunately, I had experience with feral creatures from the demon realm—I'd never tamed D, but he'd become mine as soon as I fed him.

I reached into my back pocket and pulled out a stick of turkey jerky. It was slightly smushed and a little burnt, but it would do. Peeling back the plastic, I bit off a small piece and held it over the tiny black mass. The button-nosed muzzle poked out and sniffed the jerky before snatching it out of my fingers.

Three...two...one...

The ball uncurled to reveal the most adorable little furry black face, four legs ending in delicate paws, a rounded body, perky tail, and a pair of tiny wings. Wide green eyes looked at me expectantly. I broke off another piece of jerky and held it out to the creature. After the third piece, it was eating out of my hand and purring.

It was a kitten. A demon realm kitten.

"Oh, my god, that is the most adorable thing I've ever seen," I said, voice low and soothing.

"Jane," D said, warning and amusement in his voice. "You have to take it to Cooper."

Cooper, full time summoner, portal guardian, and friend to all animals from both earth and the hell realm, was in charge of taking care of injured demon animals and returning them to the hell realm. He also had a pet cadejo, a winged demon dog I'd wanted to steal since I first laid eyes on him.

If he could have a demon realm pet, why couldn't I?

Oh, right, he was batshit crazy, and something about the trait let him talk to animals. All summoners were a little nuts. Why else would anyone guard a portal to hell and control who went in and out, even calling demons that could kill them to the earth realm? But he was an expert on hell realm beasts. I'd have to let him check the furball out for any health issues.

But no way was I giving up the kitten. D knew it, which was why he was gifting it to me to get back into my good graces.

"I'll take it to Cooper," I said, cuddling it against my chest. "I'll get it treated for any injuries and then I'll take it back home and keep it forever. You're still in the doghouse, by the way." I tried to play it cool but hurt leaked into my voice.

"I know," he said quietly, his heart in his eyes. Before I could respond, he leaned down and kissed me gently on the forehead.

Then he disappeared.

Typical.

CHAPTER TWO

By the time I drove home, the demon kitty had thoroughly explored my car, my person, and nearly caused me to crash. Three times. After flying over my face, I learned the kitty was a she-cat. And I found out kitty stank of rotten eggs.

"Stinky baby. I'm going to name you Sulphur," I said as I pulled into the parking garage attached to the downtown high-rise I called home and turned off the engine. She gave me an inquisitive chirp that melted my heart, and I booped her little nose.

She hissed. It was too freakin' cute.

"Yup. You're Sulphur. Sully for short. Hungry?"

She let out an ear-splitting meow, which I took as a yes.

Sully let me pick her up, and then kindly perched on my shoulder as I entered the lobby of the upscale building covered in soot and limping. Why I didn't get more of the supernatural healing power from my celestial or demon side was anyone's guess. Who were my best friends? Ice, ibuprofen, and hot, steamy showers, and if I was lucky a healing demon-realm elixir to speed my recovery.

The guard in the lobby didn't bother looking up. Troy was used to seeing me in various states of disarray, and he'd surely heard the explosion and emergency vehicles. Like most mundane humans, he figured I was some sort of law enforcement or emergency management type. Or a spy.

Never one to ask questions, he simply smiled, tipped his hat, and said, "Jinx, you're tracking soot on my floors. I can't have that, not after I just washed 'em."

"Sorry," I said, not bothering to stop. "Send me a bill."

"Will do," Troy said, laughing. "Will do. What you done got yourself into now?"

I'd reached the elevators, so I yelled, "The usual. Dragon demons, hellfire and brimstone, end of days."

A chuckled followed me into the elevator. "You won't do, girl. Hey, do you have a cat on your shoulder? You ain't filled out the paperwork for pets, there's—"

The elevator closed. Paperwork, schmaperwork. I had tech demons for that. Speaking of...

I got off at the penthouse, a.k.a. home-sweet-home, and surveyed the state of my space. I shared the large top floor unit with the twins, who'd come with the place. Technically, it meant they shared the place with me, but the boss had made it clear the demon boys were supposed to "keep an eye on me" when I'd moved in, so I was clearly more important. We had a ton of windows, an open concept floorplan on steroids, and an eclectic mix of modern décor belonging to the twins and the second hand almost shabby chic furniture that was all mine. They were the first belongings I'd ever purchased as an adult and refused to part with them—especially my comfy couch. It fit my ass perfectly, and the neon tartan upholstery made me happy while horrifying my demon roomies.

Total win.

The mismatched chairs were done in color-coordinated skull upholstery, and I had some lovely demon-shaped throw pillows to complete the look. I'd have to get Sully a cat bed now. I was thinking zombies...

Aside from my corner and an indeterminate number of bedrooms—it was either magic or the demons I lived with were fucking with me by adding or moving doors—the large common area had plenty of nooks and crannies cordoned off into cubicles for working, playing, and for visitors. Our most recent guest, Mara the succubus, had moved out but she left a stash of creature comforts in her corner for when she came to visit. Before joining our team, she'd been a pawn in Lord Belial's game to capture me and his lover so we could join him in a new interdimensional war against celestials. And before that, she'd been a refugee from the hell realm. I hoped she realized she was truly free now. We weren't using her like her previous bosses. The twins had set up a lucrative investment portfolio for her and for the first time in her existence, she received a paycheck. She was super grateful.

Actually, she was a little too grateful.

While an equal and valuable member of our demon hunting organization, she treated the rest of us like superiors to be served in exchange for freeing her. Things worked differently in the demon realm, but she'd been on earth long enough to know we humans didn't do the whole hierarchy servitude mafia-style thing here. Old habits die hard, as did deeply ingrained beliefs. We'd keep working on Mara, killing her with kindness until she knew how much we valued her.

"Mrrp!"

Sully, who'd been fidgeting and digging her tiny claws into my shoulder, stuck her cold, wet nose in my ear and reminded me that a) she was here and b) I'd promised her food. Right. Time to find my roomies. Boice and Roice, the twin demons of technology, my best buds, and roommates from hell were at their usual spots, parked behind multiple keyboards and screens, typing away. They had less free time to pursue their usual interests these days. Like the rest of us, they'd been caught up in cleaning up the mess caused by the recent great demon escape.

It wasn't my fault, but I still felt guilty.

The blame rightly belonged to my personal demon, the one who used to possess me. Only she'd turned out to be a traumatized and arguably insane archangel who'd been imprisoned within me as punishment for betraying her kind. Once upon a few millennia or four, she led a rebellion with her demon lover, Lord Belial, D's dear old dad.

I never asked, but I hope she wasn't D's mother. Talk about awkward.

Her fellow archangels, powerful celestial beings, quashed the rebellion and punished her by trapping her in human hosts who had celestial heritage, convincing her and the host she was a demon, and passing her around for generations before she wound up possessing me.

It was the story I'd been told. Presumably my deadbeat dad hosted her before I got her, but since he'd run off and left us, I couldn't exactly ask him.

The human host system worked—for a while—because I had celestial blood from my absentee father's side, but I didn't know any of that at the time. All I knew was that I had a demon inside of me, and demons came for bad people. I'd spent most of my life believing I was an evil person due to what I thought was a state of demonic possession.

I found out the truth right before my demon-turned-crazy-archangel opened portals to the hell and celestial realms. Mortally wounded, I shoved her and Belial, her lover and demon lord who wanted a second try at apocalyptic rebellion, into the portal and closed it, but not before some powerful unauthorized demons escaped.

The escapees were hidden on earth and up to no good, the kind of no good that could destroy a whole lot of humans and wreak havoc on the survivors. My life-saving demon grafts and mixture of human and celestial heritage supposedly gave me the power of three realms: earth, celestial, and hell. According to some cryptic prophecy written in the *Compiled Grimoires of the Wicked and Wise*, a warrior with the power of three realms would go up against Haniel and Belial in a battle of epic proportions.

Meaning it was my job to stop them.

I wasn't up to the task yet, so for now I was stuck in training. Today was the first day I'd seen any real combat. It made me hungry for more, and highly motivated to live up to expectations and clean up this mess.

Footage of the downtown devastation flashed across one of the many screens on the workstation the twins shared. I caught sight of a few phone zombies. I couldn't see what had the clueless bystanders so engrossed, but the boys could zoom in and enhance the resolution.

"Roice, could you give me a better look at what's on that lady's phone? The one in the red hoodie?"

His fingers flew over the keyboard and in less than ten seconds, I could see bouncing, colorful shapes moving along the screen, following the lady's finger. It fit with the bystander who'd been babbling about colors and shapes, but it made no sense given the chaos surrounding the lady and the other phone zombies. Amid flames, smoke, the screams of people fleeing the building mixed with sirens and police with megaphones directing people to leave the area, the lady and her fellow zombies were glued to their phones, oblivious to it all.

After a few more seconds of footage, it hit me.

"Is she playing a video game?" I asked, incredulous.

"Looks like," Roice said. "Humans are weird."

I resisted the urge to defend my species and, on whim, said. "Can you see if the others are doing the same thing?"

"On it."

"If you don't go straight to the shower and wash that swamp ass stench off yourself, I'm calling Trinity." Boice didn't look up from his computer. No doubt he was working as fast as he could on reports for Trinity so he could get to his true passion—hunting down human traffickers on the dark web and gathering blackmail material against billionaires and members of Congress.

If he wasn't a demon, I'd say he was doing the lord's work.

"Nice to see you, too, roomie," I said, stroking Sully's soft fur. Turned out the demon cat loved chin scratches, behind the ear scritches, and purred up a storm when rubbed between her tiny wings. "What do demon realm animals eat?"

"Depends." Roice said. Boice's twin kept typing up a storm as he spoke. Multiple screens flashed with footage of the mess downtown. I hoped none of the cameras caught me. I'd have to do something truly degrading in exchange for having Boice erase any footage, like stand on the corner of Broadway and Second Avenue holding a placard plastered with "Short People Got No Reason."

"Depends on what? Ouch!" The tiny demon kitten bit my finger. I grabbed her by the scruff and got a squeak of pure indignation. "Stop it. I'll feed you as soon as the two silly demons I live with tell me what you like to eat." A wicked thought inspired a wicked grin, and I cooed to the cat, asking "Would you like to eat *them*?"

After squirming and squeaking a few more times, she finally gave up and hung limp. I kissed her little nose and said, "Don't worry, sweetie. I wouldn't feed you those nasty demon boys. We don't know where they've been, do we?

My voice had gone up two octaves, which seemed to fascinate Sully. Her large eyes blinked slowly, which I understood was a sign of affection in earth cats. I'd never had a pet growing up. We couldn't afford it. I was so going to make up for lost time and spoil Sully rotten.

Turning my attention to my roommates, I was surprised to find them staring at me, jaws agape, with identical looks of shock painted across their faces. Boice wore a gray T-shirt with a cartoon demon holding a phone. The caption read, "Help, I'm being attacked by demons! Yes, I'll hold." Not to be outdone, Roice's green T-shirt read, "I tripped and fell into some feelings. I'm okay now. I brushed that shit off."

They were so immature.

But they weren't normally rendered speechless by yours truly.

"What?" I put Sully on my shoulder, but she decided to climb on my head and dig her claws into my scalp.

"Where did you get that?" Boice asked, pointing a shaking finger at my head. His voice squeaked at the end, sounding a little like Sully.

"Get it out of here before it kills us all!" Roice jumped out of his office chair and pointed at the itty-bitty fluffy kitten on my head, too.

Too flabbergasted to say anything else, I said, "D gave her to me. She was wandering around the burning building. We couldn't just leave her there."

Imagining what the tiny creature must have been through made my heart hurt. Presumably she'd been sucked through the same giant hell realm portal that let the powerful rogue demons loose on earth. The team had found more than a few hell realm beasts and terrified lesser demons who'd been going about their business one night, living their lives—probably not in peace, but in the familiar terrain of the hell realm—only to be ripped away from all they knew and tossed into a new and frightening world. Poor Sully had probably still been with her mother cat and a slew of littermates. No way I could've left her to fend for herself.

I shook off my confusion. Hands on hips, I narrowed my gaze at my roomies and asked, "Why are you being so weird? It's just a kitten."

Boice rose from his chair more slowly, his gaze never leaving Sully. "That's not a kitten. It's a Motiaummerr. They're one of the deadliest species in the hell realm."

A Moti-what?

The twins put the table between me and my allegedly deadly fluffball and kept backing up. I'd never seen them act this way before. They were demons for crying out loud, and not your garden-variety tempter demons, who while formidable enough, weren't all that powerful magically speaking. While young in demon terms, appearing circa the Industrial Revolution, they were technology demons and quite powerful. True, their talents were in the domain of all things mechanical, technical, and digital, but the twins were far from helpless despite their preferred glamour. Lanky and a bit on the homely side, with greasy hair and exaggerated features that made them look like eighteen to twenty something juvenile delinquents, no human would give them a second glance.

Beneath the glamour, they were fearsome and armed with physical and magical weapons.

Sully yowled and took flight, using my scalp as leverage. I'd have to keep her nails trimmed. The boys squealed and ducked beneath the table. It was too funny.

I stifled a giggle. "She's the size of a softball and she purrs."

"You don't know what you're dealing with, Jinx. You should really put it in an enchanted cage and get it to a portal before it destroys everyone in a five-mile radius." Boice's voice came from beneath the table.

I sighed. "Portals are all closed right now, dumbass. Besides, how can that—" I pointed to the demon cat who'd landed on my favorite loveseat, fallen over, and promptly started biting her own tail— "be deadly? She was perfectly well-behaved in the car, except when she started flying around and blocking my vision and I almost wrecked. Twice. Okay, three times." Not my best argument. "But it wasn't her fault. She was just scared, poor thing."

"It's not full grown," Roice said, peeking out from under the table. "They're only moderately dangerous when they're young."

Rolling my eyes, I walked over to my sofa, scooped up my kitty, and then plopped down with her on my lap. She stared up at me with inquisitive eyes and began purring loudly. Cuteness made up for the stench, and I rubbed her until she flopped over and closed her eyes.

"Stop calling her an 'it.' Her name is Sully and she's a good kitty," I said, offended on behalf of my little cutey.

Suddenly struck by of inspiration, I said, "We can train her! If she's destined to grow up and become a deadly demon creature, she'd be an asset to the team. We need all the help we can get."

Roice stood and looked at Sully with a wary curiosity. "I don't know if Motiaummerrs are trainable. They're not native to our part of the hell realm. All I know is they're supposed to be dangerous."

Boice stayed under the table.

"Who told you they were dangerous?" I asked. He didn't often speak of the hell realm. Both he and his brother had spent most of their lives working on earth under the supervision of our former boss, Sameal, a.k.a. The Angel of Death. Or maybe Demon of Death? He wasn't too clear about the specifics, and he'd gone AWOL before I could ask him.

At any rate, I always assumed the tech demon bros hadn't enjoyed their time in the demon realm, though they defended demon kind against propaganda spread by celestials. It was the reason demons were depicted as savage and evil while so-called angels came off as benevolent and beautiful in human religious texts.

The victors controlled the narrative, and celestials been pushing it since recorded human history.

Boice emerged from under the table. "Mother used to tell us about the creatures who lived in the great forests separating our province from the demon realm cities. We weren't supposed to go exploring because those creatures were dangerous."

Boice and Roice had a mother?

I didn't say it out loud and was glad when I noticed the sad expressions on the boys' faces. Of course they'd had a mother. Everyone had a mother. I just couldn't picture it. Why had I assumed they'd magically spawned from some portal in the hell realm?

My cheeks heated in shame. Some friend I was.

Prejudice was an ugly thing. I'd gotten over a lot of it after getting to know a lot of demons. True, as a demon hunter, I tracked down those who did harm in the human realm, but most demons on earth were refugees just trying to survive. They weren't all that different from humans. I knew it, but stereotypes still invaded my thoughts from time to time. It was a me problem. I'd have to work harder on it.

"You never told me about your mother." I kept petting Sully, who'd fallen asleep on my lap. I used the other hand to pat the sofa. When the boys shook their heads, I waved my hand at the chairs across from my sofa. With an abundance of caution bordering on comical, they walked slowly to the chairs and sat down. Each on the edge of the seat, presumably so they could get up and run away from Sully should she wake.

Or maybe they didn't want to plant ass on my new throw pillows.

I resisted the urge to roll my eyes.

"So," I said, keeping my gaze focused on Sully. "Will you tell me about your mother? If you feel like talking, that is."

We sat in silence for what felt like an hour. It was more like five minutes, but resisting the urge to fidget, meet their gazes, or draw my blade and force them to talk made it feel like an eternity.

At last, Roice spoke. "She was tough, fearsome, beautiful, and deadly."

Was. Oh, dear. She was no more, then.

"When our father, the Lord of Warfare, was called to join the legions in the last war between the great demon kingdoms, she was left to raise us and protect us from roaming demon soldiers—many deserters—and demon wildlife."

Boice took up the story then. "She was called Narcalla, Chief

Demoness of Ingenuity, and we worked together to create defenses, borrowing ideas and materials smuggled from the earth realm."

My neck snapped up and I stared at them, the pieces falling into place. "That's how you became tech demons!"

The twins nodded. Roice said, "When our father returned from the great war, he decided we would be safer and more likely to thrive on the earth realm with its machines and inventions that functioned better than many magics in the demon realm. We'd developed ways to merge magic and machines by then, so our talents would be of more use on earth. Our parents took us to a portal to meet Sameal, who would grant us sanctuary in exchange for service—it was a good deal," he added when I made a face.

Whatever. Deals with our former boss always had big strings attached, and he liked to leave out important details. It was how he'd fenagled ten years of service out of me without keeping his end of the bargain and finding D for me. Worse, Sameal convinced me D was dead even though he knew good and well that D was alive and in the hell realm, held against his will by his father.

If I ever found the bastard, I'd make him pay for it.

I took a deep breath and put aside my anger to focus on the twins as they re-lived what was no doubt one of their worst memories. Instead of stewing, I needed to be ready to listen and offer what comfort I could to my companions. They deserved my undivided attention and unwavering support.

"You made it through the portal, obviously...what happened to your parents?" I asked quietly.

My question was met with silence. The twins sat motionless in their chairs, eyes on the ground and blinking rapidly. Roice swallowed hard, and Boice put a hand on his shoulder. Crap. Nothing good could have happened.

At last, Boice finished the story. "We were intercepted at the portal. The higher demons who rule don't like to lose assets. We made it through. Our parents didn't."

His voice was flat and matter of fact, a wound too deep and old for fresh tears. It was okay. I'd cry for them. I was crying for them, I realized as I tasted salt from a tear that had traveled from my eye to my lips. I'd lost my father when he walked out on our family. It wasn't the same as a death, but the loss had devasted me. Hard to imagine the loss of both parents at once, no doubt by violent and horrific means.

"We decided to make sure other demon refugees wouldn't have to go through the same thing." Roice's voice was hard, but not bitter. Instead of succumbing to despair or wreaking havoc on the earth realm, the twins had channeled their awful situation and pain into doing good on earth. They'd made Mara feel welcome, settling her in and feeding her when I first brought her home after a night of terror at the hands of my boss's not-so-gentle interrogation.

I swallowed hard. I could learn a thing or two from these remarkable creatures.

"I'm sorry," I said. It wasn't enough. No words could heal the wound or make up for the loss. "I'm...glad you both made it. I think your parents would be proud of the demons you've become."

"Thank you," Roice said. No hiding behind snark or shrugging it off with jokes. The boys were just that. Boys. Lost. Just like the rest of us. But we'd all found each other. It was the one good thing that had come out of our mess of an occupation.

I slid Sully off my lap and tucked her against a pillow. Then I rose, walked over to the chairs between the twins, crouched down, and opened my arms. They fell into me, and we held one another so tight for a long, long time.

Boice and Roice let go and I occupied myself with stroking Sully's soft fur while they wiped their eyes.

"I'll go get a litter box and some kibble," I said. "Will you watch her?"

"Sure," Roice said, tentatively running a finger along her back. "We'll give her some water and see if she likes the laser pointer. Maybe see if she likes human food."

"And make sure she doesn't destroy the penthouse," Boice added, following his brother's lead and stroking Sully's fur. "Or die trying."

I laughed. "You might be more convincing if you weren't scratching her ears." They didn't hit me with any snappy comebacks, engrossed as they were in petting and pampering kitty. Sully purred and rubbed her tiny body over the twins' gentle hands, offering her own brand of comfort. I knew they'd come around. She was another refugee. They'd never turn her away.

I had just grabbed my keys when my phone—and the twins'—buzzed with an emergency alert. It was Trinity. We were under attack.

"Go!" the twins yelled in unison. "We've got this, you go save the day."

CHAPTER THREE

The knife whizzed past my face, grazing my cheek as I bent to avoid being stabbed in the forehead.

Damn it. I might get a scar for my stupidity.

My demon attacker threw the next blade. Distracted by vanity, the sharp edge nicked the side of my neck. Hissing in pain, I crouched low and put all my energy into situational awareness.

Sloppy. I needed to get my head in the game. I had to find the demon who was trying to kill me. No celestial powers came to my rescue this time. I was on my own with my wits and less than reliable demon powers.

At least I could still call upon enhanced vision.

Reaching out with my newly acquired senses, I scanned every nook, cranny, and shadowed corner for demon signs. His scent was concentrated near the oil drum at my two o'clock, but I couldn't get a visual. My own demon blade wasn't helping. It glowed a brilliant crimson no matter where I pointed, as if I were surrounded by a horde of deadly hell realm invaders. But that wasn't possible. According to Trinity's intel, there was one demon, and if I wanted to get out of this hellscape—metaphorically speaking, since we were on earth—I needed to find and defeat him.

My knife's glow flickered, and I blocked the third incoming blade with my wrist guard, my movements slow and lacking the former grace and finesse I'd had when working in harmony with Hannah, but at least my reflexes were still on point. It sucked, but I didn't have time for self-pity. I had to learn and master a completely new way of fighting, one that involved demon skills acquired from my grafts, powers I had yet to fully understand, let alone master.

Only this time, I controlled the demon powers. Or, rather, I *could*, in theory, control those powers once I figured out how.

I was no longer possessed, no longer shared my body with a sentient partner upon whom I'd come to rely. Since I'd lost my personal demon-slash-archangel-in-disguise, I was all on my own except for the power I truly owned, was born with, but didn't work any better. What good was celestial power if I couldn't figure out how to tap into it? It normally manifested when I was in mortal danger in a combat situation. Too bad it wasn't here to save my ass now.

Something hit the back of my head hard enough to ring my bell and make me faceplant on the gym floor. It was covered by blue mats, which did little to soften the impact. My knife skittered across the floor. I'd dropped it while falling. Stupid.

But one of his discarded knives was close. I stretched my fingers out and managed to pull it closer, tucking it under my body and out of the demon's sight.

When I could manage a solid breath, I said, "What the hell, Sam?"

I didn't wait for an answer. Sam, aka Marquess Samagina of the hell realm, had seemed like a gentleman, at least as much as demon was capable, when I first met him. He was a handsome devil, with silky, jet-black hair, a neatly trimmed beard accenting high cheekbones, and olive skin a few shades darker than mine. In traditional hell realm robes, he looked like royalty. Clever, generally chivalrous, and totally smitten with my former demon hunting colleague and new boss Trinity, one could mistake him as a lightweight dandy.

But I'd seen him in deadly combat. And during mandatory training, he showed his true, lethal powers, dropping gentlemanly behavior to become a snake mean, sneaky bastard determined to kick my ass six ways to Sunday.

Once again, I was stuck in a dimly lit gym decked out with a variety of obstacles and hiding places my attackers could use to murder me—oh, no, excuse me, so they could *train* me to fight all manner of demonic entities. It was more of a re-training since I used to fight in harmony with my personal demon.

I'd skipped a few sessions in favor of sneaking out to do fieldwork, so Trinity lured me here by faking an emergency call and siccing her boyfriend on me, the sneak.

Quiet laughter echoed around me. Another trick from my demonic attacker, one designed to distract me. I blocked out the noise and focused on my other senses. A whiff of Sam's unique scent wafted from behind me. He thought he'd disarmed me, but I still had a knife. Now all I needed was a plan.

"My dear, if you wish me to unleash hell upon you, I'm more than willing. But first, you must master our current lesson."

This totally sucked.

I was allegedly some kind of badass warrior with the power of three realms and was supposed to use them to stop the next war between celestials and demons that would take out inhabitants of earth in the crossfire.

Given my current performance, we were doomed.

I hated these training sessions. It was all in the name of saving my life the next time I faced an actual enemy demon combatant and working my way up to saving the world. No pressure. I hated that even more.

Sam enjoyed it way too much, the jerk.

"Giving up so easily?" Sam's voice was closer now, louder. He'd taken his time approaching me in case I was faking injury to lure him in so I could attack. Smart demon.

Concentrating, I tried to harness the senses that connected me with Sam's demon nature—heightened sight, hearing, scenting, and tactile sensitivity that let me know his general location by subtle changes in the room's air currents.

It was one of the abilities he'd given me when he, along with my fellow demon teammates, gave me pieces of their essences to save my life.

I sifted through the information. As far as I could work out, Sam was crouched behind my left foot, just outside of kicking rage. Great. From where he was sitting, he'd have a rather unflattering view of my bleeding and bruised body face down on the floor, weak and defeated. Or maybe he was just ogling my juicy booty.

"What are you hiding, demon hunter?"

Crap. His voice echoed all around me, so I was no longer certain where he was. Demons were good at tricking human senses. Had he moved, or was he throwing his voice? Did he know I'd managed to grab one of his knives?

Maybe I was going about this the wrong way.

I focused on channeling demon power from another source. Mara, my favorite succubus and newest team member in our Nashville demon-hunting operation, used glamour and the deepest desires of her victims to bespell them, but she could also use her glamour to warp reality in other ways. Even powerful demons like Sam weren't immune.

Most material demons could change their appearance to blend in with humans, but a succubus took it to a whole other level.

I rolled slowly onto my back, concentrating on concealing the knife. I stole a glance at my right hand and almost screamed. Instead of making the knife disappear, the glamour had created an illusion of severe damage with blood, gore, and protruding bone. Ick.

"Be still, Jane." Sam's chiding tone was gone, replaced by unnatural calm that almost hid worry. "I'll fetch some healing elixir."

Sam turned his back on me and started running for the medical kit we kept in the gym. It contained standard first aid and emergency medical supplies for humans along with a variety of demon-realm salves, elixirs, and potions. Damn it, why couldn't I get a handle on the glamour thing? Mara and I had been working hard. I was okay at disguising my facial features and changing hair color, but, like the botched disappearing knife trick, I couldn't reliably direct it to my will. My face changed, but not in the specific manner I was going for. And that was when it worked.

Demons made it look so easy.

But I wasn't a demon. I was a half-human, half-celestial—thanks dad —woman with parts of seven different demons intwined with her body and spirit. That made me officially the weirdest person on my demon hunting team and possibly the planet. All I ever wanted was to be normal, and now I was so far from normal that the life I'd always wanted was permanently out of reach.

But I was still alive, and I had a job to do. Time to stop wallowing.

I hadn't managed the glamour I wanted, but the end goal of distracting Sam had worked even better than I planned. His back was to me while he rooted around in the med kit.

Use every opportunity to your advantage. That's what I'd been taught.

I rose slowly and soundlessly, which was harder thanks to bloody cuts and a jacked-up knee, and threw my knife at Sam, hitting him between the shoulder blades.

Had this been real instead of a simulation, the demon would be fully incapacitated.

Sam turned to face me, his gaze wide with shock.

Then he graced me with a charming and beautiful smile. "Well done! You were already proficient at tactics. That was excellent use of glamour. You would have bested me even if I had gone for the kill."

The Marquess walked back to me and turned around, allowing me to retrieve my practice blade from his back. It was mostly made of earth realm steel with only a fraction of demon steel for demon detection, so he was in no danger. Demons healed quickly, and his armor and padding from the mundane human world offered protection.

I pulled the knife and cast my gaze down at the floor, shuffling my feet. Very unlike me, but I couldn't claim credit for something I hadn't done on purpose.

"It worked on accident," I confessed, my voice bitter. "I meant to hide the blade, not turn my hand into a bloody stump."

The warm hand that landed on my shoulder felt good. I looked up at Sam, who managed to project an expression of kindness and affection minus sympathy. Good. If he'd gone for pity, I'd have punched him in the gut.

"I may not have been perfect or your intention, but you managed a lethal strike. You are improving with every session, and you have only been training for eight weeks. Patience is not your strength, but you might grant some to yourself." He handed me demon salve. "Go home now, and rest."

I nodded. Not that I believed him. Patience was a luxury I couldn't afford.

And I had no intention of going home to rest. I had some research to do with the twins. They'd sent me a text message during my beatdown session with Sam. After analyzing the footage, they discovered the phone zombies at the site of downtown carnage were all playing the same video games.

A video game. In the middle of a demonic terrorist attack. Too weird to be a natural phenomenon. One stupid human I could believe, but more than ten? Something was up, and it was likely demonic. Mind control was kind of their thing.

We finally had our first solid lead on the escaped demons, and I wasn't technically allowed to go into the field. Trinity knew me well enough to guess I'd go after the powerful demons I'd accidentally unleashed without her permission.

I already had. If she found out, she'd be furious.

She was just trying to keep me safe, to make sure I was ready.

I *knew* that.

But thanks to demon grafts from my roommates, the twin demons of technology, I now knew how to hack into almost any computer system. That was the one and only demon skill I'd mostly mastered. If we could identify the game or games the looky loos had been playing, we could track down the demon or demons making and distributing them. From there, we could track them. After this morning's act of extreme demonic aggression, I had to do more than hide out at HQ and train. I needed to find the head honcho demon responsible for that prelude to mass destruction and take them out.

I needed to do a little more investigative work using my informants on the street, and I needed to get my partner on board with the plan.

There was someone else I could call—should call. A familiar stab of pain and regret tightened my chest as it always did when I thought about him. This morning's run-in with the dragon demon was the first time I'd seen Demoriel since the disaster following the battle that unleashed some of hell's most powerful demons on earth.

When he'd come back into my life during the investigation that led to the great unleashing of demons, D had worked hard to reconnect and rebuild the friendship we'd forged as kids and then later as almost lovers. We had come so far in healing our broken relationship, but during the battle, I learned that he'd lied to me. I couldn't trust him. Not yet. Maybe not ever.

But then he'd shown up to protect the citizens of Nashville from the dragon demon, and to protect me. He hadn't abandoned me. That had to count for something. And he'd given me Sully. I hope she hadn't eaten the twins. I was already in love with the little bundle of fur, wings, and teeth. She was the best gift anyone had ever given to me.

And she was a gift from D.

I quashed that thought. I couldn't afford to dwell on lost loves and lies of omission. I had a mission to complete.

Going it alone was my former MO, but I'd learned the hard way to bring back up on any mission. D wouldn't always show up to save my ass.

I only hoped my partner Lacey Green would let me live long enough to talk her into joining me in an unauthorized investigation.

It was late by the time I made it back to the penthouse, too late to pay a visit to my partner. That would have to wait until tomorrow. Probably for the best. I still stank to high heaven with such a foul stench that even offended my demon cat. Like she hadn't smelled horrible just a few hours ago. The twins had bathed and fed her, which left her calm, cool, and judgey.

Typical cat.

After a long, luxurious shower, I settled down on my couch with Sully on my lap and downloaded what I hoped was the game the phone zombies had been playing. Boice and Roice had added some layers of encryption and developed a cypher to keep yours truly from gathering unauthorized intel. Bastards.

Okay, they were just following Trinity's orders and protecting me, but still—what harm could come from testing out a game and seeing what all the fuss was about? I'd never gotten into video games as a kid. After being possessed by Haniel, I tended to bork most electronics I touched. Now that she was gone, I didn't have nearly as much trouble with computers, household appliances, and cell phones. Good thing, too. I'd almost single-handedly blown our smartphone budget over the past decade.

I cooed at Sully and waited for the download. Her belly was distended from feasting on pizza, leftover Chinese takeout—including the veggies, and deli meat. What did Motiaummerrs eat? Apparently anything and everything they wanted. It was a miracle she hadn't exploded.

"Where did you put it all," I asked, gently rubbing her tummy.

She groaned and then began wriggling. I understood. Tacos and salsa were my downfall, leaving me bloated for a day or so after overeating. Still, it had to be magic. She'd eaten ten times her body weight in food. What was she doing with all those calories?

My download completed and I opened the App. A smiling cartoon greeted me and bounced around, her oversized tits jiggling suggestively while text flashed across the screen explaining how the game worked complete with backstory. The cartoon shimmied as the first level loaded. Geez, I hoped it came with an adult content warning.

The goal was to arrange a series of gems, gold bars, and other valuable objects into patterns that cleared a path for coins to fall or to release valuables trapped in bank vaults. Boosters were available for purchase, or you could earn them by watching stupid ads. Guess that was how they made their money, but seriously, it was so...mindless.

Still, this was a vital part of our investigation, so I'd just have to bite the bullet and complete a few more levels. Maybe then I'd get the point of this. The gems were pretty, though, their sparkle mesmerizing. And I had to admit, blasting the vaults to release a small virtual fortune with a particularly clever combo move was satisfying. Totally mindless but satisfying.

"Did you seriously stay up all night?"

Boice's voice seemed far away and muffled, like he was talking to me through a door. And what was he talking about? I'd only been playing for an hour, two tops.

I made a couple of dumb moves in the game and failed to make it to the next level.

"Damn it! You broke my concentration."

I pulled my gaze from the screen and had to blink a few times to focus on my pyjamas-clad roomie who was looming over me. He held out a steaming cup of coffee. I put the phone down and took it, though for some odd reason I didn't want to let go of the phone. I had to will my fingers to release it.

"Thanks, but you know I only drink this stuff in the morning," I said, taking a sip. "I'll be up all night if I drink this late."

Boice's brows furrowed. "Um, it *is* morning. You *have* been up all night. What gives?"

Holy guacamole! As my muddled senses came back online, I realized the penthouse was flooding with light from the rising sun. I had the mother of all headaches, and my neck was stiff from hunching over my phone screen for hours.

I'd become so engrossed in the stupid, mindless game that I'd lost time. No wonder I was freaking exhausted.

I groaned as I shifted on the couch, muscles sore as if I'd run a marathon. Not surprising, since I'd fought demons yesterday in the field and in training, but the demon elixir had cured that, right? Something weird was going on.

"You okay?" Boice asked, genuine concern in his voice.

"I think so," I said. "But I think we need to do some digging into this game. When it was released, who released it, how many downloads there have been and where. Whatever else it does, this game made a slew of folks ignore explosions and disaster all around them and made me lose more than eight hours."

I pointed at my phone, reluctant to touch it. "This is a lead."

CHAPTER FOUR

Lacey lived in a southeastern suburb of Nashville on the border with Williamson County. It made her commute to our downtown HQ and hunting grounds longer, but she preferred a quieter life outside of work. Her townhome in one of the newer planned communities was three stories tall and full of character thanks to conscientious builders who varied brick color and landscaping to distinguish each home rather than going for cookie cutter identical and bland. The neighborhood was vibrant, filled with restaurants, offices, and a dog groomer who catered to the million and one pooches co-habitating with the hip young residents.

I was more of a city gal myself, preferring the asphalt jungle to trees, woods, and bugs, but to each her own.

Plenty of friendly neighbors surrounded my partner, but she didn't get too close to anyone outside of the demon-hunting community. None of us did. Secrecy was key, as was keeping the public safe from collateral damage that came with our trade. I had my roommates, and since I'd been outed as a demon hunter to my family and my sister Megan had started working for our organization, I had my family, aside from the strained relations with my mother.

Yet another thing I needed to work on.

It wasn't her fault, or mine. My stupid disappearing deadbeat celestial of a father had screwed the entire family over by walking out on us when Megan and I were kids. Mom and I were working to mend fences. It would take a while. But at least I had family by blood and found family. Lacey had withdrawn from the team.

She was alone.

Her only company was Simon, her personal demon. Simon was a mammon, an immaterial greed demon who'd latched onto Lacey thanks to a shoplifting compulsion but now worked with her to catch rogue demons. Simon was awesome, but she needed more.

She was my family by choice, too.

She needed to stop isolating herself in self-imposed exile. She needed people, a community, and a kick in the ass to spur her into action.

I was determined to get her out of the house and back into the field with me. After the fallout from our last mission, I wasn't the only one who needed to get back up on the proverbial horse. Lacey had been used by our former boss's henchman-turned-traitor to sneak Belial's messenger through an unsecured portal to earth. Barbatos, the mole in our organization, took over her mind and body without her knowledge or any memory of what she'd done. Demonic possession was insidious, and I hated the immaterial tempter demons who inflicted it on their victims.

It was a lot to process, and probably left her with a scorching case of PTSD, which was much worse and more long-lasting than the broken nose I'd given her while she fought to keep me and the rest of the team from securing the portal. Guess she was still mad about it since she refused to return my calls and had sent death threats via text if I didn't leave her alone.

Death threats weren't such a big deal. It was how she rolled.

But her texts lacked the usual colorful emojis, expletives, and creative punctuation I'd come to expect from my partner. And she'd missed our last two team meetings. Trinity was going to come for her soon, and I wouldn't wish that on anyone. She'd had Sam kick my ass in yesterday's training session. Who knew what she'd do to Lacey?

I strolled along the sidewalk, smiling at a couple walking a pair of adorable Pitbull puppies whose butts wagged with canine enthusiasm at the sight of a new friend. The couple complimented my ink—another gift from my demon grafts—and I gave the dogs a good rubdown and accepted slobbery dog kisses before climbing the stairs to Lacey's condo.

Peeking through the windows on the doorframe didn't show me much. It was dark inside, cloaking the foyer in shadow. I sighed. She was home. I could sense her demon, and Simon never went anywhere without his mistress. Simon's demon graft helped me with research and tracking. Along with the skills I'd acquired from Boice and Roice, Simon's online investigative prowess helped me channel my inner hacker and dig up a lead on one of our demon targets.

The twins and I hit gold with the cell phone zombie angle.

I was ready to follow this fresh lead, but I needed my partner to do it. Maybe I could convince Simon and Lacey to let me in for a chat in exchange for the intel I'd gathered. Simon got a thrill from mining data to sniff out demons in hiding, something he hadn't been doing since Lacey went bye bye. And Lacey needed to get out of her funk and get back to work. Maybe I could convince Simon to take a look at what I'd put together, and then I'd use my charm and powers of persuasion to get Lacey on board with my sneak-off-and-do-some-detective-work plan.

One of the shadows in the foyer flickered, and I caught the shape of a wing. Could've been a trick of the light, but I suspected it was Simon on guard duty. The immaterial demon's preferred shape was raven-like. Only this time, he was bigger.

Much bigger.

Before I could blink, phantom talons shot through the door and directly at my face.

I ducked, grateful the mundane couple and their pooches had moved along so they didn't see me wrestling with Simon. Immaterial demons were invisible to normal humans, so I probably looked silly. Or crazy.

Or maybe I looked like I'd run into a ginormous spider web, which would be a pretty good cover story. I put a pin in it before attempting to throw up some glamour.

"Hey, Lady," a concerned male voice had me spinning around in a panic. "You okay? Might want to check that thing for rabies."

Rabies?

Then my eyes and ears caught up with my powers and I realized I was holding what looked like an angry chihuahua who was growling, thrashing, and attempting to bite me.

"Ouch!" What I assumed was a couple of talons pierced the sensitive flesh of my fingers, though the illusion made it look like the horrible, chubby little ball of fur and rage was biting the crap out of me.

Having no idea how long the glamour would last, I forced a smile for the nice young man walking a pug.

"Simon's just cranky. I'm returning him to his mommy," I said, glaring at the indignant demon who's apparently realized he looked like a small, yappy dog. "Last time I dog sit for the little monster."

The man laughed, but his pug started growling. Demon glamour fooled humans, but animals paid attention to instinct and senses we humans traded for bigger brains and upright walking. He looked at his pug and frowned. "Jenkins. What's gotten into you?"

I laughed a little louder than I meant to and put Simon under my arm in a football hold, squeezing the hell out of him so he'd stop stabbing and fighting me. "Must be catching." I used my free hand to press Lacey's doorbell, holding it so the annoying buzz would bring her to the door.

"Come on, Simon," I said through gritted teeth. "You're upsetting the nice man and his dog. Why can't you be a nice dog?"

"I'm not a dog," Simon hissed. "Give me back my true form and put me down before I consume you!"

Fortunately, the human didn't hear Simon, but he gave me the look of holy-guacamole-crazy-lady-alert and backed slowly away, leaving me and the stupid demon on the front porch of said demon's home, waiting for his jerk of a mistress and my unreliable partner to open the freakin' door.

"I curse you to the pit of devoured souls, you wretched half-breed!" Simon screeched.

"If you don't stop mauling me, I'm going to exorcise you straight back to hell without a penny to your name, you little hobgoblin!"

I liked Simon better before he could talk, or rather, I liked him better before he could talk to me. I had some of his essence in me, too, and it allowed me to communicate with the little greed demon. He'd always been friendly in the past. I had no idea what set him off, but it worried me. Having learned the hard way what I thought I knew about demons and the rules under which they operated wasn't always correct, I wondered if he could really consume me.

"Leave." Simon assumed his inky black immaterial form and flew to perch on the stair rail. The air of menace surrounding him had me shivering, but something in his voice didn't match. He sounded...scared.

"Nope, not leaving. You didn't say, 'Simon says.'"

He snorted, but I wasn't sure if it was because he got the joke or he was just exasperated. I got that a lot, but at least he'd stopped stabbing me. My tattoos, which were connected to my demon essences, glowed and swirled as I healed. I was grateful for the mojo. It worked whenever one of my demon donors injured me, unlike most of my new powers.

"My mistress is unwell."

I opened my mouth, ready with a snarky reply, but paused. As far as I knew, Lacey's nose and the rest of her body had healed after battling Haniel and Belial at HQ, but unwell didn't just refer to physical wounds. I suspected trauma and PTSD. Everyone on the team was reeling from the double whammy of physical injury and psychological turmoil, but maybe it was worse for Lacey.

"Okay. You're protecting her." I didn't make it a question.

His talons, longer and sharper than any earth realm raven's in spite of being immaterial, clicked on the railing as he did that bird hop thing from foot to foot. I wondered if he had a material form, too, like Sam. Before the attack at HQ, we demon hunters had been schooled in demon classes. The lesser demons, tempters with limited powers granting them the ability to latch onto humans suffering an excess of one of the seven deadly sins, were allowed on earth and granted refugee status so long as they behaved. They fit neatly into categories of immaterial and corporeal we'd been told by our former boss, a powerful demon in charge of policing lesser demons on earth and who used me and other demon-possessed or attached hunters to track down rogues.

Our boss had lied.

Then, he'd disappeared, supposedly on the hunt for Archangels, aka high-ranking celestials, to form an alliance with us to capture the escaped demons and figure out how to stop Belial and Haniel once and for all.

Whatever. It was the oldest story in the book. Wise jackass mentor trains girl, me, wise jackass mentor lies to girl, and not-so-wise jackass mentor disappears just when he could do something useful. He sucked big time.

Shaking my head, I focused on Simon, who'd grown more fidgety, ruffling his smoke-like feathers and blinking rapidly. Yup. He was hiding something, but he seemed to be done attacking me. Hopefully he'd talk.

"Are you protecting her from me? From the team?"

"No."

I threw my hands up in the air. "Well, then for the love of lollipops, why did you attack me?"

He cocked his head gazed at me intently. It dawned on me then. Lacey must have sworn him to secrecy. She must have told him to keep out visitors, too. I wasn't asking the right questions. He could answer me, in a roundabout way and without breaking his word, if I figured out what to ask.

"She's not physically ill," I said, going for the low-hanging fruit. If she were, Simon would heal her. "So she's what, depressed, anxious, wallowing?"

Simon's gaze widened after the last word.

"Wallowing? Really? Why?" I asked.

He just stared at me. Right. He wasn't allowed to tell me.

"Ugh, this is ridiculous. Just go get her to open the door so we can talk. There's a lead on one of the escaped demons and time's a-wasting. I need to do something, but I won't do it without backup. I don't have Haniel anymore and, my demon and celestial powers are unreliable. I need Lacey, and I need you, too."

I hoped he'd listen. Lacey, like me, didn't do well sitting on the sidelines. If she was wallowing, getting her out to investigate would take her mind off it.

And if she wanted to spill the tea, I could listen.

Before Simon could answer, Lacey burst through the door, decked out in her combat gear—in broad daylight—stormed down the steps, and started stomping toward my car. Simon and I froze, jaws dropped, and watched her red curls fly around her head to the rhythm of her fury. When she reached my car, she jerked the door handle. Since I'd locked the car, it was an exercise in futility.

She turned her gaze on me, red-rimmed eyes full of misery and determination, and said, "Well, what are you waiting for? Let's go."

CHAPTER FIVE

We drove out of Lacey's neighborhood in silence, Simon perched on dash in front of his surly mistress. Once I got to the highway, my partner finally spoke.

"Where are we going?"

"Downtown."

"Because that's where we can follow up on our lead." She stared out the window, sniffling.

"Yeah..." I said, treading lightly. "I mean, we can go for hot chicken, too, but I figured some surveillance couldn't hurt."

She sighed. "Figured you show up sooner or later. I decided it was better to be useful with you than do bullshit paperwork at HQ until Trinity decides I'm fit for duty."

Boy, did I know the feeling. Hopefully this outing would cheer us both up.

Suburbia gave way to midtown hospitals, parks, and expensive houses, blending into high rises, hotels, and even more expensive condos and flats like the one I shared with the tech demons, streets teeming with tourists sporting cowboy hats and fanny packs, party buses with "woo hoo" girls, and music venues ranging from the hallowed ground of the Ryman to dive bar honky tonks.

As we approached 2nd Avenue, I clued Lacey in on the intel.

"Did you see the news about the explosion downtown yesterday?"

"Yeah. I wondered if it was demon related. I texted Trinity, but she's not telling me anything."

"Join the club. Anyway, aside from the whole unexplained explosion in a highly populated area that screamed demon, some people in the vicinity were acting weird, and not just a few. There were at least two dozen people standing around, engrossed in their phones."

"Filming?"

Lacey perked up. Good. "Nope," I said. "Check your email."

She fished out her smart phone and scrolled. The twins and I stayed up half the night researching after we discovered what was on the phone zombies' screens. On all their screens.

"They're playing video games," she said, incredulous. "People screaming and running away from an exploded, burning building, sirens wailing, police and paramedics flooding the area, and these fools are playing video games?"

"Plenty of fools out there, but not usually all in one place and doing the same foolish thing. And after losing more than a few hours playing it myself, I'm convinced there's demon magic behind it." I stifled a yawn and fought exhaustion, as well as the urge to crack my sore neck.

A ran a hand over my face and picked up where I left off. "We identified the game and traced it back to the company that released it. It's a new game development subsidiary of a larger company, and the subsidiary recently opened branches downtown Nashville and in Franklin." Franklin was one town over and within our jurisdiction."

Lacey grinned. "Did those offices open within the past two months?"

"Bingo," I said. "Lots of demon activity around the downtown location. Great place to set up shop. And there's been an uptick in the number of demons in the area since the game company opened shop a few weeks after the great escape from the hell realm portal."

Lacey chuckled. "You and your buddies hacked into Alexi's field reports."

"I had to," I said. "D and I neutralized a demon attack downtown yesterday. It's what caused the explosion."

"You did that?" she asked, sounding a little incredulous and a little impressed.

"Don't tell Trinity, okay?"

She snorted. "If I ratted you out, you'd return the favor. We'll keep all this on the down-low. There are probably more illegal demon operations in or near the city, but this one is our best lead right now. So how do you want to do this? Scan for red?"

A sweep of the office with demon steel was a good place to start. In addition to making great demon-fighting weapons, the knives were our go-to demon detectors. They had the benefit of detecting other paranormal creatures, too. For the most part, the other entities weren't on our radar, but it was good to know when they were around. They could be demon targets or sometimes formed alliances with rogue demons, so we kept track. Demon steel glowed red for demons, blue for celestials, green for gouls, yellow for mythical/elemental creatures, and white for vampires. The brighter the glow, the stronger the creature.

It sometimes glowed purple for me thanks to my weird mix of demon grafts and celestial blood.

"Have you been out scouting for demon signs?" I asked, trying to sound casual.

Lacey snorted. "No. Just Alexi. He's been doing the lion's share of the work since Trinity benched you and me."

More like the wolf's share, since Alexi Volkov harbored a wolf demon courtesy of his bastard Russian mob boss father. He was great in the field. Smart, powerful, and cunning, he used the demon wolf's strength and senses to fight and trap rogue demons. When he wasn't demon hunting, he made delicious, infused vodka and did what he could to boost our team's morale.

Someone needed to return the favor. He had issues—like the rest of us. Harboring a demon and working as a demon hunter did that to the best of us. The beating our team took during our last mission left him as traumatized as the rest of us. And since he was the only member of our team currently in the field, I was afraid he would break under the strain.

Another reason Lacey and I needed to be back in action.

I turned onto Commerce Street and entered the garage, swearing I'd remember where I parked. This time, I meant it.

"What else do we know?"

"My roomies are trying to hack into the company's system, but it's tight. They're frustrated. It would be funny under different circumstances. Anyway, the company's called ZenMax Media. Took some serious hacking and less-than-legal channels to find out who owns it. We traced a series of private companies to someone named Bella Gore, but we can't find out anything about her. ZenMax's CEO is supposedly some hotshot who has a finger on the pulse of gaming trends. They had their first independent launch not long ago and the game went viral. Same game the phone zombies were playing. Crystaldoom. They say it's more addictive than SweetieCrash."

I wasn't a gamer—not until last night—but even I'd heard of Sweetie-Crash. It was banned in schools and offices around the globe, but the ban hadn't curtailed the hours of screen time rabid fans devoted to it or stopped demand for new versions.

"Good strategy for mind control," Lacey said. "What kind of master demon can do that, and why? We're working under the assumption the escaped demons and celestials want war, since that's Belial's endgame, so are the demons looking to brainwash humans into fighting for their side?"

"All great questions. We're going to do some surveillance and then go undercover to find out." I pulled into a parking space, wedging my car in the tiny space between an F150 and a Hummer. Why the hell did people park their big ass cars in spaces marked "compact?"

"Is there a patron demon or tempter demon associated with addiction?" Lacey asked. It wasn't one of the traditional seven deadly sins, but it might fall under the broad category of gluttony. Or maybe lust—not the sexual kind, but lust for some pleasurable activity taken too far?

"Never heard of one, but the boss left out a lot of intel when he trained us to hunt and capture demons." Like the fact that some demon species could switch from corporeal to immaterial, like Sam, and others could teleport, like D. Make me wonder what else we didn't know.

Scary thought.

Killing the engine, I waited for Lacey, but she just sat there, maybe thinking or maybe zoning out, getting lost in whatever was making her so unhappy.

She shook her head, pulled down the visor and sighed as she looked in the mirror, wiping her eyes and trying to tame her red locks. "No use speculating until we know more. By the way, Trinity's still got Alexi on surveillance—which means we might get busted—but if you can glamour us, we should be able to give him the slip."

I respected the hell out of Trinity, the brains of our operation. Unfortunately, she was proving to be overly cautious and conservative in her approach to our demon hunting operation. Sure, our targets were bigger, badder, and more powerful, but we couldn't just hide out and keep watch. Boots-on-the-ground investigation was what this situation called for, and it was high time we got started.

"Okay," I said. "I'll try. Not sure how long I can hold it, but if I can tap into Mara-style glamour, I'll make us to look like gamer geeks. We should be able to sneak past Alexi and go undercover. We just need to make sure he doesn't catch our scent."

Lacey flinched when I mentioned Mara. Uh oh, was that the source of her misery? She and Mara had a thing going on. It started out as flirtation, but before Lacey went AWOL from the office, they'd seemed closer. Maybe they were having relationship issues? Since intimacy with a succubus could literally suck the life out of humans and demons, it was possible.

Yikes. It sucked, and not in the fun way.

I liked Lacey, and Mara had become an invaluable member of our team and a friend. If it was just the logistics of fun time without the risk of life and soul, we could work on finding a solution. The twins might know how to help.

D would know how to help, but our relationship problems and my pride were obstacles I wasn't quite ready to tackle, so I couldn't ask him.

Putting the issue aside, I closed my eyes and focused on the appearance I wanted to project—young and trendy gamer girls. The magic flowed from me and filled the car. Simon squawked, breaking my concentration.

"Will you shut up?" I said through gritted teeth.

"Fine, but you both look weird. Maybe you should stick with chihuahuas."

Snarky demon.

I glanced in the mirror and squeaked. Yeah, the reflection staring back at me was odd bordering on alien. Lacey didn't look much better, but at least her features were in the right proportions, if not all in the right places. Damn it, I needed to get better at this.

After a few more attempts, Lacey looked great. Slight alterations to the appearance of her bone structure, height, and clothing along with changing her red hair to blond made her unrecognizable.

I looked...almost human. A little too Anime on the features, but we were infiltrating a gaming company. It should work.

"I took the liberty of submitting a job application for Jinx under a pseudonym." Simon's voice emerged from Lacey's phone where he spent most of his time in the field. He was fantastic on the web, and the Internet fascinated him. I was pretty sure he'd explored every nook, cranny, and dark corner. "Anita Dickenme has an interview tomorrow at 11:30 am for the position of game tester."

I scowled at the phone containing the little jerk of a mammon. Lacey coughed to cover her laugh. It was nice to hear her laugh. She could use a haunting from the ghost of her old self. Too bad it was at my expense.

"Anita Dickenme? Really?" You'd think after spending so much time online Simon could come up with a normal name.

"A chihuahua? Really?" He answered. Jeez, how long was he going to hold a grudge? And it was his fault. "I found it on a name generator site. It was the best option."

"Fine," I said. "Let's check out the building for demon signs and see who's going in and out."

We walked past the front of the office, which smelled of demon, though only faintly. Maybe they were using a concealment spell, or the powerful demon or demons in charge could be off site. Lacey stepped inside, pretending to be a lost tourist looking for directions so Simon could scope out the corporate office-scape. It wouldn't do for me to waltz in the day before my job interview. I decided to keep my current disguise since it was easy to hold, weird as I looked.

There was a bar next door. I went inside, ordered a margarita, and pulled my knife out to surreptitiously check for demon signs along the wall the bar shared with the office.

No red, but I caught a brilliant flash of blue and growled.

Celestial.

There was a celestial here, one who might be interested in fighting demons without worrying about "trivial matters" like human collateral damage. Or worse, feeding off the misery of the survivors.

Not on my watch.

Besides, I had a bone to pick with the celestials.

The bar was mostly empty of patrons. Who was the so-called angel in disguise?

Not the bartender, and not the old man in overalls and a trucker's cap sitting at the bar. I'd been well away from the bar when my knife started glowing. Not the family sitting in a corner booth loudly planning their itinerary for the rest of the day. That left a middle-aged man nursing a beer at a table near the front, and the young co-ed with an expensive hair- cut, decked out in a mini-dress, cowgirl boots, and a giant diamond on her right ring finger, standing by the window.

The co-ed caught my eye and smiled, lifting her glass filled with amber liquid before she beckoned me over.

Bingo.

Seemed I'd been made, too.

I approached her with caution, glad I'd added six inches of height to my glamoured appearance. At five foot nothing, people, demons, and other non-human entities towered over me and often used their height as a weapon. I used it to my advantage, too. Being underestimated had won me more than a few fights. It had also made me scrappy.

But for this encounter, I was happy to be at eye level with the celestial.

"So," she said, her voice smoke and honey. "What's a bad girl like you doing in a place like this?"

"Same as you, I suspect" I answered, sipping my drink. She was hot, or at least the form she chose was hot. I'd been studying up on celestials since I found out I was half celestial, and I learned they could alter their appearance to blend in with humanity as well as demons could using the same form of glamour. Rumor had it some were even better than succubi and incubi. It should have made glamour easier for me. Then again, I'd only had a few months to practice.

Maybe the co-ed could give me some tips.

She smiled, showing off perfectly straight, bright white teeth. "Well, maybe we can help each other out. We didn't get a chance to finish our last conversation, but we can't talk here."

"Last conversation?" I'd only ever met one celestial, as far as I knew, and that one had looked like an old hippy grandma.

Wait a minute...

Before I could blink, the bar and everything around us disappeared.

CHAPTER SIX

My head spun and I would have fallen on my ass if the celestial hadn't caught me. We were surrounded by a haze of mist and unnatural quiet. While I couldn't see more than a few feet in front of me, there was enough light to show me the celestial Cassie, looking much as I'd last seen her in the guise of a friendly grandma serving fresh baked brownies.

She was glowing. Show off. I almost asked where she'd left her wings.

My glamour had apparently disappeared since I had to look up at her. Bummer. I'd have to spend more mental and metaphysical energy rebuilding it, assuming she took me back to the bar.

"Where are we?" I asked, striving for casual boredom. My racing heart and rapid breathing probably gave me away.

"Nowhere, or rather, in between," Cassie said, smiling.

I snorted. "Cryptic much? What does that even mean?"

"It means we are neither in your world, the demon realm, or mine, but in the space between. More importantly, we are in a place where we may speak frankly and freely without being overheard."

I suspected she wasn't worried about being overheard by humans, but...

"Overheard by demons, or by your angel buddies?"

Her smile widened. "You're cleverer than I gave you credit for, Jane McGee. Stopping Haniel and Belial's invasion of earth was no small feat. And you survived, which was even more surprising. I see you've gone through a few...changes."

She looked me up and down, ogling the tattoos that marked my demon grafts as they shimmered in blue, red, and for some reason unknown to me, gold. Her lack of disapproval surprised me. In fact, she seemed pleased.

I shrugged. "It wasn't just me. My team of *demons* and *humans* stopped the invasion. I would have died if the demons on my team didn't give me these grafts. The only celestials around weren't exactly useful. Where were *you*?"

Aside from Haniel, my boss Samael, aka the Angel of Death, was the only celestial who bothered to help, and he played for both sides as far as I'd been able to work out. Boice and Roice were staunchly anti-celestial, blaming the angels for tarnishing the image of demon-realm entities in human myths and histories. They claimed celestials were arrogant snobs who thought themselves above sentient creatures from other realms.

So far, I'd seen little to prove them wrong.

"Some of my fellow celestials don't care what goes on in your realm. As far as they're concerned, demon hunters like you are responsible for cleaning up the mess on earth by capturing the demons who escaped. Others are working behind the scenes to negotiate for peace."

"Like you?" I couldn't hide my disdain. Humans and demons on my team were working on the front lines risking life, limb, and soul while cowardly celestials refused to get their angelic hands dirty. "Not as much risk working behind the scenes, and there's plausible deniability. You can switch loyalties like you switch your glamour."

Cassie shook her head. "I'm part of a faction dedicated to a more... active approach, like you."

Anger welled within me, along with the power that was part of my celestial heritage. Normally, it gave me a bubbly sensation like it had when I fought the dragon demon. This time, anger turned bubbles to boiling lava, threatening to crack through my façade of calm.

"I am *nothing* like you." My voice was low and guttural. It echoed through this so-called space between and had the mist scattering in its wake. "I'm out here busting my ass to stop this war with my team. We're battered and emotionally shattered, but we're still fighting. What the hell are you and your kind doing?"

Suddenly, the space transformed from blank and foggy to something more familiar. We were in my backyard, or rather, the backyard of my childhood home, complete with the rickety, rusty old swing set covering a dingy sand pit. My mom still lived there, but the landscaping had changed from barely above the poverty line drab to chic cottage core.

"Nice illusion," I said to Cassie, who'd traded the friendly grandma smile for a decidedly sterner elder stateswoman look.

"It's not an illusion. This is your past. You need to understand how all this started. I risked more than you know to retrieve this information and even more by sharing it with you."

Before I could come up with another snarky remark, I spotted a tall man with olive skin, dark hair, and handsome features coming around the corner of the house. Gulping, I watched as the man I barely remembered called for me. My five-year-old self ran outside in a tiny jumper, lopsided pigtails bouncing as she started skipping. She was smiling. She looked happy.

I looked happy.

This was before, then. Before I became possessed by Haniel, who I thought was a demon, one who'd chosen me because I was a bad child, the spawn of evil.

This was when my life had been normal.

I did not want to see this, but I couldn't look away. I was standing in the middle of it, like a director or camera woman, somehow able to pan in and out as the vision dictated. A shiver ran down my spine as an unnatural cold filled my soul instead of the red-hot rage I expected.

My rage and hatred were cold and bitter.

I hated my father, a celestial who'd duped my mom into marrying him and who'd left after she bore him two daughters, but not before giving me the curse of my demon/archangel in disguise. *He* was bad, the spawn of evil, not me. If I ever found him, I'd stab him through the heart with my demon blade, cut off his head, and present it to my mom, showing her I'd avenged us for his sins.

He didn't look evil now, though. He looked...sad.

"No," I said. "Whatever this is, stop it. I'm not interested in any trips down memory lane."

Cassie looked at me with sympathy and tenderness that I didn't trust. "You need to see this. It's time you learned the truth."

The man, my father, lifted this tiny version of me into his arms and spun her around as she giggled and squealed. He smiled at her...at me, with what looked like love. I didn't want to believe it, didn't want to be standing in the presence of the celestial creature who'd conjured this image as she fed on my misery. It's what angels did, or so I'd been told. I'd seen nothing yet to convince me otherwise, and my misery was what had allowed me to trick Haniel into dropping her guard during the battle at HQ. When I was dying, I let my misery out, let it call to her, and she'd answered the call before I sent her back through the portal to hell along with Belial.

I wasn't going to feed Cassie.

Looking away from the scene, which paused like a movie, I met Cassie's gaze and tapped into my celestial power. Fueled by anger, it answered my call and did...something to Cassie.

Cassie flinched, then looked away. "It isn't what you think. Our nature is to relieve the suffering of others." Before I could call bullshit, she said, "But I shall respect your wishes and your boundaries."

I stared, unsure what to believe. I didn't sense her power, so I assumed she had, in fact, backed off. Very un-celestial like behavior, but my sources were more than a little biased. According to my roommates, celestials were masters of propaganda, painting themselves as divine and benevolent in human myth and legend while literally demonizing species from the hell realm.

Then again, demons could have their own propaganda, and they had their own biases. And I had my own prejudices

I nodded, as close to a thank you as I could muster and looked back at the frozen scene of me in my father's arms, carefree, happy, and normal.

Cassie did some celestial version of unpausing, and my father stopped spinning me, hugged me close, and dropped to the ground so I landed in his lap. I wriggled and protested, but he placed a long, elegant finger over my lips to shush me.

"They're watching," He whispered in child-me's ear, but I could hear clearly in this time and place. Celestial visions had good sound quality. "And listening."

"Who's watchin', Daddy?" I whispered back. I didn't turn my head, but my gaze darted around.

"You can't see them. Not yet. But they're out there. We have to be quiet."

He bounced child-me on his knee while he spoke, still smiling, presumably acting "normal" for whoever was watching. Child-me giggled. It was a good distraction. Five-year-olds had the attention spans of gnats. Child-me stopped looking for unseen voyeurs and focused on having fun.

"I have two gifts for you, but you can't tell anyone about them."

Child-me stopped giggling and looked up at our father, dark brown eyes like his wide and excited. "Presents?"

"Yes." He'd turned child-me around and propped her butt on his raised knees, so her head was above his. A pang shot through my heart, and I had to steady myself. I'd forgotten about that—the way he used to hold me. The celestial vision triggered the memory.

Propaganda or no propaganda, celestials were cruel.

"When do I get them?" child-me asked.

He gave child-me a mock stern look. "When you swear to me you'll never tell anyone. Not your mother, not your sister, not anyone. Understand?"

Child-me nodded with maniacal enthusiasm and held out her hand, pinky up. "I pinky promise, Daddy. Mama said I not supposed to swear."

He entwined his pinky finger with the child's and did...something. Child-me froze and went wide eyed. I wanted to rip her off the bastard's lap and take her far away to safety. His gaze held hers, but something stirred within. Red sparks swirled and danced in the depths of his dark eyes. He pulled child-me closer until her forehead touched his. Child-me seemed immobile other than her eyes, so like his, which rolled and blinked frantically with terror.

The red sparks disappeared from my father's eyes just before they appeared in the child's gaze.

In mine.

This was when he'd given me Haniel, and the beginning of what would become the destruction of my childhood.

My evil bastard of a father released child-me and placed his hand on her head, muttering something in an unfamiliar language. Not of the earth realm, and not demon, which left celestial. Did Cassie understand it? I wouldn't ask. My back was turned away from her and I used every ounce of my self-control to stop my body from trembling.

I couldn't stop the tears running down my cheeks.

Child-me shook her head and looked up at our father, confused, but no longer terrified. He must have used celestial magic to make her—me—forget. He smiled at child-me, lips trembling, and child-me smiled back. "What about my present, Daddy?"

"I gave you the first," he said, hugging child me close. "Here's the second."

He slipped a tiny ring on the child me's finger. The metal circle caught the light in a few places, but others were dull and tarnished. On it was mounted the figure of a man with a long beard who wore a crown of a what looked like several pairs of bulls' horns. Battered as it was, child me clutched it to her heart as if it was the most valuable treasure in the world.

It had been my most valuable possession for years, at least until child-me realized Daddy wasn't coming back.

I'd stopped wearing the ring after I realized I was demon possessed. I didn't deserve to wear such a treasure, foul and evil as I was. It sat in a box hidden away in a safe at my downtown apartment, resting next to the picture of the man who'd abandoned me.

I held back a scream, knowing if I unleashed my rage, it could destroy the world.

My father spoke again. "Someday, when the time is right, you'll remember this: demons are red, angels are blue, and prophets wear green when they speak to you. This ring," he said after swallowing hard. "It will help you when you need it most. Don't lose it."

The illusion faded. Cassie spoke from behind me.

"I'll leave you now. You may use this space for respite. Take as long as you need. When you are ready, say *reditus*, and you will appear as you were in the bar. There is more you need to know, and more I need from you."

I rounded on her, power blazing from deep within the core of my being and attacked.

CHAPTER SEVEN

Cassie recoiled, then produced a shimmering shield, deflecting the phantom spear I didn't remember conjuring, let alone throwing at her. I collapsed, falling on my butt in the sea of nothingness made by a so-called angel who was worse than any demon I'd yet encountered, including Mephisto, Barbatos the Traitor, my Demon Boss, and Belial.

She didn't drop the shield, but her voice was gentle when she spoke. "What I need from you is an alliance. I want in."

I snorted, but she kept making her case, "You and your team need my help to defeat the escaped demons and Belial. And you need me to negotiate peace between humans and celestials. I will train you in your celestial powers, share information, and assist as and when I can. You still have the ring?"

I nodded, unable to speak. Just as well since Cassie wasn't done talking.

"I do not know what it is for or what it does—yet—but the ring must be important if your father left it with you. As for the rest...prophets were sacred and revered in the early days of humanity, guides for both humans and celestials in our quest for survival. Be on the lookout for your prophet."

Jeez, I was so sick of this shit. "I'm sure he'll be super useful, since prophets are known for being straightforward and not at all cryptic." Yeah. I was bitter.

"It's more than we—you—had to go on before. And you will be privy to any other information I gather."

Surprisingly, I believed her. I didn't trust her motivations and I knew she had her own agenda, but the intel was good if not entirely interpretable. Yet. I wouldn't be waiting on any prophets, but I was damned sure going to find out what dear old dad's ring did.

I turned and met her gaze. "Fine. I'll do you the same courtesy on one condition. I want you to help me find my father."

She paled and took a step back.

In a flash, I was on my feet and holding another spear. "You know where he is, don't you?" She did, and she was going to tell me so I could find him and kill him.

"I only know where he was, not where he is now, and I wouldn't tell you now even if I did know. But if we form an alliance, I'll help you," she said, holding up a hand to stop me from interrupting. "If and only if you promise not to kill him, assuming he can be killed."

Fat chance. I'd find a way to kill him. By all that was sacred and profane, I *would* find a way. "Why can't I kill the celestial bastard who sired me? And why are you so keen on working with me and my team, anyway. Celestials haven't exactly been involved in earthly matters for the past few millennia near as I can tell."

Cassie sighed. "I'll help you because we want the same thing, Jane. Peace on earth and an end to the brewing war between my world and the demon world. You are the key. And we need your father to tell us why he freed Haniel and hid her inside of you. It is the key to discovering how you will defeat Belial and Haniel to restore peace to the three realms, as was foretold."

I laughed. "Oh, you got the memo, too? I hope whatever cryptic angel book you got your prophecy from makes more fucking sense than the demon version. The one I heard doesn't mention my deadbeat dad." I felt a little more like myself, hence the snark, but there was a huge crack in my armor I'd need to repair after I processed all I'd learned today.

Cassie lowered her shield enough to meet my gaze, taking her time. Smart celestial. I was half-tempted to plunge my phantom spear through her eye, but she wasn't the proper target.

I didn't make a habit of shooting the messenger.

No matter the pain she'd caused me with that unwanted trip down memory lane, it was the memory and the awful truth I needed, even if it left a raw, gaping wound in my soul. Cassie wasn't my friend, but she wasn't my enemy, either.

The real enemy was my father. Always had been, especially since I now knew he was somehow involved in this current mess—escaped master demons and celestials on earth and preparing for war.

I took a deep breath and willed the spear to go away. I wasn't sure where it went, but it probably involved metaphysics and physics well above my paygrade.

And my math skills.

Cassie lowered her shield and stood up straight. "My source is probably even less clear than yours, but you are the warrior. You must succeed, and I must help you, or everything and everyone I hold dear will be destroyed."

I stifled a giggle. Cassie frowned. "Sorry," I said, not meaning it at all. "You must not spend a lot of time on earth. Nobody talks like that anymore. Maybe I should teach you how to blend in better."

Instead of getting annoyed, Cassie simply nodded, as if we were having a perfectly normal conversation rather than me throwing shade on her communication skills. I'd have to add understanding sarcasm to my list of things to teach the angel, assuming I decided to work with her.

Who was I kidding? I was totally going to work with her because she could find my dad.

She knew it, too. But I still didn't know what not-so-dear old dad had to do with my role as the warrior destined to stop a war between the hell, celestial, and earth realms or some shit.

As if reading my mind, Cassie said, "Your father kept Haniel imprisoned for millennia. Then, for reasons known only to him, he pulled her out of her celestial prison cell, imprisoned her within himself, and came to earth—"

"So he could what? Seduce my poor mom, sire me and my sister, and put Haniel in me? That makes no sense. I was five, and powerless. And why did he choose me and not Megan?"

I wouldn't wish my fate on anyone, especially my sister, but it was a fair question. She was the eldest, the proverbial heir, and I was the spare. So why me?

Wasn't that always the question...

Cassie scowled. "It's rude to interrupt, but you are correct. Nothing about his actions makes any sense, but they triggered the events leading to Haniel's escape—not to mention the escape of those demons you're chasing—and her reunion with Belial to restart their rebellion.. We need to know why your father suddenly left with Haniel. We need to know if he was acting alone or one someone else's orders, or who he was running from."

Okay. That made more sense. I'd get the information out of him—maybe even let D take a crack at him using some brutal demon realm interrogation skills—and then I'd kill him. Or maybe I'd let mom kill him. We could kill him together as a mother-daughter bonding thing, and I'd even let Megan join in. It was a messed-up thought, but it suited the situation perfectly.

Of course, I'd have to be on better terms with D before I could get him to interrogate dear old dad. And I'd have to wait until Cassie found father dearest. Yet another problem I had to solve while being warrior extraordinaire and tracking escaped demons, training to get a handle on my new powers, fixing my broken teammates and team leader, and mending fences with my mom and sister.

Man, what a long to-do list.

Getting back on track, I said, "It's a reasonable line of investigation. Assuming I form an alliance with you, a temporary one with very specific terms, what do you want from me?"

Before she could interrupt, I held up a hand, "Maybe you don't want war, but you want something else. If there's one thing I've learned from The Arbiter, aka my former boss, celestials aren't all that different from demons in terms of paying the piper."

She glowered at me. Oh, had I hit a nerve? I'd have to remember for future encounters.

At last, she sighed and sent her shield to wherever angels stored their celestial weapons. "I need the Sigillum Dei. It's important."

What. The. Actual. Hell.

The Sigillum Dei, a powerful artefact granting the wielder power over all creatures except Archangels but could summon Archangels and could send any demon or celestial back to their own realm permanently? *That* was what Cassie wanted. Because she could totally be trusted with so much power?

Not going to happen.

I lifted my middle finger, said *reditus*, and disappeared from the space between.

CHAPTER EIGHT

Apparently time worked differently in the space between since everything the bar was the same as when I'd left it—minus Cassie—and no more than five minutes had passed according to my phone. A quick look in the mirror behind the bar showed me my glamour was back in pace, too. I slapped a twenty on the table, making the assumption Cassie hadn't paid her tab, and stepped outside to wait for my partner.

Lacey and Simon emerged from her reconnaissance mission about thirty minutes later with a layout of the building and details on the demons who appeared to be managing it, all low-level tempters representing a variety of sins. No sign of any powerful demons. Crap. The big baddie who was really in charge wouldn't be so easy to find, but I couldn't help the pang of disappointment stabbing at my gut.

Which was better than the pang of sorrow lodged in my heart.

With nothing else to do, I offered to take Lacey for lunch. She shook her head, which was weird. We always hit a drive through after stakeouts and surveillance missions. Her refusal was more telling than her surly attitude.

"Just take me back home. We'll regroup tomorrow before you go undercover for your interview," she said once we were in the car and had traded the maze of downtown streets and midtown businesses for the beginning of the suburbs.

"Okay, what gives?" I said, pulling off the road and into the parking lot of a strip mall that just happened to have one of the best hot chicken joints in the city.

Lacey turned to me and glowered. "What's it to you?"

Oh, for the love of lollipops... "What's it to me? I'm only your partner and your best friend. That not enough?"

We stared at one another, but she dropped her gaze first.

"Look," I said. "While you were checking out the demon gaming office, I got zapped to the space between—don't ask what that is because I don't totally understand—by a celestial who showed me the worst day of my life. It did a number on my head, and I'd like to talk about it. I'd like you to talk about whatever's eating you, too. I'll even go first. And..." I added, going in for the kill, "I'll throw in a ginormous bowl of banana pudding."

Our favorite chicken joint had the best desserts, and Lacey had a sweet tooth big enough to attract a glutton demon had Simon the greed demon not already called dibs on her.

Lacey fiddled with the hem of her shirt and muttered something.

"What was that?"

"I said I want peach cobbler, too. And I want dirty bird fries and mac and cheese."

Damn, with so much sugar and carbs, whatever was going on with her, had to be bad.

"Deal."

I shared all my recent trauma over damn hot chicken, fried to perfection and paired with potato salad, baked beans, and extra pickles. To her credit, Lacey listened intently, offered sympathy, and, even better, offered to pull out my father's toenails with pliers when we found him.

She really was a great friend.

Then I told her about Cassie's request for the Sigillum Dei.

"Hmm," she said between bites of fries. "Sounds like the celestials want their toy back. Probably afraid you'll give it to the demons." Thank goodness we'd entrusted the Sigillum Dei to Trinity and her demon companion Sam, who'd used their encyclopedic knowledge of demon concealment magic—and more than a little know-how with cutting edge tech—to safeguard the artefact. No one else on the team knew where it was, so there was no way Cassie could get it from me.

I nodded, licking the grease off my fingers like a barbarian, but seriously, you did *not* waste hot sauce this good. "Tempting, but I don't think any good can come of anyone using the Sigillum Dei. If I knew how to destroy it, I'd have done the moment it landed in my cold, dead hands."

Lacey rolled her eyes. "You didn't actually die. If you had, you wouldn't be here stuffing your face right now thanks to demon grafts because they don't bring back the dead. And anyway, we need to artefact to send all these freakin' demons and celestials back where they belong."

"Technicality." I sopped up extra hot sauce and chicken drippings with a slice of bread. "The point is, we need to be on the lookout for other celestials snooping around for it, not to mention celestials who actually want a war with Belial and his demons. I'll bet the city is crawling with them."

Lacey shrugged. "Not our department, but you're right. I take it you're going to work with the angel?"

"Yeah, but I'm going to run it by Trinity first. No secrets," I said, staring pointedly at Lacey. "That was how the boss—the old one—did things and it got us into this mess."

Lacey smirked. "Okay, no secrets except sneaking out to do fieldwork."

I arched an eyebrow and waited for Lacey to finish her bite of dessert number one before inviting her to talk.

"Fine," she said. "It's Mara. No, scratch that. Mara is who and what she is. It's me. I'm the problem, and I don't know how to not be the problem."

I snorted and helped myself to a giant spoonful of dessert number two. "Well, that explains everything. Not. I double dog dare you to start making sense."

Lacey pulled the dessert plates out of my reach and smacked my hand with her spoon. Totally uncalled for. I'd have to report her to HR for inappropriate field behavior.

"Point taken." She arranged our stack of lunch plates with meticulous precision, probably so she could gather her thoughts into something coherent. I got it. Relationships were a bitch to navigate. Relationships with demons of seduction had to be even more trying.

At last, she spoke. "Mara has to feed. She can't feed on me without permanent damage to my soul since I'm only human. So, she has to hunt skeevy people and...do things with them before she feeds on them. I mean, she's a succubus, so I get it. She can't help it. It's what she has to do."

Oh, wow, put it like that, and I could see the problem. Succubi used their powers of seduction to feed on their prey. Since my team had first encountered her in Nashville, hungry, miserable, and on the run from more powerful demons in the hell realm, we'd offered her conditional sanctuary. She had to feed on the life energy of entities in the earth realm —the vast majority being human—but we made her promise to only feed on depraved individuals who harmed others but evaded justice.

Then, she'd been used by one of Belial's minions in a failed ambush and capture attempt on yours truly. It was how the succubus had come under the protection of our demon hunting team.

When she'd helped us turn the tables and kill the minion who'd used her against her will, she'd cemented her place on our team. I considered her a friend. She and Lacey had become more.

Lacey was young and reasonably progressive. Though I didn't make it a point to pry too deep into her sex life, I didn't think sharing her lover with other people—especially the worst of the worst humanity had to offer—would be bearable, probably like being in love with a sex worker. Sex work was real work, but it could be tough on a relationship. It would take a strong, patient, not-at-all-jealous, trusting, and secure person to not only tolerate it, but to accept it and still be happy.

"But you don't like it," I said. "You don't like sharing Mara?"

"No, that's not the problem," she said, waving her hand in dismissal. "It's not the seduction and feeding part. I get it. It's not personal. It's dinner."

Okay, now I was really confused. "If the idea of sharing Mara doesn't bother you, then I don't get it. What's the problem?"

Lacey put her head in her hands and rubbed her eyes. "She has to be around horrible people all the time. I'm the only nice person she'd ever spent time with, other than you and the rest of the team."

"That's a good thing," I said, my voice gentle. "You're really good for her, and aside from whatever's going on between you two, she's good for you, too."

Slamming her hands on the table, her fiery gaze met mine. "That's the problem. She's so used to being treated like shit, she put me on a holy pedestal and she's basically worshipping me. It's not right."

Oh, holy wow, had I ever gotten it wrong.

I could've kicked myself. Lacey Green was many things, but petty and jealous weren't part of her makeup. She defied explanation and expectations. It was why she was so good at her work, and why I liked her so much. Mara's need to feed wouldn't bother her. But the whole pedestal thing? Different matter entirely.

I could see it. Whenever I ran into Mara, she was always so ingratiating and grateful, and being what she was, she could anticipate what I wanted and needed—what anyone wanted and needed—and become that thing. She was an ear to bend, always first to pick up the duties none of the rest of us wanted around HQ, serving us food and drink and dazzling us with her presence and essence.

Did she do it out of obligation? What if she thought we wouldn't like her if she didn't serve us?

Something else could be bugging Lacey, too. Like me, she always wondered what she'd done to attract her demon. She struggled with the idea she was somehow bad, tainted, and corrupt, and so she deserved to be in the world of demons. She had the same ugly voice in the back of her mind that I had. I told us we were where we belonged.

Because we were evil.

No. No more. We were done. I called bullshit on that stupid, self-loathing notion.

The celestial power I'd learned to recognize and sometimes tap into welled within me, fueled once more by anger. Lacey wasn't evil. Had she made mistakes? Sure. She was human. But did the fact she'd been targeted by a greed demon and thrust into the world of demon hunting make her evil?

Hell. No.

Lacey had dropped her head back in her hands. I wasn't having it. I channeled the celestial power within me, taking it down a few notches this time, and spoke.

"Look at me." My voice held a strange timbre. It made Lacey jerk her head up and take notice.

Well, now, wasn't that interesting?

Not that I'd ever abuse my power to get my partner to follow orders, because that would be wrong.

I put a pin in the thought and focused on the task at hand. "You are *not* evil. You deserve happiness. You are worthy of happiness, and you are worthy of Mara."

She let out a shaky laugh. "Since when did you start quoting cheesy motivational posters?"

"Stop deflecting," I said. "You are worthy. You deserve happiness with Mara. And you know what? I'm going to keep saying it until you stop and really think about it. Because eventually, you will believe me."

"It doesn't work like that," she said. "I think...I think I might need therapy."

It was my turn to laugh. "Duh. You do. I do. We all do. And Trinity's got someone lined up to work with us. Someone in the community," I said, meaning demon-hunting-in-the-know-about-the-supernatural-world community. "You'd know that if you showed up for meetings."

I had more than a few issues with Trinity's leadership, especially her conservative, overly cautious approach to investigations, but the decision to bring a counselor on board was necessary and a brilliant leadership move on her part. I'd had one session with the former demon hunter turned psychologist. She'd impressed me with her bearing, knowledge, and overall peaceful vibe, and had taught me a few tricks to deal with panic attacks.

I was due another session, but Lacey could take my spot. My partner needed more immediate help to save her relationship with Mara.

I pulled out my phone and texted Lacey Dr. Khatri's contact information.

"You should have Mara go, too. Maybe if she starts to believe we'll like her even if she stops acting like a servant, it will help your relationship, too. I know it will make her more effective in the field."

I contemplated getting another order of desserts. Amateur psychology and celestial bullshit always made me want to stuff my face. It was better than drinking or drugs.

Lacey narrowed her gaze and said, "When are *you* going to talk to her?"

I put on my best look of superiority and said, "Already did one session. As soon as I can squeeze in an appointment between training sessions, I'll go work on my daddy issues. And mommy issues, too."

"Uh huh," she said. "Just don't forget to work on your Demoriel issues."

Ugh, she had to go and bring that up. I still wasn't quite ready to deal with D, but my heart ached for him. We'd lost ten years already, and if one of us didn't cave to reach out to the other, we might lose even more precious time.

I might lose him forever, and I didn't think my poor, battered soul could bear it.

"Don't worry," I said, firing off the text message I'd avoided sending for too long. "I'll work on my Demoriel issues with Demoriel."

Just two simple words, but they were all I could muster.

Let's talk.

CHAPTER NINE

I arrived at HQ bright and early to check on our newest recruit who also happened to be my sister. Had to check on her. I wasn't avoiding the ass-whooping waiting for me in the gym, I was being a good sister. Really.

Since discovering what I did for a living and her own celestial powers, she decided to come work with the team. I didn't find her in the gym or hanging around the staff lounge. Instead, I found her in a spare office, staring at a computer screen with a slack jawed expression that could only mean one thing.

Mandatory online training.

I shuddered, remembering my first mandatory online training and stood behind Megan's chair while one of a bazillion video modules loaded. Poor Meg. I doubted she was prepared for hours of mind-numbing—not to mention ass-numbing—boredom. Or maybe not. I'd been a field agent for ten years and had encountered each and every species, variety, and manifestation of tempter demon a dozen times over.

This was all new to Megan.

I sat down next to my sister and twirled in my chair, wishing Lacey or my roomies were around for an office chair race. Megan wouldn't do it, the goody two shoes, even though she'd still be able to hear the video. I was sure there was some psychological study out there that proved rolling chair races improved memory and retention. Trinity should really look into it. I'd bring it up in our next staff meeting.

"Could you not," Megan said. "I'm supposed to finish this online training today and you're distracting me." She didn't bother to say hello. I got that a lot.

I spun around again. "I think we need to combine office chair races with mandatory online training, and I need some scientific studies to back up my argument."

Megan sighed and hit "play," making the screen come alive with cartoon demons explaining the ins and outs of their species. "The only thing that needs scientific study is you. Did you skip your meds today?"

Wow, looked like someone was a Grumpasaurus rex today. I expected that level of smack talk from Lacey, but from Megan? Ouch.

"No. I may have mixed them, but I never skip. But seriously, why even bother with this? Everything we thought we knew about tempter demons is wrong, or at least not entirely accurate. What we really need is a course on higher demons, you know, since they've started showing up on earth and making threats and stuff."

"Don't say 'and stuff.' It makes you sound like an idiot. And definitely don't say 'and shit' either."

It was like she could read minds.

"Anyway," Megan said. "I've been put in charge of updating the training materials with all the new information we got from your last case, which means I have to review the current material. It's tedious, but at least I'll get caught up with the rest of the team."

A cartoon demon wearing a lab coat and glasses stood in front of a chalkboard—like anyone used those anymore—and pointed as letters magically scrawled the names and powers of common tempter demons. For convenience, the demon professor categorized them based on the seven deadly sins, because Catholic tradition was nothing if not precise and meticulous.

Demon Professor ran down the immaterial tempters, Maces, Levis, and Belphs, which covered wrath, envy, and sloth, respectively.

According to what we now knew was outdated or incorrect information, these demons couldn't assume a corporeal form and relied on possession of the physical body and/or the mind of the target to lead said target down the path of self-destruction while getting a tasty soul meal in the bargain.

The video droned on with the lecture, moving on to corporeal and immaterial demon classes. "Corporeal demons cannot become immaterial or possess their victims and must rely on persuasion and cunning. They often work in concert with immaterial demons with complimentary agendas and compatible sins. Thought to have been created by demon lords at the dawn of humanity's rise, tempter demons provided a gateway to the earth realm to promote infiltration and eventual conquest. Celestial beings unleashed their own creations, the so-called virtues, to counteract tempters, though modern humans largely fight the effects of the seven deadly sins by other means, including science, medicine, religion, New Age mysticism..."

We'd found out the hard way that several demons could be both corporeal and immaterial, switching forms as easily as donning glamour.

The rest of the information was still accurate. Succubi and incubi were lust incarnate, shapeshifting into whatever the target most desired and tended to work well with fellow corporeal demons of gluttony, Beezelbubs—Bubs or Bubbas for short. Nothing paired better than food and sex. Mammons of greed and Egos of pride rounded out the list.

I stopped listening and pondered the lack of virtues in our operation —literal and metaphysical. Our former boss had balked at the notion of working with so-called angels who represented virtues that corresponded to the vices embodied by demons, at least based on celestial propaganda. But why? In light of the brewing war between realms, having more intel on beings from the celestial realm would come in handy.

Maybe Cassie could help.

There had to be a connection between celestials and demons, just as there was a connection between virtue and sin. I didn't think it was as simple as one being the polar opposite of the other. Sentient beings were too complex. But there was...something.

Yet another mystery to be solved.

"Well," I said, getting up and pushing my chair back to its proper location. "I'll leave you to it."

"Gee, thanks," Megan said. "What's your plan for today?"

"Don't be too jealous," I said, resigned to my fate. "I've got my own mandatory training session to complete, and mine leaves bruises."

The wolf grabbed me from behind, his jaws snapping at my exposed neck. Luckily, he only came away with a scrap of T-shirt.

Unfortunately, it was my favorite T-shirt. The top line read, "Relationship Status," and below were a series of boxes labeled, "Single, Taken, Waiting for a Demon in a Trench Coat." The last box showed a horned demon with an open trench coat sporting a pair of heart-covered boxer-briefs to cover his naughty bits.

He'd bitten the demon right in his underwear. Super rude.

I spun around, landed a kick in the beast's stomach, and growled right back at him. "That's for my T-shirt."

Red sparks danced in the wolf's golden eyes. Uh oh. Not good. The wolf demon was in the driver's seat. The man who was supposedly in charge of his canine demon had gone bye-bye. It made no sense. I hadn't hit Alexi that hard. The wolf demon-possessed Russian giant was the gentlest soul I'd ever encountered and always maintained control of his beast. In fact, our training sessions together had been fun, playful, and almost relaxing until now.

It dawned on me, then. All this time, Alexi had been going easy on me. He wasn't anymore.

Scratch that. His wolf demon wasn't going easy on me.

Either the stress of too much fieldwork was getting to him, or his wolf demon had had enough. Crap. I was so going to get a beating.

A giant paw with sharp claws slashed at me. I didn't dodge quite fast enough and got four scrapes across my flank for slowness. But I ducked low and swiped at the wolf's legs, knocking him onto his back. Good thing he'd been on his hind legs instead of four feet. The beast was so much stronger than I was, at least without full access and control to my new demon skills.

And he wasn't messing around.

He leapt back to his feet—all four this time—and snarled, showing me a mouth full of long, sharp teeth.

Throw me a cape and call me Red Riding Hood because I was seriously freaked out.

I had some more turkey jerky I could use as a dog treat in my pocket, but that might really piss him off. Most demons had no sense of humor, especially the animal variety.

What I needed was a plan.

One of the advantages being five foot nothing was it gave me mad gymnastic skills. I was theoretically smarter than the wolf demon. He ran on instinct and rage without Alexi in charge to balance him out. It gave me an option. Risky, but if I didn't do something soon, the wolf would wear me out.

Violating the cardinal rule of dealing with predators—never run from them—I spun on my heel and took off at a sprint across the gym. Agony flared from the gashes on my side, but I pushed through the pain. The wolf howled and gave chase. He was fast, but I had a head start and didn't have as far to run. Legs pumping, breaths controlled, I made for the wall, wolf hot on my tail.

Three, two, one...now!

I ran up the wall and executed a flip that let me land on the wolf's back with enough force to knock him over. Before he could snap his jaws, I had my demon blade at his neck. The wolf stilled but didn't slap the floor with his paw to acknowledge my victory and his surrender.

I didn't let go.

"Alexi? You in there?"

He growled, glaring at me with yellow eyes. Damn it, I did *not* want to play dominance games. I liked Alexi, but not in his current state as an angry, predatory demon wolf.

Something inside me let out a low, feral growl. The something was hungry, angry, and...territorial. She snarled and snapped at the wolf demon beneath her. He was not her master, not her alpha, and she would make certain the male wolf knew it.

I leaned down and put my fangs against the wolf demon's neck.

Fangs?

Her voice blended with mine, much as Hannah's used to when she possessed me. It was familiar and oddly comforting. I shared her intensity and resolve.

"We are not your prey. We bested you. We are alpha."

Holy guacamole. Alexi's grafts had given me a wolf demon.

No, not a real one, but my phantom fangs pierced the tough skin of his neck, drawing blood. Good blood, hot and sweet. Transparent demon wolf claws grew from my hands, making me drop the knife. My she-wolf wanted to tear into Alexi's wolf's flesh and feast on it, muscle, bone, and marrow.

Ew! Bad girl.

"You are not my alpha, she-wolf," Alexi's wolf said in a growly, feral voice. "I made you. You are part of me."

Alexi's wolf bucked and threw me off his body. I landed on four phantom feet and my wolf roared in rage. She knew, as I did, that we could not defeat Alexi's wolf. I didn't think he could defeat us, either, which left us in a bit of a pickle in terms of hierarchy.

"Alexi! Jane! Down!"

The command, delivered in a familiar, authoritative voice, made the Alexi's wolf go limp. If I hadn't been facing off with him, he probably would have rolled over. Neat trick. Trinity would have to teach me. Then again, maybe it only worked for her since, as team leader, she was his alpha.

Oh, maybe that was the issue Alexi's wolf had been experiencing as we battled.

The essence of the phantom demon wolf I carried was dominant. Duh. What else would my wolf be, especially one created by Alexi's very dominant demon wolf? But it meant Alexi's wolf was now unsure where he fell in the hierarchy and what my place was. My wolf howled and locked her gaze on Trinity's. A challenge.

Bad idea.

"Agent McGee. Get your wolf under control." Trinity snapped. Uh oh. I was in trouble.

After a few agonizing moments of mental gymnastics and negotiations, I took a deep breath and visualized my beast, just as Alexi had taught me in anticipation of my demon wolf's appearance. In my mind, I sat on a hill in the middle of a green field surrounded by forest. The sun was setting, and as shadows fell along the land, a golden wolf emerged from the trees, assuming the same flickering, ghostly form she'd manifested when we sparred with Alexi. Her transparent fur shimmered in the waning light, as did her eyes. She snapped and snarled inside my mind, and...sulked?

Why was she pouting?

Oh.

It took a while, but I got it. She'd finally come out to play after months of fighting to emerge, and now I was locking her away again.

Wait, maybe I could make this work to my advantage and solve the problem with Alexi. In my mind's eye, I approached the shadowy figure of the wolf and knelt before her in my human form, remembering to keep my head higher. Alexi had told me the key to controlling a demon wolf was to remind it who was in charge. I was the alpha in our relationship, and I decided when and where she could come out.

"She-wolf," I said, meeting her gaze. "I am your protector, your guide, and your alpha. Yield to me, and I will keep you safe."

Yellow eyes stared at me, unblinking, as the wolf snarled and showed me her teeth. In the real world, I kept my breathing even and focused on staying calm, while in my mind I kept my gaze locked with the demon wolf's. After a long moment, she dropped her gaze. I grabbed her muzzle and pushed until she lowered herself to the ground, rolled over, and gave me her belly.

"Good girl," I said in my mind. "Very good girl. I am your protector, and you are my defender. Together with the he-wolf, who is your packmate, we will defend the innocent. Trinity is my alpha, and Alexi's alpha, and your alpha. Alexi and I are...littermates. We are equals. He and his wolf will run with us and hunt, and together we will make the demons we hunt our prey. We are pack, now and forever."

I let go of the wolf in my mind's eye. She rose, ears perked and tail wagging tentatively. It was strange to see on such a terrifying beast, but I found it oddly charming. I reached out and ran my palm along her head and down to scratch her behind the ears. The she-wolf nipped at my fingers before licking them.

So. Freakin'. Cool.

I couldn't wait to go running with Alexi. Maybe Sully could join us. Holy guacamole, I had *two* pets now!

I opened my eyes and saw Alexi in his human form. He grinned at me and gave me the thumbs up. I saw a bit of the wolf still lurking in his gaze, and I let my wolf come to the surface, her gaze meeting Alexi's wolf without challenge. If I had a tail, it would be wagging.

Nah, my entire ass end would be wagging. I'd always wanted a brother.

"I'm calling her Zer," I said to Alexi. "She can't wait to play with Volk." Volk was the name of Alexi's demon wolf. It was the Russian word for "wolf." Alexi's dad, who'd named the demon wolf, wasn't very creative, but Alexi hadn't bothered renaming him.

"Zer" meant gold in my father's language. I'd learned a bit of the language when I was kid and studied it whenever I could once I started demon hunting. The language and culture were a part of his human aspect, or guise, but I embraced it. My middle eastern roots were mine by birthright as a human, and I wouldn't let my anger at my father steal that joy from me.

The celestial part still felt alien, but in time I might learn to embrace it, too.

Alexi chuckled. "Our wolves will have many adventures together. Congratulations on finding Zer."

The big Russian teddy bear beamed at me. I hadn't seen him this happy in a long time. It made sense. He wasn't so alone now that his graft had given me a wolf demon. He had a pack now. We were like family. I hoped he'd always wanted a pain in the ass but lovable little sister, since that's what he'd be getting with me.

Before I could get too caught up in the moment, Trinity's voice brought me back to reality.

"My office. Now."

"Can't I shower first?" I whined. I should probably take care of those nasty wolf claw wounds on my side, too. Since I'd come to reality, they hurt like the dickens.

Trinity gave me a death glare, magnified by her glasses. She was rocking her favorite royal blue suit today. Add in a tight bun, high heels, and her flawless dark complexion, and you had high level executive girl boss badass. Said girl boss had the power and mojo to back it up, too. And it seemed she was not best pleased with me. Par for the course.

That sucked. I figured she'd be happy with my progress.

"Okay, okay," I said, wincing as I held up my hands in surrender. "But if you don't let me pee, one of those new office chairs is going to get a golden sh—"

"Jinx!"

Ha! I got her. She wanted to laugh. I could see it through the eyeroll. Plus, she called me Jinx instead of Agent McGee. And even thought I did need to pee, for Trinity and this rare moment of laughter, I'd hold it.

CHAPTER TEN

After a long elevator ride to the lowest floor of HQ, I followed Trinity down the hall to her office, glaring at the desk outside where Barbatos, our former boss's executive assistant, used to sit. Someone had cleared it of Barbatos's personal effects, few as they were. I hoped they'd burned them along with his body.

And if his soul or essence had returned to the hell realm, I hoped it was somewhere writhing in agony.

His betrayal had gotten all of us into this mess—loose rogue demons, pissed off celestials, Haniel and Belial reunited and plotting their next move, and earth caught in the middle. As a mole in our organization, Barbatos had played the long game, biding his time and learning our secrets so he could betray us to Belial.

Yeah, he could rot in hell.

Trinity glowered at the desk before opening the door to her office. She'd taken it over after our boss went AWOL and had redecorated it to her taste, though the rows of screens that monitored portals, broadcast local and world-wide news, displayed the rise and fall of stock markets, and one that, to my utter delight, showed HGTV were still there.

HGTV was new. Trinity must be in the market to renovate or redecorate, or maybe she just liked the hot guys doing the renos.

I wasn't complaining.

How had she done it in such a short amount of time? The place had been destroyed during the disaster that let the demons out of the portal Haniel opened.

Weapons clashing, energy pouring from the portal. Blood. So much blood. My blood. Can't think. Head injury. Haniel holding me, cradling me as I bled out. Dying. I'm dying. My strength couldn't fail me. Have to close the portals, but I'm tired, so tired and fading, fading, fading...

Oh, crap. I needed to snap out of it. I didn't have as many panic attacks as I did in the beginning, but this office was a trigger. I'd nearly died here. And now I was on the floor, cradling my head in my hands and struggling to breathe.

"Jinx?" Trinity's voice was gentle, and it grated on my nerves. I didn't want pity.

"I'll be fine," I said, panting. "Just fighting PTSD. How you holding up?"

She frowned and offered me a hand so I could get my ass off the floor, but she didn't say anything. We were all in therapy or soon-to-be in therapy—fortunately, not group therapy—dealing with the trauma of our last mission while working hard to sort out the mess said mission had made. Trinity didn't talk about personal stuff to anyone except Sam and our shrink, as far as I knew. If she wasn't sharing with me, I wouldn't share with her.

I practiced my deep breathing exercises and played the five things I can see, four things I can hear, blah blah blah game to stop center myself. I'd already named the screens and Trinity's desk, so I focused on the rest of the room. The metal bookshelves were filled with our former boss's personal library along with new additions from Trinity's stash. The Great Big Book of Uselessness, a.k.a. *Compiled Grimoires of the Wicked and Wise*, sat on Trinity's desk. She and Sam had been studying it, hoping to find out more about the vague prophecy they'd discovered during our previous investigation. A large version of the prophecy hovered over the desk in enchanted glowing letters.

In the days of the great ancient war, Belial was defeated, and his allies exterminated or banished. Should the banished one, the one who has long slumbered, awaken, this Fallen of the Host of Seven is she who has the power to open the gates to the Realm of Darkness.

To defeat her, a Warrior forged in turmoil must rise and battle the Harbingers of Doom, which are Seven Sins and Seven Virtues.

The Warrior will lead seven into battle; imbued with the Power of Three Realms, they will stand against two.

Arbiter and Intercessor, in Harmony or Discord, will decide the course as they should have long ago.

With the Warrior, or against the Warrior, to stand or fall with the Steadfast or the True.

Okay, it wasn't totally useless. I was the warrior who had the power of three realms—earth, celestial thanks to dear old Dad, and demon thanks to my grafts. Those were definitely part of the forged in turmoil thing since I'd almost died getting them.

Haniel, the archangel disguised as demon who formerly possessed me, was obviously the "banished one" who'd awakened and opened the gates to the Realm of Darkness. She was also the Intercessor—all of these larger-than-life entities had at least three names and a slew of titles, probably just to confuse us mere mortals—and would either come around to the side of our former boss, a.k.a. the Arbiter a.k.a. Sameal the Angel/Demon of Death or would be against him. And they would be with or against me and the Steadfast or the True.

Ugh. I needed a flow chart. Or maybe a Venn diagram.

No point in counting on Haniel or Sameal. Fifty-fifty odds sucked, and there was no way to predict what a celestial or a demon would do. The last piece of the puzzle, however, was a bigger mystery.

I plopped down in the chair opposite Trinity, focusing on the squeaky noise the leather made as I wiggled my ass. Trinity pushed her glasses up to sit properly on her nose and stared at the prophecy. I stared, too. Panic had faded, only to be replaced by frustration. The stupid prophecy gave me a headache every time I looked at it or thought about it.

I started with my usual opening. "It says 'Steadfast or the True.' I figured it means our team, but are we the Steadfast or the True?"

Trinity shrugged. "Demons are precise in their language. Barring any translation errors, I take it to mean the Steadfast and the True are two different groups, though this is a much older form of the common demon language than I've encountered. We're still working on a more accurate translation."

"Okay, let's assume two different groups. Which is our team?" I asked.

"I have no idea." Trinity threw her hands up in the air as she spoke, clearly frustrated. "If it said 'damaged' I'd know it was our team."

She wasn't wrong. "Maybe it means we'll have an ally?"

"Or an enemy," Trinity said, pointing at the prophecy. "To stand or fall with the Steadfast or the True could be interpreted as a you—the warrior—standing or falling, either with the Steadfast or the True."

"Why does one have to be an enemy?"

Trinity sighed. "Because our track record and bad luck suggest we're going to be fighting multiple enemies on multiple fronts. We already know we're fighting demons and celestials. They're the Harbingers of Doom."

My brain hurt. I changed my mind. This prophecy was totally useless. But it made for a great segue. "Speaking of celestials, we have a potential ally and informant from their side. My old pal Cassie the friendly neighborhood angel showed up earlier today with an offer I couldn't refuse."

Trinity narrowed her gaze at me. "She showed up, huh? Was that before or after you snuck off with Agent Green for an unauthorized stakeout?"

Uh oh. Play it cool, Jinx.

"During. And before you hand me my ass, we didn't engage any demons. It was a strictly observe and report mission. It gave Lacey something to do other than mope about her love life, and it got me an in with an angel. Plus, Simon got me a way into the demon-run video game company so I can do some recon. I have a job interview tomorrow."

Trinity put her head on the desk. Thankfully, she didn't start banging it like the last time we met. "You can't go into the field until you've learned how to fight again. You aren't the same as before."

"No kidding," I said. "But I managed to glamour myself and Lacey, and I beat Sam last session and Alexi in today's training. Not completely helpless here, and I'm good for infiltrating and intel gathering. I promise I won't fight."

Trinity jerked her head up, eyes wide in disbelief. "You won't fight. You? Trouble follows you wherever you go, and fight is your middle name. No. We can't afford to lose you."

"You can't afford to keep me sidelined!" I got up from my chair and started pacing. "We have a lead, and we need to follow it. Better yet, it's here in Nashville. Who knows where the other six escaped demons have gone?"

Trinity waved her hand dismissively. "Don't worry about it. They're all here in Nashville. They can't leave. Neither can any archangels who escaped the portals."

What. The. Hell.

That was news to me. I stopped pacing and stared at her. "And when were you planning to share with the rest of the class?"

Trinity sighed. "It's strictly need-to-know, and you didn't need to know. Neither does the rest of the team. Honestly, if you weren't so annoying, I wouldn't have let it slip."

Let it slip? This was important information that defined the scope of our investigation. And what was keeping them confined to Nashville anyway? A barrier would take a lot of power to establish and maintain. No one on the team had the kind of power necessary to pull it off. We couldn't even keep the tempters from leaving the city, let alone more powerful demons. And we'd never been in charge of regulating the comings and goings of celestials, which would likely take even more power and magic.

Wait a minute...

Oh, no. She didn't, wouldn't, couldn't. I hopped up on top of the desk, earning me a death glare, loomed over Trinity, and asked in a low, menacing tone, "What did you do to keep the demons in Nashville. Trinity...did you strike a bargain with a demon?"

Her face turned to stone. It would take a wrecking ball to get anything else out of her, and I didn't have one. But she was right. I was annoying, not to mention determined, enough to channel my inner chisel and chip away at her vault of secrets.

I didn't need to. Her silence was answer enough. Our fearless new leader had made some sort of demon bargain to keep our supernatural invaders trapped in the city. That kind of magic would require a steep price. What had she bargained away to get it? I'd find out, and the team and I would do whatever it took to save Trinity from the consequences of her deal.

In the meantime, if she *wanted* to keep it a secret...

I hopped down from the desk, much to the detriment of the wounds on the side of my body, and sat back down, smoothing the wrinkles out of my pants and mourning the destruction of my T-shirt. Then I turned my most charming, brilliant smile on Trinity.

"I'll make *you* a deal. You let me go undercover—a strictly fact-finding mission—and I'll keep your secret and will do my best to avoid any and all combat until you deem me fit for duty."

I even saluted. I was so good.

Trinity stood, stomped over to me, and got in my face. She had to lean down, since I was so short and because I was seated. Too bad for her. I'd had a lifetime of experience with looming intimidation tactics. I was immune. I kept my face neutral and tried not to laugh.

"That's blackmail." Trinity said through gritted teeth. "You have no idea how precarious our position is. I'm doing everything I can to keep us hanging on to every advantage by the tiniest threads before this whole thing unravels."

Trinity was good with metaphors. I even pictured each team member hanging onto the frayed edges of a torn cloth dangling from her left hand, a cloth decorated with lots of cute little cartoon demons and angels. In my vision, she held her demon steel knife and balanced the stupid prophecy book on her head, too. Like a boss.

But her eyes were full of such sadness and despair. I wasn't the only member of the team carrying the weight of impending war and doom on my shoulders. Trinity carried all that along with the responsibility of keeping me safe so I could save the world. She was keeping all of us safe while asking us to risk life, limb, and soul while fighting demons and celestial.

I almost backed down.

But a temporary reprieve would do little to ease her burden. The sooner we started capturing and banishing the rogue demons, the sooner Trinity could set those burdens aside and have a well-earned respite.

"It's not blackmail. It's bargaining," I said. "We've worked with demons long enough for you to know the difference. If it makes you feel better, we can have Sam draw up a contract."

Assuming Sam knew what she'd done. I suspected not. He was super protective, and he had a great deal of magic of his own, but I doubted he could manage a barrier. And he'd 'never have allowed Trinity to strike a bargain with a more powerful demon. Sure, he was a Marquess of the hell realm, but in the demon world, he ranked beneath demon lords and dukes. If he could manage that kind of power, he would have used it to trap or defeat Belial and Haniel during our last battle. Instead, we barely managed to shove the two wicked lovebirds back through the portal even with him fighting alongside the team.

I arched a brow, and her gaze went wide. Yup. I figured I'd worked it out. She'd made a deal with another demon and hadn't told Sam, her demon lover and best friend. Secrets were lies of omission. It was the issue between me and D, and it made my heart hurt to know it would come between Sam and Trinity sooner or later.

But I couldn't afford to go soft. I needed to be in the field, and I wasn't above being a cold, calculating bitch to get there.

We stared at each other for a long moment. Trinity was doing the best she could and was a natural planner and protector. I *knew* that. I knew she wanted to keep me safe. But if I didn't do my part to stop the demon hoard holed up in Nashville, none of us would be safe.

"I'll take Lacey," I said. "She's combat ready, and so is Simon."

Trinity spun on her heel and went back to her desk, fiddling with the already perfectly stacked papers sitting on top of it in neat rows. I held my breath. She was the boss. I'd gone behind her back and against her orders on a stakeout, and she had to be pissed. That was understandable, but she shouldn't be surprised. I had a well-earned bad reputation I was working hard to repair by being a team player and training and doing compliance shit. It had to count for something.

"Take Megan, too."

My jaw dropped. I was too flabbergasted to speak and punching my boss would not help my case.

Before I could recover, Trinity said, "Your sister's ready for some field work. She's a quick study, follows the rules, and I *know* you won't take any risks that might put her in danger."

I stood still, trying to think of an argument, but Trinity gave me her death glare and said, "I'll expect a full report tomorrow. You're dismissed."

CHAPTER ELEVEN

I sat in the bland, boring waiting room, fidgeting and trying not to stare at the demon sitting across from me.

He didn't seem to have any problems ignoring me. Rude.

He was just a garden variety tempter demon, and not a very powerful one. Meanwhile, I had seven different types of skilled and powerful demon inside me—and it didn't even happen the fun way. Not that I'd want the fun way, at least not with all of them.

Just with Demoriel.

The jerk still hadn't answered my text.

A woman's voice shook me out of my musings. "Mr. Ben Derhover?"

I giggled, earning a frown from the lady at the door who looked up from her clipboard, her smart red framed glasses lending her a disappointed principal look along with the pinstripe suit. I got that a lot. But come on, it was a giggle-worthy joke name.

The demon disguised as a human dude bro, complete with a backwards ball cap, T-shirt that read "It's just a game, Bro" flanked by cartoonish consoles, stood up, stretched, and shuffled toward the smartly dressed human resources hiring manager. His gait was wrong, a dead giveaway the dude was a new demon who hadn't mastered the art of passing for human. Based on the way he moved, his true form was likely something used to walking on all fours. Creepy.

At least his glamour was decent.

He wasn't the only new demon hanging around the ZenMax office, which heightened our suspicion that the company was a front for one of our rogue demons. If dragonesque warriors and demon kitties managed to get through the portal before it closed, why not a fleet of lesser demons? And being proverbial fish out of water on earth, those lesser demons might be inclined to latch on to a bigger, badder demon looking to invade and conquer the earth realm.

Pinstripe smiled as the demon dude bro lurched over to her and didn't seem taken aback by his weird walk, attire, or general slacker attitude—or his name for crying out loud—but maybe it was because he was interviewing for a game tester job.

Or maybe all lesser demons crawling out of the woodwork went with stupid names. I'd have to ask Simon if he's put out a find-your-human-name site for demons on the web since he was the smartass who'd come up with my undercover name.

He totally got the twins to help.

Demon dude bro followed pinstripe through the door, leaving me alone in the waiting room to fidget and contemplate how I could weasel my way into a job.

Crap. I was overdressed. True, I'd wore jeans but had insisted on a silk blouse and blazer because, hello, job interview? Boice and Roice had laughed their snarky little asses off. Bastards. No matter. I'd totally put them in their place. Since I'd gotten some of their essences in my demon graft healthcare package, too, I knew a lot of their secrets. After I rattled off a few account numbers and links to videos of some of their more dubious entertainment endeavors from the 90s—a hip hop boy band with the two nerdiest geek demons to ever crawl out of hell—they'd helped me work with my sometimes-functioning demon glamour.

They suggested I go with pink hair, younger looking features, and they gave me a pair of the most blinged-out cat ear headphones for my undercover gig. The headphones were equipped with a sophisticated hidden comms system that would let Lacey and Megan listen in and would let me communicate with them if I got into a jam.

I was totally keeping the headphones.

I was totally going to send links of the Daemon Boyz's 1995 performance at EXIT/IN to the rest of my demon-hunting team, too. Pretty sure they bribed the owner to let them on stage. Lucky for them, Nashville audiences were too polite to throw beer bottles at the stage, but they did get hit with a few beaded bags and one fanny pack.

Best use for a fanny pack in my humble opinion.

I pulled out a power compact from my oversized pink bag and checked my face in the mirror. It was still just...wrong. How did Mara make it look so easy? According to the succubus, it was as simple as thought and appearance. Meanwhile, I had to fight to shift my face into some semblance of normal bordering on uncanny valley. The eyes were too uniform, the nose too narrow, and even though I'd tried for a gap in the front teeth to give my disguise a bit of character, it didn't help.

After all that work, I just looked creepy. Guess I shouldn't have been so judgy about gamer bro.

The disguise would have to do. Maybe it would help me blend in. Assuming our lead was correct, a powerful demon or demons were involved with ZenMax and were probably only hiring lesser demons. My shitty glamour and obvious demon scent should make me blend right in. They'd released a game called Munchie Madness, a cross between classic Pac-Man and match three games, which had taken the city by storm in a matter of a month and a half. Not so coincidentally, it had taken off within a few weeks of the Great Demon Escape of Nashville. According to the company's website, they were launching in Nashville first to work out any bugs in the game before their global release.

An odd choice—unless, of course, the company was run by demons confined to Nashville.

I wasn't a gamer, but Boice and Roice assured me the business model for ZenMax was odd. Instead of creating "gotcha" games that hooked players and then required cash for frequent upgrades, Munchie Madness was free and had decent expansion packs available at no cost.

It also had parents, teachers, employers, and all other productivity driven authority figures up in arms because it was so damned addictive and had players shirking their required work and life activities. In other words, brewing chaos. It was suspicious enough to warrant an investigation. The fact that the tech demon brothers couldn't hack into their system was even more suspicious. Having lost several hours playing their latest release pretty much sealed the deal. This was not a normal company run by humans.

"Miss Anita Dickenme."

It took me a moment to remember the ridiculous name was my alias— my roomies supplied me with all the requisite documents, accounts, and an online history to shore up the identity for the ridiculous moniker Simon concocted. Pinstripe had returned to fetch me for my interview, hopefully with one of the higher-level managers in the organization. If the manager was a demon, I would do my best to gauge its power, get hired, and infiltrate the organization.

It would be easier to ask Trinity for forgiveness than permission, and I still had her secret as a bargaining chip.

I stood, smoothed my silk blouse before remembering I was supposed to be a slacker, and covered the misstep by tossing my hair over my shoulder and plastering on what I hoped was a winning smile. Pinstripe raised a brow but didn't run screaming. Either my glamour was holding, or she was used to weird faces. Or she was a demon in disguise. Whatever. She wasn't the one I needed to impress.

I followed Pinstripe through the door, which led to a large room filled with cubicles. Most were occupied by clones of Dude Bro demon lounging in office chairs while engrossed in whatever was flashing across their smart phone screens, presumably a new version of Munchie Madness or the next game in the pipeline. Around a third of the gamers were slack jawed and eerily still except for their fingers and gazes darting back and forth over the screen—kind of like the humans at the explosion who were glued to their phones.

Crap, I hope I hadn't looked like that when I was playing.

Others all but vibrated with unspent energy, legs bouncing up and down, feet tapping, and bodies shuddering in response to their games. Or maybe they were jacked up on whatever was in their drink bottles. It was so jarring compared to the game zombies. What was the connection between the two responses, and what were the demons in charge getting out of it, and how did it fit into Belial's larger plan?

I wished I could use my demon knife to see if any of the entities in the cubicles were human, but it was too risky with my unreliable glamour.

A few of the gamers in cubicles were surrounded by what had to be soundproof windows. They slammed their bodies against desks or threw chairs at the windows, their mouths contorted as they screamed.

"Don't mind them."

I'd fallen behind, staring at the violent gamers as my demon senses churned with revulsion. Torture. That cinched it. Demons were definitely involved in the operation.

Pinstripe offered me a sympathetic smile. "They're method actors working on sound effects for characters in an RPG we have under development. The position we have in mind for you won't be quite so...intense."

I shook my head and turned my gaze back to her, my lips curling into what I hoped looked like a smile of genuine relief. "Good to know," I said. "But I'm not a lightweight. I finished Dark Souls faster than the guys in my group."

I pushed a little bit of succubus charm into my voice, something I'd recently managed to master thanks to Mara's training sessions. It worked better when my target was receptive. Since Pinstripe didn't want me paying too much attention to the "method actors" who were probably lesser demons or humans being tortured for power, I'd get better results.

But I was so going to stop the torture before I left the building.

"Impressive." Pinstripe looked me up and down. "We're testing a wide range of content and concepts, so you'll be asked to try out some of the girly stuff, but rest assured, we are equal opportunity," she said, her voice full of reassurance. "Be sure to note anything that seems too gendered on your survey form."

Nodding, I pushed a little more charm into my voice and said, "By the way, who am I meeting? I'd like to talk to someone in upper management if possible. I have some ideas and a demo game I designed."

My partner's voice hissed through my headphones. "Don't push too hard or she'll get suspicious. And a powerful demon will see past your glamour and blow your cover."

Whatever. I *had* done this before. I didn't need Lacey, or my sister, who was presumably listening in, to tell me how to do undercover work. Pinstripe smiled as if pleased. "You'll be meeting with our head of product development. Wait until you sign your contract agreement and NDA before you bring up your game."

"Thanks for the tip," I said, wishing I could say told-you-so to Lacey.

Pinstripe walked me out of cubicle-ville and to a bank of elevators. "Go to the sixth floor, sixth office on the right. You'll be meeting with Judy Labrador. Show her you have hustle, and you should get in."

Sixth floor, sixth office...where was the other six? It was a little too on the nose. I'd be sure and mention that to my roomies when I got home. For now, I made my way to the sixth floor and exited the elevator to find a bright space filled with natural light pouring in through the executive office windows and filtered by glass walls and doors. I checked to make sure the coast was clear and risked pulling out my demon knife, glamoured to look like a smartphone, and walked around as if a little lost.

Nothing.

I'd expected brilliant red, but none of the offices I passed made my knife glow or even give a flicker of light. Were they hiding their demonic essences? The demons who'd slithered out of the portal were certainly powerful enough to pull it off, but why bother? My essences were demonic in nature, as were the essences of the lesser demons interviewing for jobs. No need to hide from us. They were clearly recruiting from the supernatural population of Nashville, who'd know they were working for demons. Ordinary humans couldn't sense them, so I failed to see the point.

"Jinx, whatever you're thinking of doing, don't. Just go in, talk to the big wig, get hired, and get out." This time it was my sister's voice scolding me through the headphones. Megan was so overprotective, which was kind of funny. She'd only recently started working for our demon hunting organization. I had years on her.

Guess it was a bossy older sister thing.

"Oh, I'll go talk to the big wig. Then I'm going to get those tortured souls out of cubicle hell." I turned away as I spoke into the mic connected to the headphones.

"What?" Lacey barked.

"Jinx, don't do it!" I winced and resisted the urge to yank off my headphones. Jeez, Megan didn't have to be so loud. If she kept it up, I'd get a migraine before I even got to the interview.

Or she'd blow the magic that kept everyone but me from hearing anything.

I turned down the volume instead so I wouldn't have to listen to my screaming babysitters and strolled down the hall to office six. A tall woman with blond hair piled on top of her head in a messy bun paced back and forth, hands waving as she spoke. Conference call. Perfect excuse to wait outside and get a sense of her. She was probably a demon. I didn't have confirmation from my knife, but after years in the field, I'd developed good instincts. Dressed in executive black from turtleneck and tailored blazer to pencil skirt and high heels, she didn't move like a human.

I'd caught her off guard. Good.

"Pretty sure the big wig is a demon," I whispered into my mic. "Can't confirm with demon steel, but she's clearly not human."

"How do you know?" Megan asked. For once, it wasn't a snarky question, or one filled with skepticism. Megan was in full on learning mode. I had to turn the volume back up.

"Moves like a predator," I said. "Kind of like a big cat. And she hasn't blinked once since I've been watching her."

"That's so creepy. Like Hannibal Lecter."

Common misconception, and one that drove Boice and Roice crazy. They'd given me more than a few lectures on celestial propaganda. I wouldn't wish one of those on my worst enemy, let alone my sister. "A few serial killers are demon possessed, but most are just evil humans. Don't ever bring up demon serial killers with the twins are around."

"Roger that. Can you get some video?" Megan asked. "I'm in charge of updating our training modules."

Lacey growled. Grumpy much? I'd have to check in with Mara and see how things were going on her end. Since I'd introduced them—because I was a totally awesome matchmaker—the least I could do was work to get their relationship back on track. It wasn't interference. It was my moral obligation.

"In. Get hired. Out. Now."

Okay, Lacey was all business. Probably for the best. I walked closer to the door and started pacing, playing with my hair, and generally trying to get the attention of the big wig, Judy Labrador. That might take a while since I could hear her yelling through the glass.

"Not good enough. She needs more."

A male voice answered. "We're doing all we can, but we can't risk another incident. We need better storage."

"There's nothing wrong with the storage," she said, her voice icy. "I designed the system myself and it's perfect. Your team just isn't working hard enough. They don't understand the vision."

"We're pulling more hours than the designers crunching for the new release! I can't—"

She cut him off, her voice volume rising along with the hairs on my neck. Yup. Definitely not human. "I don't want to hear those words anymore. Do, or do not. There is no try. Is there anyone on your team who doesn't believe in me? Does anyone think we're not going to change the world?"

Wow. Total megalomaniac. And she was quoting Yoda? Kudos for being a quick study on pop culture references, but it was still freaky.

"No, ma'am," the voice said, tone flat and defeated. "We're all committed. I'll speak with the team."

"I'll do it myself. Later" she said, turning her gaze on me. Intensity and the zeal of a fanatic burned in her unblinking eyes. A chill ran down my spine, and I imagined this was how a deer felt when it locked eyes with a mountain lion. "Right now, I have a new candidate to interview."

She motioned me in. It took more strength than I bargained for, but I opened the door and entered her lair.

"Hello," she said, her voice lower than most women and as intense as her gaze. "My, but you are adorable, aren't you? Are you ready to show me what you're bringing to the table?"

"Absolutely," I said, flashing my most winning smile.

"Splendid."

Quick as a snake, she tossed something at me, and I braced for impact and my doom.

CHAPTER TWELVE

I caught the Smart Phone by reflex and glanced at the screen.

Then, I fell into wonder.

Colors. Crimson, azure, verdant green, lemon yellow, creamy orange, plum purple, and many others. Too many to name, but I wanted to. I needed to see them all, experience them, capture them all and keep them for my own. So many colors danced in front of my gaze.

Beautiful. I'd never seen anything so beautiful, so peaceful, so perfect.

There was too much noise buzzing through my headphones. Screaming voices. They made the colors dim. It wouldn't do. I shook my head until the headphones slipped to my neck. That was better.

My fingers moved on the screen, and it made the colors and shapes fly. They danced faster and faster and faster, igniting my senses. Blue tasted like cotton candy and sounded like the tinkling of bells. A red strawberry greeted me with a burst of notes as it fed me nectar sweeter than honey. Gold blanketed me with the warm rays of the sun on a summer's day and sang me a lullaby as I curled on a candy apple green lawn, tart and delectable.

The colors and shapes filled the space around me in every direction, covering my skin and absorbing into it to fill me with joy and wonder as music filled my ears, rainbows of flavors danced across my tongue, and the scents of roses, lilies, baked apple pies, and warm mocha lattes wrapped me in a ball of complete contentment. Everything I loved, all I'd ever longed for, it was right here, in this place and in this space.

There was nothing but the shimmering hues and shades. Never would I leave them. I had to keep them moving. I reached for a symphony of plums and almost caught them, but something tugged at my mind, trying to pull me away from the colors.

Pain shot through me, pulling me away from the joy of the colors. I was on the floor in...where was I? It was a bright room, but not as bright as the colors. It didn't matter. I had to focus on the colors and keep them moving so I could taste harmony and hear silver.

My fingers paused and the colors slowed down, the music faded, replaced by distant thunder, and sugar turned to sand on my tongue. Sadness poured out of the shapes and colors, and they faded to gray, their sparkle gone.

Agony ripped through me.

No, no, no, I couldn't let them fade. I needed the colors, the sounds, the tastes and textures. If they went away, there would be nothing but despair.

Awareness crept along the periphery of my consciousness. Heart racing, sweat pouring into my eyes, blurring the colors and shapes. I went numb, bereft of joy and so empty, and then went rigid with so much pain. All I had to do was keep moving the colors and shapes and the sadness would disappear, the pain would go away. A scream of frustration tore from my throat. Why was my throat so dry?

My head ached, my limbs shook, and my skin was glowing for some reason. There was something important about the lines and patterns on my skin. I couldn't remember, the thought just out of reach, but there was something I should be doing.

A tiny golden berry kissed me with such sweetness. Its song beckoned, promising me tranquility and happiness if I just focused on it, loved it, craved it, and gave myself over to it.

Tired, so tired. I needed the colors. Why were my fingers refusing to obey me?

A voice broke through my confusion, a woman's low alto. I knew that voice, but I couldn't place it. My concentration was shot.

"No, this won't do. It won't work! Her soul energy's a mess, too volatile, and she kept fighting extraction. What is she?"

Another familiar female voice answered. "I thought she was a demon, ma'am, I swear. I mean, look at her. She's obviously using glamour and she used succubus charm to give her a leg up on the interview."

A vision of a pinstripe suit popped into my addled brain. That was the second voice. Pinstripe. There was something I should remember about her. She'd brought me...somewhere.

"Well, if she's not the problem, what the hell is going on with the collection? Did Research clean and sterilize this collection unit? I've told them a thousand times we cannot afford contamination. Look at this!" The shrillness and volume hurt my ears, deepening my confusion, but I knew that voice. Her voice. Who was she?

Think, think, think...Labrador. It was her name, the name she'd chosen. But why? Most people didn't choose their names. They were given names by parents. My name was...what was my name? I'd chosen my name, too.

Nothing made any sense, and my thoughts were all muddled. The abnormally low register of Labrador's voice was filled with frightening intensity. Dangerous. She was dangerous. I was in danger, but I couldn't quite remember why. My head was pounding, and flashes of color kept invading my thoughts. It was hard to focus.

Why was I here? Danger made sense since I was on the freaking floor writhing in terrible pain. Had a demon kicked my ass?

Demons. I was a demon hunter, Jinx McGee, demon hunter, but I wasn't supposed to be hunting right now because...there was a reason. Wasn't ready for some reason. Trinity said so. That was right. I needed more training. I'd come here to investigate. I wasn't supposed to engage. No fighting demons.

It was coming back to me in bits and pieces.

Pinstripe and Labrador were still arguing about collection units and cleanliness and what I was supposed to be. I needed to focus and do something before they decided to take me down to some lab and dissect me or something else equally horrible. Like torture. Torture? There were...people...no, demons being tortured here. Or maybe both? Torture was wrong. I was supposed to stop it.

I'd have to get off the floor first.

"There's human and demon sourced soul energy in there! How are we supposed to screen suitable donors if we can't get a clean sample?" Labrador's voice had gone up an octave—which put her in the baritone range—and she was yelling. "And there's some other contaminant. Who prepared this collection unit?"

"I don't know. We'd need to scan the bar code—"

Labrador cut Pinstripe off. "Mistakes and excuses, it's all I get from these people. What is it about the vision, the importance of this work they don't get? They're not getting it, and that's why they're screwing up and not working hard enough. We need a new team in research. Pronto."

"Judy, you've already replaced your R&D team. Twice. Corporate appreciates your dedication, but they're not going to keep investing if—"

"I'm not doing this for corporate. I'm doing this for Bella!"

An unearthly shriek rang out. I rolled into a fetal position and covered my ears, which had to be bleeding by now. I opened my eyes and had to close them against the brilliant light surrounding the entity formerly known as Pinstripe. But Pinstripe was gone.

In her place, a monster roared.

Holy guacamole, she looked like something vomited from the nightmares of H.P. Lovecraft.

From a head that reminded me of an octopus, only with one giant eye in the center, sprouted tentacles lined with more eyes. The tentacles whipped about wildly as an unearthly voice sounded from...somewhere. The thing didn't appear to have a mouth, which as probably for the best. My addled brain was at its limit, and I didn't think I could handle teeth with eyeballs.

But I wasn't so far gone that I didn't recognize the monstrosity floating in the room with me and Labrador.

This wasn't a demon.

It was a celestial.

Some call them angels—some being people who didn't know them very well. This was a Biblically accurate angel, which was utterly terrifying and scarier than any demon I'd ever seen.

And I'd seen some scary, ugly-ass demons.

Crap. I hoped I didn't turn into *that* one day.

Cthulhu's hideous cousin, a.k.a. the celestial who'd shed her human disguise, stopped screaming in favor of chewing Labrador, who was presumably another celestial, a new one.

"I don't care about your little side quest, and neither does corporate. The only thing we care about is getting a weapon capable of obliterating the enemy. That is your primary directive, and if you fail to deliver, the board will replace you and you'll be buried so far into the pit of agony your suffering will pale in comparison to the enemy you're aiding and abetting."

Labrador vibrated with rage, fists clenched and radiating power. Damn, I did *not* want to see her true form.

My head fully cleared, and reality hit me. Deep in the heart of a powerful *celestial's* lair and on the verge of having my cover blown, I was writhing on the floor doing my best impression of a goldfish that jumped out of its bowl and now had to flop on the kitchen counter.

Right. Think. These weren't demons. They were celestials, and they were apparently building a weapon to obliterate the enemy—presumably the demons running loose in Nashville—but Labrador had some side project to help Bella, who was an enemy.

Whose enemy?

Most of it made no sense, but I keyed in on "weapon" and figured it was linked to the soul energy they'd sucked out of me with a freakin' video game. The celestials were still arguing, which gave me the chance to orient myself and examine my surroundings. A cylinder that looked like a cross between a blood collection tube and a Victorian perfume bottle sat on Labrador's desk, full of glowing...stuff.

The stuff had come out of me. And it was volatile.

Made sense. I myself was rather volatile. Trinity said I couldn't fight demons. She hadn't said anything about celestials. I'd found a loophole if I could summon the strength to use it.

I slowly pulled my headphones back over my ears, only to be greeted by screams that did nothing to help my aching head.

"Jane! Come in Jane! What's going on?" My sister. Crap. This is not how I wanted her first field mission to go. "We have to go in!"

"No," Lacey said, her voice strained. "Not without backup. Simon, go in there and get my partner."

Good. Megan couldn't come in here. They'd tear her apart. Simon would do nicely for what I had in mind. I called to him through his essence embedded in my graft and did my best to show him what I needed him to do. When I sensed his proximity, I mustered my purely human strength and speed developed from over a decade of training, snatched the cylinder, and bolted out of the room with celestials hot on my tail.

CHAPTER THIRTEEN

Running on adrenaline that wouldn't last much longer, I was in no shape to fight. Screwed. I was so freaking screwed if Simon didn't show up soon. Racing past the elevators, I flung open the door to the stairs and slid down the rails. Pulling out my knife would be stupid on this unexpected carnival ride, so I channeled my rage and horror into conjuring some celestial magic.

Please work, please work, please work.

I could really use one of those shields Cassie pulled out of her ass.

Instead of a shield, I managed something that looked like a cross between an umbrella and a mushroom. Ridiculous? You bet. But it deflected the magical spears and bullets of light flying out of Pinstripe's bazillion eyeballs as she chased me down six flights of stairs.

I flung open the door to the first floor and leapt into the air as the angel monster flew out after me, landing behind her. My demon steel's blue glow was blinding, but it scored the celestial's golden flesh and took out one eyeball.

Too bad she unleashed another one of those unearthly shrieks, which were extra weapons in her arsenal. I ducked and rolled, barely avoiding a tentacle that had sprouted daggers between eyes. Skidding across the polished floor, I activated the noise cancellation function on my head-phones. It didn't completely block out the ear-splitting screams of the terrifying creature, but it helped me focus on not getting ginsued.

Somehow, I'd managed to hold onto the container of my soul energy, which could probably cause another explosion like the one from yester-day. Yeah, I'd put two and two together and come up with an explanation for the carnage. Guess there were no OSHA or safety standards in celes-tial weapons manufacturing.

I had no idea how explosive my mojo was, and I didn't intend on finding out or letting the terrifying angel brigade get their tentacles on it again.

Thanks to Lacey and Megan, the lobby was almost empty. No collat-eral damage to unwitting humans. Many of the demons who'd been lounging in cubicles ran, dematerialized, or flew out of the building while I ducked, leapt, and twisted to dodge tentacle knives, using my mush-room umbrella shield to stop the ugly monster from shanking me. I'd managed to take out a few more eyeballs, but all it seemed to do was piss her off. My strength wouldn't last, but I had to keep her busy until Simon arrived, and I'd sent him on a little side quest first.

A ping sounded behind me, and the elevator doors slid open.

Shit. Labrador had arrived.

I backed up against the wall so Pinstripe couldn't stab me in the back and watched as Labrador turned that creepy, unblinking gaze on me. I didn't need to worry. Pinstripe focused on the other celestial, too. Smil-ing, she transformed into a bizarre collection of wings covered with eyeballs straight out of horror film. Every unblinking eyeball locked onto me with predatory intensity.

What was it with angels and eyeballs?

"Naughty, naughty little devil, aren't you? Or maybe a fallen angel... but with a dash of human? I've never met a creature who was all three, but there's a legend about one. Tell me, are you Sameal's little pet come to play warrior? If so, you're way out of your league."

Sameal's pet? Nope. I worked for Sameal, a.k.a. my AWOL boss, at least until he went bye bye. I was his least favorite employee, biggest pain in his ass, and still most likely to get the job done while being a total smar-tass. A pet I was not.

But she was probably right about being out of my league.

"I came here expecting to find some demons up to no good, not two ugly ass celestials making weapons and torturing other beings. Not very angelic of you. You already blew up one downtown building. I'll bet this," I said, holding up the container, "can do some damage to your little opera-tion. Still think I'm playing?"

Pinstripe, who'd been creeping closer to me with those knife-laden tentacles, froze, her bazillion and one eyeballs widened. Good. Labrador's wings shuddered and her gazillion eyeballs blinked rapidly.

"Give it back. Bella needs it."

Labrador floated closer. I raised the container above my head. "Nope. It's mine. You stole it from me, remember? Move one more inch closer and I'll smash this bundle of volatile energy and blow us all to Kingdom come."

Labrador stopped. My gaze darted back and forth between the two celestials, which did nothing at all for the pounding in my still-aching head. I was so tired. Maybe I should chug the contents of the container like an energy drink. Was it even a liquid? I always thought of magic as immaterial, but maybe it had some physical form like electricity?

"It appears we've reached an impasse." Pinstripe dropped the freaky eyeball-laden appearance and resumed her perfectly polished HR profes-sional appearance. No overt signs of injury, but she favored her right side, holding her right arm close against her body, weight resting on her left leg. Celestial glamour couldn't hide the injuries I'd inflicted with demon steel, it would seem. And demon steel appeared to work as well against celestials as it did against demons.

Good to know.

I put a pin in that for later and add it to Megan's training updates. If there was a later...

Labrador morphed back into her blond emo human guise and glow-ered at me. "If you smash the storage unit, you'll destroy yourself, too."

"Maybe," I said. "But I'll take you with me, and then what will happen to poor Bella?"

Labrador screamed and shook. Oh, for crying out loud. A tantrum? Really? I was fishing, but she seemed fanatical enough to take the bait. See, I was still investigating. Trinity would be so proud. We needed to know who this Bella was, and why she could possibly need weaponized soul energy. Obviously, Bella wasn't the top-level boss of this operation if they were keeping her secret from "corporate," presumably fellow or higher-level archangels. Then again, wasn't ZenMax's owner named Bella?

Couldn't be a coincidence.

Whoever Bella was, she meant something to Labrador. Something personal.

"Stop this foolishness at once!" Pinstripe yelled at her colleague. Labrador flinched as if struck and then settled. Looked like Pinstripe was the one in charge. Pinstripe turned to me and said, "Bella does not concern you, nor do our activities. We're here to destroy the demons you unleashed. Give me the storage container and I'll let you leave with your life and soul intact."

I raised a brow and glanced at the container. Pinstripe flashed an evil grin and said, "Mostly intact. You'll recover. We'll eradicate the demons on this plane. Everybody gets what they want, and no one gets hurt."

I cackled like a mad woman and said, "Right. No one gets hurt except the humans you drain, demons you torture, and anyone in the blast zone when your little experiments go wrong. Not on my watch."

Pinstripe waved a hand dismissively. "Casualties of war. And make no mistake, we are at war. If we don't neutralize the demonic threat now, millions more humans will suffer and die."

I didn't believe for one second that Pinstripe gave cherub's ass about the suffering of humans or their deaths. Hell, she'd probably get a nice misery meal out of it. But maybe I could get more information if I pretended to negotiate.

"How do you even weaponize soul energy?" I asked, lowering the container. "I want to slaughter demons as much as you, but I won't take out humans in the process. If you can weaponize this stuff, you can find a way to point it directly at demons and not innocents."

Pinstripe smiled. "I'm sure we can come to some sort of mutually beneficial arrangement. If you find the demons for us, we can target them with our weapon."

"How?"

"That, my dear, is a trade secret."

Okay, Pinstripe wasn't going to budge. Not surprising, but I had to try. "Fine," I said. "I'll run it by my team. But the cylinder goes with me. Consider it my insurance policy."

Pinstripe opened her mouth but was interrupted by an ear-splitting shriek like an eagle's cry echoing through the lobby. I grinned. "Thanks for the interview. It's been...interesting, but I'm afraid the position doesn't really suit me."

Simon swooped down and grabbed me by my shoulders. The celestials shifted back into their unearthly forms and gave chase, but right on cue, Sam and Alexi burst through the door and attacked. I caught a glimpse of Alexi's demonic wolf fangs tearing into Labrador's wing and Sam with a blade in each hand running at Pinstripe before we flew out the door and toward our getaway car.

Simon dumped me unceremoniously on the pavement beside the vehicle. What the fork? I cradled the container against my chest as panic rushed through me.

"Yo, asshole! Explosive here. How about taking it easy on the landing?"

Lacey and Megan burst out of the van and started barraging me with questions and checking me for injuries.

"What happened?"

"You weren't supposed to fight, you idiot—"

"You're carrying a bomb?"

"—could have been killed. What were you thinking?"

I ripped off my headphones and plugged each earhole with an index finger before shouting "Enough! I'll explain later but we need to get out of here now."

We piled into the car. Before I could buckle in, Megan tackled me in a bear hug, almost cracking my ribs.

"Ouch! Take it easy. I'll be okay. Just a little dinged up, so take it easy with the boa constrictor action."

Someone else jumped into the car and cast a glowing shield around it. I'd seen that shield before. Megan yelped in surprise and Lacey spun around with her knife at the ready. Before I could tell them to stand down, Cassie, my chronically late guardian angel, appeared and unleashed a burst of magic. It covered the area in a thick haze of fog and seemed to slow the celestials pursuing us.

"Drive!" the angel yelled. "It won't hold them for long."

Lacey sped down the street breaking about a gazillion traffic laws, but I wasn't too concerned. Any cops would be too focused on rushing to the ZenMax office to worry about us, and we were close to HQ. When Megan let go of me, she started working the complicated communications equipment in the van, presumably letting the team know we were coming in hot and to prepare for lockdown.

"Are the twins at HQ?" I asked.

"They are, and we called Mara and Demoriel in. They've alerted Cooper and Demoriel sent his buddies to help guard the portal in case the demons you pissed off try to escape."

I took a deep breath and leaned back in the seat. "That won't be a problem. They aren't demons." I glared at Cassie. "They're celestials, and they're making weapons to destroy the escaped demons and any humans who get in their way."

CHAPTER FOURTEEN

"Drink this," Mara said, holding a cup of some warm, nice smelling liquid against my lips. Exhaustion overtook me five minutes into the drive to HQ, so my partner and my sister had to drag my ass into the building and down to the lower-level bunkers. Lacey and Megan had then dumped me unceremoniously on one of the comfy couches and left to shower. The twins greeted me with insults about my appearance, but they congratulated me on taking on the angel brigade. We were scheduled for a team meeting and debrief, but I'd given my roommates the CNN version, complete with vivid descriptions of the eyeball laden celestial beings with tentacles and wings.

"Told you they were ugly as all get out," Boice had said after I gave him a rundown of the action.

"No joke," I said, running a hand over my aching head. "They had great glamour and concealment magic, though. I didn't get any signs of their nature or powers until they whammied me with the phone."

"Don't forget conniving and cruel," Roice added, plopping Sully on my lap. She still smelled nice, so they'd either have bathed her again or she had a naturally pleasant smell when off the streets and out of the hell realm. Kitty curled up on my lap, purring up a storm and licking cuts and bruises on my face.

Cassie, who stood apart from the team, grimaced, but didn't argue.

I took a sip of Mara's magical healing tea and mustered a smile for her. "Thanks. You're the best."

Mara beamed. "No, you are, you and this team and this world—"

I held up a hand and leveled her with my gaze. Time to nip this in the bud. It may or may not be able to help Mara and Lacey's relationship, but I would help Mara become her own person—demon—instead of fawning over all of us for showing her a modicum of decency.

"You are a valuable part of this team, a part of this world, and you need to learn to take a compliment. We love you for who you are, not what you can do for us."

Her cheeks flushed red, but she nodded. "Right. That's what Lacey keeps saying. I'm sorry."

Ugh, and there she went apologizing. Again. We'd have to break her of that habit, too, but later.

Sully mewed in protest after I stopped petting her. She climbed up my torso and curled herself in the crook of my neck, her warm weight and soft fur draining away my anxiety. Wowzers! I had an emotional support demon cat. How cool!

"You should listen to Lacey," I said. "She loves you, you know, but she needs a partner, not a servant. You owe it to yourself and to her to find out who you are, who you want to be, and what you want."

"I know," she looked away and fidgeted with the hem of her shirt. "It is difficult to change. I've been an instrument of fantasy fulfillment for so long. It feeds me, but more than that, it was my purpose in the hell realm. The reason for my existence."

"Must be tough." Trying to find a new purpose in a new and unfamiliar world was something I could relate to. "For the longest time, I was a demon-possessed demon hunter. Now I'm...something else. I thought being free of Hannah—Haniel—would make me feel, I don't know, normal? Like I was the only on in charge of my life."

Huh. I'd shared that last little nugget to encourage Mara to open up, but the unexpected tightness in my chest was very telling. I'd been so busy training and fighting to get back into the field, and it wasn't just because I had a big job ahead of me. I'd thought I was human, a human possessed by a powerful demon, but still human.

But I wasn't. I'd never been fully human.

I hadn't wanted to deal with the loss of who I'd been when I'd had Hannah, and I sure as hell didn't want to be alone, truly alone, with my own thoughts as I contemplated who and what I was now. Not normal, that was for damned sure. But I was even less human than I'd been before with just my unknown celestial heritage. Now I really and truly had demon in me. Three different aspects in one person seemed like too much.

Some of what I was feeling—pain, confusion, and worry—must have shown on my face, since Mara gave me an empathetic smile. "It can be scary to be in charge. To not know what you're doing, what you're supposed to be doing, or even what you want. For me, sometimes it's just easier to be what I was."

I looked away. "You hit the nail on the head for sure."

"It's not all bad, though," Mara said. "I may not know what I'm doing or who I am, but I've found I still want to fulfill needs and desires—not carnal, but other needs—for Lacey and for all of you. I've never had friends before. It feels...nice. Doing things for you is not about feeding or fulfilling a purpose. It's just...well, it just is."

I took her hand and squeezed. "Tell that to Lacey. And...tell her what *you* need and desire."

Since we were sharing, and since Mara was in fact easy to talk to and a good listener, I said, "And, full disclosure, I never had friends until I joined the team either. I get it. You find something like this, like a family, and you don't want to lose it. You'll do anything to keep it. But you don't have to worry. We've got your back, just like you've got ours. That's what friends do."

Trinity, who'd been hanging out in the corner of our conference room and checking her phone, cleared her throat. I'd have been embarrassed about all the deep conversating, but I figured Trinity could stand to hear it, too. She was our leader, but she was still a member of the team. She needed to lean on us, especially considering whatever bargain she'd made to keep our demons and possibly celestials confined to Nashville had gotten her into a jam.

She didn't have to go it alone. I'd make sure we got her out of whatever horrible deal she'd made to give our team a fighting chance to capture the escaped demons and stop a war between them and celestials that could destroy humanity.

Trinity looked between me and Mara and gave us a status update. "Sam and Alexi are on their way back now. Cooper's staying put. He'll be safe in the forest with his furry friends, or so he says. The rest of Nashville's summoners are holed up in various safehouses."

Thank goodness. Cooper was a little off, and a little scary, but he was an insanely powerful summoner and he treated guarding his portal with deadly seriousness. Guarding the portal had nearly cost him his life during our last mission. He'd reinforced security measures and probably had every earth realm and demon realm animal in the vicinity patrolling.

And since he wasn't coming here, I didn't have to worry about him trying to take Sully away.

Not that I'd give her up now. She'd claimed my heart the moment she looked at me with those big green eyes.

True, she'd slid back down to my chest and was currently digging her claws into my boobs, but I still loved her. I'd just have to give her a claw trim.

"Good. We can have a debrief after Lacey and Megan wash up, and after Demoriel gets here," I said, trying to act casual. I wasn't worried about him. He was tough, resourceful, and more than a match for a couple of freaky angels.

I wasn't worried, and I wasn't pining for him. Nope. Not me.

I'd dropped Mara's hand, but apparently it was her turn to dole out reassurance. She plopped down on the sofa next to me and put an arm around my shoulder. "He'll be here soon. You should talk to him. Tell *him* what *you* need."

"No fair," I said, leaning against the succubus. She was warm and soft, and I was so tired. "You don't get to use my own advice on me."

Sully had retracted her claws and moved to my lap, made herself comfortable, and resumed her deep, rumbling purr. All I wanted to do was sleep, and maybe dream. Maybe the colors and shapes would come back, those wonderful, amazing, brilliant colors would take the away my exhaustion, my pain, all the stress and worry and weight of the world on my shoulders. I could put it all aside and get lost in the bliss of the colors and let all my cares drain away...

Sully hissed, then growled, snapping me back to reality. I gasped and scooped the cat up as I stood, my legs trembling and my body shaking. I wanted those shapes and colors and the escape they promised, and it terrified me. Between facing off with powerful celestials and running for my life, I'd put the euphoria and terror of the celestial's trap and its sweet Siren call in a box to deal with later.

Later was apparently now.

CHAPTER FIFTEEN

"Jinx?" Mara stood and put a warm hand on my shoulder, anchoring me. "What's wrong?"

I wanted to tell her I was okay, she didn't need to fuss over me, but the words were stuck in my throat as I struggled to breathe. Panic attack. Great. As if I didn't have enough PTSD fodder thanks to nearly dying, losing my almost life-long connection with Hannah, daddy issues, mommy issues, and demon grafts for which I was grateful but still made me feel like a stranger in my own body, now I was dealing with terror or possibly withdrawal from a freakin' video game.

No, not a video game. An insidious mind-controlling, soul-sucking device created by a batshit crazy celestial to power a weapon of mass destruction.

"Breathe, Jinx. Focus on breathing. You're safe." Trinity's soothing voice crooned to me, and her warm arms embraced me while Mara hummed a beautiful, peaceful melody and Sully purred. After a long, agonizing moment, I remembered to breathe.

"What happened to her?" Trinity asked quietly.

"She got up close and personal with a celestial draining device and barely made it out intact." Lacey had finished showering and arrived just in time to see me in the middle of a totally humiliating flashback. Crap. I was supposed to be the warrior, the strong one, the one who would get us all out of this mess.

Instead, I was a mess.

"What can we do for her?" Megan asked. They were all speaking in low whispers and acting as if I couldn't hear them, like I wasn't there.

"I can help," Cassie said, tentatively. "If she'll let me, I can take some of this burden from her."

The angel's voice and her offer brought me out of my panic attack long enough to say, "No!" I heard a commotion and raised voices. The twins, Lacey, and Mara were yelling at the angel, flinging accusations and more insults. It wasn't exactly fair to take out their frustration on one member of the celestial species, but I got it. Did Cassie know about the celestials in charge of ZenMax all along? If so, she hadn't told me. Not the best way to build trust.

"She needs grounding."

I opened my eyes and was at once relieved and terrified to see Dr. Khatri approaching me with a calm, controlled aura that gave me peace and pissed me off at the same time. This was private. Patient-doctor confidentiality. The good doctor wasn't here spilling the rest of the team's struggles for everyone to see.

Dr. Khatri must have guessed what I was thinking and feeling, since she shooed Trinity and Mara away, took me gently by the arm, and led me to one of the small rooms surrounding the central space of the bunker. Before escorting me inside, she turned to address my colleagues.

"I'll expect to see each one of you in individual sessions tomorrow. This team has been through major trauma, and none of you can keep fighting without addressing it. Jane already has a head start. It's why she survived today and why she'll get through this. Follow her good example."

Dr. Khatri wasn't much taller than me, which made me like her a little bit better. With large brown eyes that seemed to gaze right into your soul, dark hair pulled back into a tight bun, and a compact, muscular body, she was also tough as nails. A former demon hunter from California, she'd put herself through graduate school and earned a degree in psychology after retiring from the field at age forty. I had no doubt she could still hold her own in a fight now at age fifty-something. But being strictly human with only a little bit of magic from her maternal ancestors, fighting was too risky. These days, she traveled to centers of demonic activity—and probably celestial activity, too, based on what I'd learned today—to take care of demon hunter mental health.

Most centers were located on the east and west coasts of the United State, but Nashville became a hotbed in the early 1800s when the Bell Witch, who wasn't a witch at all but actually a pissed off Mace, or demon of wrath, ripped open a portal to the hell realm and went on a rampage against the locals living near her cave. Since then, about a half dozen portals had popped up in Tennessee, that we knew of, most of them around Nashville. Demons on the hunt liked highly populated areas, and demons on the run needed an urban population where they could blend in and go unnoticed.

Our team was trying to contain the current great demon escape crisis while also trying to avoid mass panic in the community. We'd warned the other demon hunting and regulatory operations in the country, who'd get the word out to the wider world, but we told them we had the situation under control, which was decidedly true. Dr. Khatri, who figured we weren't being entirely honest, showed up at HQ about a month ago and started working with us on mental health and morale.

I hated to admit it, but she was just what the team needed.

I let the good doctor lead me into the dark room and didn't fight as she eased me down onto the bed. I closed my eyes and let the quiet and dark envelop me. My breathing wasn't under control yet, but I wasn't hyperventilating anymore. I'd kept Sully, or rather, she'd kept me since she refused to let Mara pull her out of my arms. The demon cat settled herself on my chest and licked my face.

Grounding. Right. Focus on what I could feel, smell, taste, and hear. Since my eyes were closed, no need to worry about what I could see.

"I feel a sandpaper cat tongue on my skin, smell stinky cat breath somewhere between rotten beef and old tuna salad, taste bile, and hear a cracking, rasping voice I assume is mine. How's that for grounding?"

Dr. Khatri snorted. "You're deflecting, but not bad. How's the heart rate?"

I didn't know why she bothered asking since she'd already grabbed my wrist and started measuring my heart rate herself. I opened my eyes and my gaze landed on Sully, who was doing her best impersonation of a Halloween decoration. Back arched, fur sticking up on her head, down her back, and along her tail, wing spread to make her look bigger—which was totally adorable and not at all menacing, bless her fuzzy heart. She growled, and that was more impressive. My kitty must have been feeling protective since she hissed and swatted at the doctor.

"Hush," Dr. Khatri said, giving my cat a stare down. "I'm not hurting her. Make yourself useful and purr."

Sully glowered at her for a few more seconds, gave her one more dirty look, and then began licking her front paw and running it over her face for a cat bath. When in doubt? Wash. Sully wasn't admitting defeat, just acting bored and haughty. Cats were all kinds of awesome.

Still, considering my roommates' reaction to Sully, I figured I should warn Dr. Khatri not to press her luck.

"Careful doc," I said. "According to the twins, she's a Motiaummerr, one of the deadliest species in the hell realm."

Dr. Khatri put a hand on my forehead then shoved a digital thermometer in my ear. "Well, the deadly creature in question is currently licking her nether regions, so I think I'm safe for the moment."

I turned my attention back to Sully who was, indeed, licking her lady bits with one small leg hiked up in the air. She stopped when she noticed me looking at her and chirped inquisitively.

"Sulphur Springs McGee, that's not very ladylike," I chided. Sully gave me a slow blink and then resumed her tongue bath. Clearly, I had failed to establish dominance and using her full name didn't have the same impact on the cat as it had on me during my misspent youth.

But Sully was purring, and the soothing sound and vibration calmed my body and mind.

By the time the doc finished her brief physical exam and checked me for injuries beyond visible cuts and bruises, I was mostly back to normal. My body no longer shook, I could breathe, and I could think.

"Doc?"

"Yes?"

"Is it true what they say about addiction? Is just about people trying to self-medicate?" I was grasping at straws and trying to rationalize how easily I'd fallen into the celestial trap.

I'd never had a problem before. My love of tequila aside, I hadn't overindulged since one staff meeting we had after I made a stupid deal with our boss that started all our current troubles. I would find out how a powerful demon—Belial's messenger and minion—got through a local portal without detection and send him back. In exchange, I'd become team leader for a short time and got access to the grimoire to aid in my investigation.

It had also put the lives and souls of my mother and sister on the line. My boss's twisted, evil logic dictated that a threat to my family would be better motivation than simply saving my own neck.

After such a tough day at the office, I'd needed a drink or three.

During the investigation, I'd reconnected with my childhood companion and almost boyfriend Demoriel, uncovered a boatload of secrets about demons in general and the demons on our team, and it all culminated in finding out my personal demon was a celestial and the former lover a demon lord, Belial, who wanted to mount another rebellion in the hell realm and start Demon versus Celestial War 2.0 on earth.

Keeping a clear head was a job requirement now, so I hadn't had a drink since, and I'd never done drugs. Since I thought I was demon possessed, self-control was key. No recreational drugs, especially hallucinogens. While I did love comfort food, especially tacos, the rigors of training kept me busy, healthy, and didn't give me a lot of time to binge eat.

Come to think of it, the rigors of training had kept me so busy, I barely had time to think. Nope, scratch that. I'd actively avoided thinking or being alone with only my thoughts.

Oh, good grief and crap on a piece of toast, I hadn't given myself time to process everything I'd been through.

Dr. Khatri hadn't answered my question, but the knowing smile on her face made me think she'd been giving me time to have this little epiphany. It irked me a bit, but it was fair and made her a totally effective therapist. Still, I wasn't going to talk until she gave me an answer.

Her smile widened. I frowned. After what felt like an eternity but was just enough time to make start squirming, she spoke.

"The self-medication hypothesis is one theory developed to explain the association between mental illness, or PTSD, and substance abuse. Based on what your partner described about your entrapment along with the field report detailing the odd behavior of humans at the scene of the downtown explosion, I'm thinking there's more magic involved than addiction in the mundane sense. Our analysis is preliminary, but the twins' research so far shows the percentage of humans affected by entrapment at the scene who had a history of addiction was no greater than the estimated percentage of people affected by addiction in the general population."

Well, that was a relief.

"But, since you brought up the subject, are you worried about self-medicating, or perhaps other unhealthy coping strategies?"

So much for relief. Man, she was good. A pain in my ass, but good.

I sighed and pulled my aching body to a sitting position. If I was going to spill my guts in a therapy session, I wouldn't do it flat on my back. I didn't do vulnerability. I was a safe person for my friends to be vulnerable with, but I actively avoided putting myself out there with anyone. The issue would probably come up in another session, but for now, my head would be on the same level as the damned doctor's.

I shrugged and played it cool, wondering why my heart was racing—again—and why I had an overwhelming urge to squirm and fidget. Ugh. This touchy-feely stuff always made my ass twitch.

"I've been keeping insanely busy with training and getting back into the field, so I don't have to think about how I almost died. How I'm no longer as human as I was before. How my deadbeat celestial dad saddled me with what I thought was a demon and then abandoned me and my family, and so I don't go crazy from being alone in my head since Hannah left. But since I have a phantom wolf-demon in my head, the last part probably won't be an issue now."

The tightness in my chest eased a bit. Wow. I hadn't meant to spill that much. I figured I'd bank some of my issues for future therapy sessions, but it felt...good, comforting even, to put it all out there.

"That's remarkably self-aware of you. Not surprising."

"Really? It surprised the hell out of me."

Dr. Khatri rolled her eyes. "Take the compliment. You've identified the problem, so your next step and homework assignment, aside from journaling about all this, is to implement some healthy coping strategies. Your little friend there is a good start."

Dr. Khatri extended her index finger within booping range of Sully. After a thorough sniff, Sully bumped her snoot against the doctor's finger and then aggressively head-butted her hand in a demand for pets, purring and chirping up a storm.

"Does that mean she's officially my emotional support demon kitty? I need you to put it in writing so Cooper can't take her away."

The doc laughed. "I recommend at least an hour per day of cuddles, pets, and playtime. Right now, I recommend some self-care, including a long shower, a healthy meal, and some sleep."

If only. There wasn't time for any of that, however, given the team was holed up at HQ, waiting to see if the celestials would mount a counterattack to get their weaponized soul energy back.

"Okay...I'll shower, but the meal will have to be a working dinner so I can debrief the team and then get busy researching the weapon—"

Dr. Khatri gave me her stern look, the one that made me feel like I did whenever I got called to the principal's office as a kid, which was a lot. I thought therapists were supposed to be soft, but I guess former demon hunters turned therapists were tough. Psychology school apparently hadn't taken the hard ass out of her.

"There will be no debriefing tonight. It can wait. You're going to take along shower, eat, and then get at least eight hours of sleep, just like the rest of the team after I do a mental health check on them."

I opened my mouth to protest but she held up a hand to stop me. "We have demon sentinels on guard duty. They're rested and ready to keep watch. This team is in turmoil. You and your colleagues aren't going to be good for anyone, let alone yourselves, unless you take time to recuperate."

Demon sentinels? Wait a minute...

"Did Demoriel show up with his magical demon buddies?"

The doc nodded. "He did. He asked after you. Maybe you should talk to him. He could help with the other part of your assignment, which is to face your feelings and talk about them."

"I thought I was supposed to do that with you."

"You are," she said, scooping up Sully and depositing her on my lap. "But I can't be your only confidant. I understand you and Demoriel grew up together and have been friends for a long time?"

I snorted. She made it a question, but I'm sure she knew about my complicated past with D and everything else about me from my personnel files. We'd grown up together because he was an abandoned demon boy who found shelter in my childhood home—in my closet most of the time—as well as food, companionship, and a kindred spirit.

Me. I was his kindred spirit and sole companion for a long time.

In him, I'd found a friend and someone who understood something of what I was going through. From the age of five until a couple of months ago, I believed I was possessed by a demon. He *was* a demon. I didn't have to hide who and what I was from him like I did from my family, classmates, and the humans in my community.

He didn't have to hide who and what he was from me, not like he did once he'd grown older and started exploring the human world. We'd had a bond that turned into more when he came back into my life. Not just attraction and lust—though there was plenty of that, at least on my end— but the bond of childhood friendship and the bond forged by outcasts who find each other share.

Did we still have that bond?

I was surprised to realize the answer was yes, at least at least for me.

Was it damaged, frayed by lies, omissions of truths, and possibly hanging on by a single thread? Yes. But it wasn't broken. We could fix it.

We had to try. I had to try.

I heaved a deep sigh and said, "D and I have some issues to work out, trust being the most pressing. Any advice?"

The doc smiled. "Always. Make a commitment to work on the relationship, and both of you need to take responsibility. Set a time to talk about what caused your trust issues, accept repair attempts, and communicate, communicate, communicate."

"Oh, is that all?" I asked, then blew out a breath. "Okay, I'll give it my best shot. D will, too, since he's been trying to make amends. I mean, he gave me a cat. That's probably the best gift anyone's ever given me."

"Good," Dr. Khatri said. She rose from the bed and loomed over me, hands on hips. "But first, shower, eat, and sleep."

I got up and put Sully on my shoulder, then I followed the doc out to the common area. Cassie was nowhere in sight. Typical. I'd track her down and deal with her later. The rest of the team had arrived. Alexi and Sam were tending to their battle wounds, Trinity was chatting with Lacey and Megan, and D was standing in the corner with a grim look on his face while the twins appeared to be ripping him a new one, probably on my behalf.

They were such sweeties. Snarky and misguided, but sweet in their own special way.

I walked over to them and handed Sully over to Boice. "Do we have food and a litter box?"

"Don't need one. She knows how to use a toilet. Just give her a boost and help her balance," Roice said, beaming. "I trained her myself."

Whoa! Smart kitty. Roice seemed so proud, and they weren't afraid of her anymore. She'd won them over. I gave her a pat on her little head and cooed to her, telling her she was the best, smartest, most special kitty in the whole world.

"She'll eat anything," Boice added, sounding equally proud and a bit in awe. "Well, she's eaten everything we've given her so far—chips, pizza, apples, deli meat. And before you get on my case, it won't hurt her. Mom told us that the little goblins will eat anything, including demons."

I hoped it didn't upset her little tummy and give her exploding diarrhea. If so, I would totally make them clean it up. But she seemed okay. As far as I knew, she hadn't had any issues with her first giant meal of human food. She meowed at Boice and then pulled her tiny body free of his grip and flew to Roice.

Aw, she'd claimed them, just like she'd claimed me.

I had the feeling Sully was going to be great for team morale. We could make her our team mascot and get her a little sweater with the company logo. I'd have to cut out hole for her wings and forelegs, but—

Boice snapped his fingers in front of my face. I smacked at his hand, irritated that he'd interrupted my demon cat mascot uniform planning. He grinned and patted me on the head. "Go shower. We'll feed her and put her in your room. We've got pizza and Caesar salad if you're hungry."

My stomach chose that moment to rumble. "Sounds great. I'll have some after my shower. Could you two give me a moment with Demoriel? Alone?"

The twins both scowled at D and crossed their arms. Oh, great googley moogley, this was ridiculous. I wasn't some fragile little lovesick ninny in need of protection. I could handle D. But the twins were stubborn, especially when they had their sights set on an enemy. Hadn't the twins asked if D and I were going to kiss and make up after the downtown explosion? Demons were so fickle. I'd have to get them to make nice with D. But not now.

Right. Time to pull out the big guns to distract them.

"You got the container of my energy?" I asked.

They nodded.

"Good. Be careful with it. According to the celestials who stole it from me, it's volatile." No surprise there. The twins didn't say it, but they were totally thinking it. I could tell. "And this might come in handy, too."

I reached into my bra and pulled out the mobile phone the scary angels had used to trap my ass. Yes, I'd been out of it and writhing on the floor in the aftermath, but I never let good evidence slip through my fingers. I was a total professional when it came to investigations.

"Nice work," Roice said, his gaze alight with interest. I hoped it was interest in the phone and not my boobs. "Thanks for keeping it warm."

I smacked his hand when he hit the button to open the screen. "Careful! I don't want your dumb asses getting trapped. Go do your sciency demony mumbo jumbo research on this and let me know what you find out. Better be quick before Dr. Khatri pulls you in for a session."

As I'd hoped, the twins rushed off to their computer stations, eager to begin preliminary analysis of the celestial technology before getting on the doc's radar. She'd called in Lacey after me, and then had stepped out of her makeshift office to ask Mara to join them. Good. Lacey and Mara could work on their issues and the twins could get a head start on figuring out how the celestial tech worked, and more importantly, how to stop it.

And I could extend an olive branch to my demon.

"D?"

Demoriel met my gaze, wariness in his. Damn. He was waiting for me to go off on him, or maybe to dismiss him. Or reject him. Fear of rejection was his Achilles heel. Had been since he'd been abandoned on earth. Once upon a time, he thought I'd abandoned him when his father summoned him back to the hell realm. I looked for him and tried every summoning technique and magical means at my disposal—though I knew now that my former boss hadn't kept his end of the bargain. He'd promised to help me find D, but he hadn't tried. He'd lied about it.

He'd lied about a lot.

Because of the boss's lies, I'd never found D, and D thought I'd given up on him.

And then I'd abandoned him as soon as we hit the first snag in our new relationship.

He should have told me that Belial was his father, but he hadn't trusted me. It stung, but I understood. Fear of my reaction had stopped him, and when I learned the truth, I'd made his fear real. He should have told me the truth, but I should have been willing to hear it and to give him the chance to explain instead of bailing.

I took a slow step closer, careful not to spook him. He'd relaxed a bit after my roommates left, but his guard was back up now that we had a bit of privacy. Somewhere inside the powerful demon man lived the lost and lonely boy he used to be, still longing for a home. It made my heart hurt. I put my own fear aside and slowly extended my arms.

"Can I give you a hug?"

Before I could blink, D scooped me into his arms and held me so tight it hurt to breathe. I didn't care. Who needed oxygen with an embrace so warm, so comforting, and so right? It was like coming home. Tension and the day's terrors faded, replaced by solace in each other's arms.

"I've missed you," he whispered, his voice hoarse.

"Me, too." I said, fighting back tears. I wished I could stay in his arms forever, but we had to do the work if we wanted to find our way back to each other. "Want to talk over breakfast tomorrow?"

He pulled away and met my gaze, his filled with humor and hunger. Heat crept into my cheeks. We both remembered our last breakfast, and what had followed. While I was eager for a repeat, sex wasn't a good idea right now. Not until we'd worked out our trust issues and worked on the relationship.

But a make out session and heavy petting could be on the table. What a delicious thought.

Before I could let the thought blossom, D leaned down and kissed me, gentle at first, tentative, leaving it up to me if I wanted more.

I did. Oh, did I ever.

I opened my mouth for him, and it was all the invitation he needed. He picked me up and spun us around, pinning me against the wall as he explored my mouth with his tongue, nipping and sucking at my lips. His hands moved to cup my face. It was tender and erotic, all good things rolled into one.

It ended sooner than I would have liked, but it was probably for the best. The room had gone quiet. I risked a glance over D's shoulder and found everyone left in the room, including my sister, pretending to ignore us while smiling or chuckling. Even Trinity smiled, but maybe that was because Sam was massaging her shoulders.

Megan met my gaze and gave me two thumbs up.

"Until tomorrow," D said. Then he spun me around, slapped my ass, and shooed me out of the room.

CHAPTER SIXTEEN

I woke up with a face full of fur. Sully had apparently decided my face was the best bed for her hairy ass and had plastered her entire body, belly down, over it. I pulled her down to my chest, earning a squeak of protest, but she settled soon enough.

Surprisingly, I'd slept very well. Every time a nightmare invaded my sleeping brain, Sully's purrs chased it away. Kitty was the best emotional support animal ever.

We cuddled until my bladder demanded I get up and take care of morning business. Sully decided to exercise her wings, flying around the bathroom and knocking toiletries off the counter and shelves before I placed her hairy rump on the toilet to take care of her morning business.

"Wait a minute," I said after scooping her off the seat and flushing. "Are you bigger?"

I swore she'd grown overnight, but that wasn't possible, was it? I didn't think earth cats grew so fast, but maybe demon cats, or Motiaummerrs, or whatever they were did. I didn't want to call Cooper and ask, but maybe Trinity had some books on demon realm animals in her vast collection.

Someone knocked at my door, so I put aside my musings about the growth rate of demon feline species and went to answer it, my stomach fluttering with equal parts anticipation and dread. Sure, hashing everything out was the key to rebuilding our relationship, but I wished we could just fast forward to the good part after all the talking and talking and crying and yelling, or just magic our way out of it.

Sadly, life didn't work that way in any realm, earth, hell, or celestial.

I opened the door to a mouthwatering sight. Demoriel with sleep tousled hair and morning stubble, wearing a tight T-shirt that hugged his muscles and flannel pajama pants low and loose on his hips. He held a tray with breakfast sandwiches and coffee. Three sandwiches.

Sully swooped down and grabbed a sandwich, flew into the closet, landed on the top shelf, and began devouring it while growling.

"Glad you brought three," I said, running a hand through my messy locks. Thankfully, my roommates had brought my go-bag with them to HQ packed with my favorite yoga pants and a T-shirt that read "Learn Latin. Talk to Demons," which had served as my pajamas. I fiddled with the hem of my shirt and looked up at him through my lashes, my lips curling into a smile.

He grinned and said, "*Adoro il tuo sorriso, mi fa battere il cuore.*"

It wasn't Latin. I'd learned enough Latin to get the gist of relevant ancient texts on demons. But it was close. Italian. Italian spoken in a deep, sultry voice like smooth Kentucky bourbon and just as warm and satisfying. He said he loved my smile. It made his heartbeat.

It made me want to jump him bones.

I was so easy.

I stepped aside and gestured for him to come in. Like all the rooms in our HQ bunker this small sleeping room was equipped with a bed, nightstand, TV, and a small powder room, but no table or chairs. It was more dormitory than hotel, but the bed was comfortable and had enough space for us to both sit without encouraging any shenanigans. Besides, we'd shared a bed before. When we were kids, we'd curl up together after Mom went to bed, and we'd fooled around in my own bed in my own home not long ago, after he'd come back from the hell realm and into my life.

Before I'd learned the truth about this dad. Belial, our enemy, the demon who wanted to capture me—and his lover Hannah/Haniel possessing me—was Demoriel's father. Not that there was any love lost between father and son, no more than there was any lost between me and my piece of shit celestial father. But D didn't tell me the truth. I had to find out when Belial attacked and almost killed me and the rest of the team.

We ate in companionable silence and sipped our coffee. I gave him a few surreptitious glances, and he did the same. We needed to talk, but where to start?

"Belial sent me to find and capture you," D said, all business. "He only sent Mephisto later after he figured out I had no intention of betraying you to him. I knew he'd send someone else, so I kept watch to protect you."

I put my coffee cup on the nightstand with excessive care. What I wanted was to fling it across the room at D's thick, stupid head.

"Protect me," I said, matching his tone. "Because I've always been a damsel in distress who couldn't take care of herself."

"That's not what I meant—"

"Stop talking, D. I'm not finished." I stood up and, for once, loomed over *him*. "So, you didn't actually escape from dear old dad using high demon magic because you're a 'decent practitioner.' He sent you. That was your first lie. Then you lied—well, not lied, you just didn't tell me you were back for a while, so I'll let that one slide—and then you didn't tell me you're Belial's son. A lie of omission."

He stared at me with his jaw clenched tight and scowling as he took his "punishment." No, I wasn't having it. D was a fighter. So was I. And when we fought each other, we were electric. I needed to get him mad enough to have the knock down drag out we were due and to talk to me and tell me all his secrets so we could put all this past us.

"If I'd come to you straight out of the hell realm, out of the hell my father put me in, told you he'd sent me to find you and bring you back but not to worry, I would never do that to you, you would have trusted me, right? Because trust is something you do so well."

D, one. Jinx, zero.

He stood up, taking away my height advantage, and started pacing. Good. He was getting worked up now. The vein on his temple was pounding, he was breathing hard, and his fists were clenched.

Oh, look at that, mine were, too, and I my own racing pulse pounded in my veins.

"Is that all you've got, D? Trust issues? Really, I expected better. Don't disappoint me."

He stopped and hit me with a death glare. "Why not? I'm very good at disappointment. I was such a disappointment to my father that he had one of his minions to dump me on earth. Or maybe it was my mother who didn't want me, whoever she was. Nothing changed when he called me back to hell. I was a means to an end. That's all. Not an heir, not a general, not a beloved son—just a tool to get what he wanted."

Oh, man. I knew Belial was evil, but even evil bastards could love their children. Then again, I thought my father loved me once upon a time.

I sighed. "Guess I'm not the only one with trust issues. Look, I get it. Your dad's an asshole of epic proportions. Mine is, too. He was the one who saddled me with Hannah, or Haniel. Breathed her right into me when I was five years old and then bailed on the family."

D stomped over to me and gripped me by the shoulders. "Your father did that to you? Your *father* used you as a vessel to imprison Haniel, one of the most powerful celestials in three realms?"

I pulled out of his grasp. "Oh, no you don't. We're talking about you right now. We can talk about me later, and we can talk about modernizing your weird, formal demony way of speaking. Now tell me, what did Belial do to you when he called you back?"

His gaze blazed with fury with a weariness beyond bearing just beneath the rage. I was already determined to destroy Belial out of duty. Based on the look in D's eyes and the awful things Belial must have done to inspire it, I'd be killing the demon bastard out of vengeance.

D's fingers dug into the flesh of my shoulders hard enough to bruise, hard enough to make my demon ink glow and my celestial power heat up to boiling. "He used every method at his disposal to break me, mold me, and make me his instrument of destruction. I hunted lesser demons, slaughtered them, and brought their corpses back to my father, and he nearly tore me to pieces with demon magic until I had to learn how to defend myself or die. I lost myself in darkness and delighted in death and destruction. It was that or go mad. Or die. But I refused to die."

Tears rolled down my cheeks as I reached for him. He pulled back and let go of me like I was a piece of hot iron that burned him. After stumbling back a few steps, he turned around as if to leave.

"Don't go," I said, grabbing his arm. "Please don't walk away from me now."

I couldn't let him leave because I'd realized something.

"You were more afraid to tell me what Belial did to you than you were to tell me he was your father, weren't you?"

D's body went rigid. Looked like the score was D, one, Jinx one. But I was no longer interested in keeping score.

I shook him lightly. "Did you think I would judge you? Or leave you? Me, the bad seed, my mother's bane and my father's dirty little secret— the kid everyone hated because they knew I was different. I was cursed and evil and the only reason a kid like me would be cursed was because I did something to deserve it. That's what everyone thought except for my sister. And you."

"You're not evil." D didn't turn around, but his voice was raw and strained as he spoke. "Your mom never thought you were evil, either. She just didn't know what to do to help you, and she was working so hard to keep your family going, there wasn't much she could do other than feed, clothe, and shelter you. And love you from afar."

D was right about my mom. I was working on healing our relationship, but old habits and beliefs died hard. I'd spent so long believing she didn't love me because I was bad, and she'd spent years thinking I'd pushed her away because she was a bad mom and that *I* didn't love *her.*

I braced myself and took the proverbial leap of faith, hoping D would catch me when I fell. "You're not evil, either, and you always accepted me and loved me just as I was. Just as I am. Just like I accepted you and loved you since we were kids. I don't know what else there is between us, or what we might become, but I do know you're my best friend. I would never abandon you, no matter what. I'm sorry for anything I ever did to make you think I might."

By now I was ugly crying. Good thing I didn't have a mirror. My face was probably blotched and puffy, nose running, and eyes swollen from too many tears. Tremors ran through my body, but I refused to let go of D and collapse on the floor.

If he walked out the door, I'd never get him back. The thought of losing him, that my stubborn pride and rash reaction might drive him away, had me on the brink of panic and despair.

D slowly turned around to face me. Fat tears rolled down his cheeks as he struggled to breathe, gasping to fill his lungs with air like a man on the brink of drowning.

"What Belial did to you, it wasn't your fault, D. You didn't deserve it."

I moved closer and he opened his arms, allowing me to collapse against him. I'd have fallen had he not caught me with his strong arms. Instead, I told him what was in my heart. "I'm sorry for what happened to you. I'm so damned sorry I didn't find you, didn't fight heaven and hell to get you out of there. I shouldn't have trusted Sameal. I should have tried harder, I—"

"Shh," he whispered, stroking my hair. "Hush. It's not your fault. You didn't do anything to drive me away. You were right. I was afraid to tell you, but I shouldn't have been. I should have trusted you."

I melted into him, shuddering as a decade of sorrow, grief, and confusion came pouring out of me, and poured out of D, too. He'd been through so much. We both had, and yet, somehow, we'd survived, and we were here. Together.

It was enough to make me believe in miracles.

"You're the reason I stayed alive," he said. "Even in my darkest hour, I knew I had to survive so I could find my way back to you."

A fresh wave of sobs wracked my body, but this time, they washed my worries and uncertainties away. We were both here. We had a chance.

"No more secrets. Wherever we go from here, let's be honest with each other. Always."

He choked on a laugh. "I don't think I have any secrets bigger than what I just told you. Except..."

I tensed, but he chuckled and kissed me on my forehead. "Confession time. I like pineapple on pizza. Black olives, too."

I burst out laughing. It was too perfect. "Gross and grosser, but I think I can live with it. Given time."

D picked me up, making me squeak in surprise. He took me to the bed gently set me down. "My intentions are honorable, I promise, but I was already exhausted when I came in with breakfast. You could use a few more hours of sleep, too. I can sleep on top of the covers, or I could go back to my room, or grab a couch..."

I patted the bed. "Too tired for monkey business, but I wouldn't mind curling up with you for a while." The request made me oddly shy. No matter what I told Dr. Khatri or myself, I could do vulnerability. But only with D.

It still wasn't easy. But when he climbed into bed beside me, turned me on my side, and spooned me, I realized being vulnerable was worth it.

Sully landed on the pillow beside me with a light thud. She sniffed D's hand, accepted a boop on the nose, and gave his finger a gentle lick, the hussy. She touched her nose to mine and then curled into herself. I fell asleep with the feel of D's arms around me and to the sound of Sully's gentle purrs.

It was a brief respite, a calm before the storm, but I would take it and savor every moment.

CHAPTER SEVENTEEN

I ran through a field full of colorful shapes and color floating above me as I ran and jumped, trying to swat them with a stick like they were giant pinatas. Sully flew by and popped ten in a row with her claws. Show off. At last, my running leap brough me close enough to hit a bright purple diamond. It burst, showering me with candy, tacos, and tiny bottles of liquor as the team cheered me on with thunderous clap clap claps.

The claps grew louder, then turned into knocks.

"What?" I grumbled, leaving my pleasant dream world for an unwanted state of being awake. "I was just about to make a margarita."

An annoyingly chipper voice traveled through the door straight to my aching head. "No time for day drinking, you and D slept in long enough. Chop chop. Staff meeting in five. Get up, get dressed, get moving."

"It's official. You're my least favorite sister."

Megan laughed. "I'm your only sister."

"Which means you can be my favorite and least favorite at the same time." I dragged the covers over my head rolled over, landing against a hard, warm body. D. I smiled. Between my demon and my demon cat, I'd had the best sleep, even if it was only for a couple of hours after an early breakfast. And I was more than reluctant to get out of bed.

"The twins stayed up all night analyzing the phone and the explosive soul goop you brought in last night. Don't you want to know what they found out about it?" Megan used her singsong you-know-you-want-to voice that never failed to get me to go along with whatever mischief she concocted when we were kids.

But she was right. If the twins had information and a lead on what to do next, like finding out how the celestial entrepreneurs were collecting and transporting the soul-sucked energy from the phone zombies to wherever they were storing it, we could track it to the storage site and stop them from building their weapon of mass destruction.

Duty called.

"Good morning, Jane," D said in a sleepy voice. He rolled over and yanked the covers off my head, then he kissed me before I could protest.

I could get used to this.

"If I have to get up, you have to get up," I said, hopping out of bed before my inner ho-bag decided to take advantage of the demon in my bed. Sex, as tempting as it was, would have to wait, and it would be better to work out more of the kinks in our relationship before getting physical again.

But it also gave me an idea. "When we solve this case, I think you should take me on a date," I said as I rooted around in my bag for clean clothes and underwear, not to mention a toothbrush and deodorant. "A real date, like a sit-down dinner, movie with a giant tub of popcorn with extra butter—you know, something normal people who like each other do.

D stretched when I looked up. Since he was still above the covers, I got a great view of his toned body, including those mouthwatering abs as his shirt was rucked up, and a hint of his glorious Adonis belt, aka a part of the male anatomy that made smart girls stupid. He grinned, flexing just a bit for me. Damn, I needed to look away before I started drooling.

"I think that's a fine idea. You'll have to let me know where we can find the best burgers in town, or steak and lobster if you prefer. How about dinner and a night out on the town dancing, or maybe we could catch a live band, or a movie, or a show at TPAC?"

I blinked hard, suddenly and irrationally emotional. I'd never had a date like that. Between being the weird girl next door and the beginning of my demon-hunting career just after I turned eighteen, I'd never had time for dating. Hookups? Sure. But an actual date with the promise of a real relationship?

"Jane, are you okay?" D hopped out of bed and rushed over to me. He reached out like he wanted to take me in his arms but hesitated. We were still a little unsure of each other, of our boundaries and what was permissible. I hated it.

Wiping stupid tears away from my eyes, I reached for him, and he took me in his arms.

"Too much?" he asked, rubbing my back. "We could start with coffee or a walk in the park. Something simple."

I laughed and thumped my head on his chest. "No, it's not too much. That all sounds...perfect. I'd love to do all those dates and more with you."

He pulled back and grinned at me. The dimple on his right cheek made my heart melt. "You pick the restaurant and time. I'll do the rest."

I stood on tiptoes, grabbed his face, and pulled him down for a kiss. Unlike D, there was nothing tentative or gentle, just raw need to claim him, to show him how much he meant to me. He caught on quick and opened his mouth so my tongue could explore him and continue the claiming. I bit his lip and then ran my tongue over it to soothe the sting.

He groaned. Good. I liked a little pain with my pleasure, too.

I snaked my hands around to grab his firm ass, enjoying the freedom to touch and tease. He picked me up and cradled my ass in his firm hands so he could give as good as he got. I ground against his growing arousal, moaning at remembered ecstasy. I hadn't had him inside of me—not yet—but his kisses and caresses promised the heights of heaven delivered in a body made for sin.

My annoying sister started banging on the door again. "Stop with the kissy face and get moving!"

D carried me over to the door, opened it, grinned at my sister's look of surprise, and kissed me thoroughly in front of her, my team, Megan's husband Brad, who'd joined us at HQ for safety and was now staring at me with his mouth hanging open, my mother—

Oh, shit. Mom.

D ended our kiss and turned to my mother, who'd been evacuated to HQ, and said, "Good morning, Mrs. McGee. Nice to see you again."

Charlene McGee, aka my mother, was poised and polished from her perfectly styled blond locks to her pressed and immaculate dress suit despite being dragged unceremoniously from her house to the bowels of HQ. They must have caught her just after work, but she didn't have the same frazzled, disheveled appearance the rest of us wore. The makeup hid her freckles, a gift from our Scottish ancestors, but she had a lovely round face, sparkling blue eyes, and pale skin that contrasted with my olive tones and dark eyes from my Persian father.

Assuming he really was Persian. He'd lied about so many things. But if his appearance had been some sort of celestial glamour, I wouldn't have inherited his features, right? I did have my mom's bone structure, which meant I didn't always get profiled by the cops and TSA. Megan had pale skin and blue eyes, so she never got hassled. I was glad since I didn't wish that sort of racist bullshit on anyone.

My mother stared at us with an expression I couldn't interpret but assumed was disapproval. She'd always disapproved of me.

Internal therapist here! You're not being fair. She doesn't disapprove of you. She disapproves of what your father did to you.

Right. I'd been working on my mommy issues, but old habits stuck to me like gum on the bottom of my boots. After my father saddled me with a demon-disguised crazy archangel, I'd become the bad kid. Self-fulfilling prophecy, but in my defense, I was only five and thought I'd become demon possessed because I was evil and had attracted evil.

I wished Cassie had shown me that stupid vision sooner, but at least I now knew the truth. And I was an adult now.

Looking back, my relationship with my mother was clouded by my own hang ups and negative self-image as much as her struggles as a single mom who'd been abandoned by a man she'd loved so much.

I took a deep breath, and instead of saying something snarky or defensive, I said, "Hi, Mom. I'm glad you're here with us. You'll be safer. I promise I'll sort this mess out as soon as I can so you can go home. I—"

Mom rushed over to me and grabbed me in a bear hug. Then she let go and started looking me over and poking and prodding me. It was weird, a little invasive, and still filled me with a strange warm and fuzzy feeling that made my eyes water. Again. Ugh, while all these feels were good for me, I kind of missed being emotionally stunted.

"Meg told me you got captured by those awful angels. Did they hurt you? Have you had anything to eat? You're too thin." Mom was crying, too. Crap.

I squirmed and looked at the floor. "I'm fine, mom. And D fed me this morning. The twins fed me last night and I got checked out by the doc."

"Good. As for you," she said, looking at D, "I'm so glad you're here for Jane. You don't let her go off on her own to fight these...things. Look out for her."

He put his hand over his heart and gave her a small, solemn bow. "Always."

She blushed. My demon made my mom blush. It was so adorable. I'd have to tease them both later. Mom turned her attention back to me and gave me an odd look. A familiar sense of panic stabbed at my chest under the scrutiny. Ugh. I really needed to get past this. Mom wasn't judging me or looking for flaws or trying to figure out what I'd been doing wrong.

Did I have something in my teeth?

"It's good to see you smile, Jane."

I was smiling. At her. Oh, poor mom. Her reaction reminded me of how damaged our relationship had been and how far we had to go. But I shook off the guilt I didn't need to carry and focused on living in the moment. And for the first time, I could be my authentic self and share it with her. It was a gift beyond measure.

"Thanks, Mom. Did the twins get you settled in?"

My mom waved her hands dismissively. "Don't fret about me. You go meet with your team and come up with a plan to stop those bad angels. I'll help with research and keeping everyone fed."

I gave her another hug and then grabbed D's hand so we could take our seats at the conference table. Lacey and Mara were sitting together, their chairs as close as possible. Good. It made my heart ache a little when I spotted Alexi sitting on his own. Megan busied herself helping the twins set up for their presentation while Brad worked at one of the computer stations day trading or some shit.

Okay, I shouldn't be so judgmental about it. As a mundane human, Brad wasn't equipped to work in our world.

Then again, neither was my mom, but she was making and serving food and checking in on everyone and doing her part. She didn't have to, owed us nothing, and by all rights could have been angry or resentful about the disruption to her life. Instead, she decided to be part of the solution.

I caught Megan glance at Brad and then away. Uh oh. I'd never really cared for Brad, but Megan had seemed happy with him. That was enough for me. But maybe the happiness had faded. Or maybe Brad was just being an ass because Megan had her own career now and wasn't at his beck and call anymore.

Brad glanced up at me. I smiled. With teeth. His gaze went wide, and he ducked his head to focus on his computer. I wondered what new money-making scheme he was working on. Megan told me he was diversifying, hopping into the hot real estate market in Nashville that booming.

"I think you scared him," D said, a smile in his voice.

"If you two are done making goo goo eyes at each other, we'll start this meeting." Boice strolled up to the head of the table and placed the phone and storage container on top for all of us to see. The container looked as full as it had yesterday with the strange, glowing substance that could be either liquid or gas. Maybe the twins hadn't made any progress on that front. They still had the phone, though.

Roice, who'd donned safety glasses, lifted the container and jabbed the top with a giant needle attached to a syringe of some sort. It was glass and had demon writing on it, so not from earth. I really didn't want to know what a needle that size would be used for in the hell realm, but the twins could have rigged it in their lab. They were always tinkering with tech and trying out different types of magic on it to help the team out with investigations and to trick us out with James Bond worthy demon-tech gadgets. I figured at least seventy-five percent of their work was team related.

As for the other twenty-five percent? Again, I didn't really want to know what else they got up to in their lab.

Roice pulled the plunger up slightly, presumably extracting a sample of the energy inside. My energy. What was he planning to do with it? I assumed I could regenerate soul energy or life force, but maybe I needed to get the stuff in the container infused back into me somehow. The process would no doubt be unpleasant and painful, and likely dangerous.

Ugh, I did not want to be one of the twins' science projects.

After Boice donned his safety glasses and placed a beaker inside some sort of transparent demon glass container, Roice placed the lid on the container and jabbed it with the needle, pressing down on the plunger.

As soon as the energy hit the beaker, it exploded.

CHAPTER EIGHTEEN

Chaos ensued.

Everything happened so fast. The beaker inside the demon glass shattered as blinding light flashed from the explosion. When I came back to my senses, I was under the table in the middle of a panic attack, panting and trying to catch my breath. It was harder thanks to the hard, heavy body covering mine.

"D," I gasped. "Can't...breathe."

He pulled his body off mine and pulled me up to my knees, checking me over for injuries while I focused on not hyperventilating. I closed my eyes and listened to the chorus of shouts and curses echoing through the room. Shouting, but no screams, no smoke, no fire or blaring alarms. We were okay, then. The explosion stayed confined to the demon glass.

A warm hand on my back helped me slow my breathing and centered me. When I finally rose on shaking legs and surveyed the room, the twins were staring at the demon glass container with their jaws agape, shock written over their stupid faces. The idiots hadn't expected the explosion, which meant they hadn't fully tested the soul energy's volatility until now. In the conference room. With the whole team surrounding the table like sitting ducks.

I was going to kill them. From the looks of the rest of the team, I'd probably have to wait in line.

Mara was calming Lacey, Alexi had wolfed out and was ready for battle, Brad was presumably hiding under his desk, since all I could see were his ass and feet, and Megan stood with her demon knife at the ready.

She was a full-blown bad ass. It ran in the family. I couldn't have been prouder.

D looked so angry I had to take a step back before I came to my senses. He wasn't a threat to me, but he might teleport to the twins and lop their noggins off. I put a hand on his arm and said, "It's okay. We're all okay. Don't murder our tech support, okay?"

D growled.

"Let me handle it. I'll replace their hair gel with superglue, or maybe put plastic wrap over their toilet. Or," I said as D's lips twitched with the effort not to laugh, "I'll cover everything in their room with aluminum foil. You can totally help."

He put a hand over mine and took a deep breath. Oblivious to their near death and destruction, the twins were busy bickering about the results of their impromptu experiment.

"I told you we should have tested it last night," Boice said, elbowing his brother.

"How could I know?" Roice said, scowling. "It didn't react this way in our other tests."

"Nice to see you two didn't blow up the place." Trinity's snark and timing left me in awe.

Our girl boss had walked in with Sam, who looked grim and a little angry. Oh dear. More bad news, or did Sam figure out what Trinity bargained away to confine our enemies to the city? I hoped she'd talk to Sam about it. The Marquess demon was powerful and clever, and he was in love with our fearless leader and scholar extraordinaire. If he couldn't figure out how to break the bargain, he could find a loophole or two to get her out of giving up whatever she'd bargained with.

I hoped it wasn't her soul.

Roice looked offended. "Have a little faith. We're professionals."

I snorted. Professionals my fat ass. I would have said it out loud, too, but I was worried they'd do another panic-attack inducing demo. It was getting old.

Trinity glanced at Sam, who produced a flask from a pocket in his fine robes. Right on cue, Mom brought out a tray full of tiny glasses and placed them on the table before excusing herself to go back to her work in the kitchen. The Marquess filled our glasses with a shot of some pale liquid, handed one to Trinity, and took one for himself.

"Please, my friends, this elixir is soothing and will calm you."

I grabbed a glass and downed it like a shot. Instead of going down with a burn, the drink was smooth, like good Scotch flavored with a hint of caramel. Warmth spread through my body along with a sense of well-being and without the buzz that came from liquor, but still pleasant.

"Okay, break's over. Time to get back to our staff meeting." Trinity turned her attention to the twins and said, "No more surprises from you two or I'll cap your supply budget permanently."

We all took our seats at the conference table and waited for my roomies to continue their presentation.

"Right. The substance in the flask—soul energy, life force, or whatever you want to call it, is pure magic. This thing," Roice said, pointing to the phone the celestials had used to drain me, "is eighty-five percent tech. Technology is our jam. The celestial magic is a little trickier, but it's not all that different from demon magic."

"We did some experimenting last night." Boice flashed a wicked grin as his fingers tapped on the keyboard that linked to the flatscreen on the wall. Instead of showing a PowerPoint presentation filled with their trademark demonic icons, a video clip waited.

Boice hit play, and we watched the twins, who'd apparently filmed themselves, tinker with the container of my soul juice. Decked out in lab coats, safety goggles, and gloves, they almost looked like respectable scientists, scientists who doubled as skinny gamer boys with spiky dirty blond hair sporting graphic tees and skinny jeans. They hooked up the storage container to some sort of tubing connected to a contraption that looked like a combination circuit board and enlarged computer chip. Screen Boice fiddled with the container, turning it upside down, then right side up before shaking it and banging it on the side of their workbench.

I gasped and Roice paused the video, a stupid smirk plastered over his stupid face.

"What part of volatile and explosive did you not understand?" I resisted the urge to bang my head on the desk. We were okay, obviously, but watching my idiot roommate play with magical celestial crap that had blown up a downtown building and caused a minor explosion not five minutes ago was not good for my blood pressure.

Unperturbed, Roice snorted. "Just wait. We haven't even gotten to the good part yet."

Ugh. These morons were going to be the death of us all. I totally loved them, but their shenanigans were completely out of control.

Real-life Roice hit play, showing screen Roice hooking up some kind of tubing to the bottom of the storage container and fiddling with other pieces of equipment unfamiliar to me. Their workspace in the conference room was clean and clear, so they must've filmed in their lab somewhere in the bowels of our operations building. Made me curious about the other wonders and horrors hidden in the nooks and crannies of HQ's lower levels.

Turning my attention back to the screen, I watched as Boice activated something that pressurized the interior of the storage container, pushing its contents down through the tube to reach the electrical portion of whatever the twins had constructed. The tiny light bulbs that were attached to the circuit board suddenly blazed to life. Movie twins shielded their eyes, and screen Roice yelled at screen Boice to back off on the pressure. Other components of the circuit board became activated with rapidly spinning gears and moving parts.

When smoke started spewing from the lights and motors, screen Boice turned off the pressurizing device.

Roice paused the video again and said, "As you can see, the soul energy can be tapped by mechanical means and used to power physical devices."

"We only used a fraction of what's in there." Boice held up the storage container and tapped it against his head. "There's probably enough Jinx juice in there to power the city for a few days."

Okay. Enough was enough.

I hopped out of my chair and snatched the container out of the demon's hand. "Stop screwing around and don't call it 'Jinx juice.' It sounds so...dirty."

Boice took a step toward me, reaching for the container. No way was I giving it back. I darted to the left and dodged his hands, ducking and coming out behind him so I could kick him in the butt. Roice took advantage of the distraction to make a grab for the container, but I anticipated the move and shoved my elbow into his gut.

"Give it back!" Boice said from the floor. Huh, guess I kicked him harder than I thought.

"That was so uncalled for." Roice wheezed after my hit to his solar plexus. Served him right.

The twins could've fought dirty using magic, but I figured they'd have a care while I held the container. While good at playing it cool, the fact that they were afraid to get rough and risk knocking it out of my hand let me know they did, in fact, have a healthy respect for the nature and stability of the energy. Or maybe the feared my celestial and demon powers.

Nah. They knew I still sucked at tapping those. It was the unstable energy.

"Enough!"

Trinity rarely yelled, but when she did, we all stopped and listened. Our fearless leader stood and glared at us. Then she closed her eyes and rubbed the bridge of her nose, a sure sign that she'd had enough of our shenanigans. "Agent McGee, please return the container to Agents Boice and Roice."

Roice grinned in triumph, but it quickly died when Trinity spoke again. "Agents Boice and Roice, you will treat the container of soul energy with the care an unstable energy source deserves, and you will find a way to give it back to Jinx by magical means when this investigation is over, aside from whatever you use for the investigation. It belongs to her."

I handed the container to Boice and sat back down, pacified for the moment. "You'd better not even think about using that big ass needle on me," I grumped.

"Why is it so volatile?" Lacey asked. "Seems like celestials would look for some other means to power their weapon. Working with such dangerous stuff puts them at risk for exposure—not just to us, but to the mundane world—and puts them at risk for blowing themselves up, too."

Boice beamed at my partner. "That's an excellent question. We think the volatility comes from Jinx's unique mixture of celestial, human, and demon soul energy. As for risks, assuming the celestial realm operates like the hell realm, which is a safe enough assumption given their use of magic, they're out of their depth when it comes to technology on earth."

It made sense. Why bother inventing machines when you had magic to do the work. The hell and celestial realms would be a cultural anthropologist's dream to study. No industrial revolution, no digital age, I imagined them as fantasy realms with feudal systems, where the greatest magic wielders ruled and fought one another for power with enchanted armies when they weren't fighting monstrosities fuel by even more powerful magic.

I'd seen illustrations of such battles in demon realm books, strikingly similar to human artworks from the dawn of human civilization through the Middle Ages. A first-hand account of the power structures would be useful to the team. Most of our refugee demons were at the lowest rungs of the ladder of power, and our former boss wasn't forthcoming with information about the demon realm that didn't pertain to our operation. Maybe I could ask D about it. No, he had too many bad memories and they were too...raw.

"Demons rely on magic for most everything, too. You humans and part humans would find the hell realm quite primitive at first glance, kind of like earth's ancient to medieval period but with better hygiene and without the dysentery." Roice picked up his brother's narrative. If they got really excited, they'd start finishing each other's sentences. "We have spells for hunting, farming, building, heating and cooling, you name it. Lesser demons trade labor or service for magic they can't produce themselves. It's why demon lords and other high-ranking demons have so many legions. Mechanical and technological devices confuse them."

"Unless they've been on earth long enough to adapt and learn." Mara said. She hadn't been speaking at meetings lately, except to agree with team members or cheer them on. It was great to see her gain the confidence to share her knowledge. We'd totally been underutilizing her.

No, that wasn't right. We'd underestimated and undervalued her. It wouldn't happen again. Not on my watch.

I met Trinity's gaze. She must've read my mind and had the same thoughts herself, since her lips curled into a small smile, and she nodded. "That's a great point, Mara. Do you think the celestials are hiring demon refugees to work the tech as well as for harvesting energy?"

Mara's cheeks flushed and she sank in her chair a bit. Lacey grabbed her hand and squeezed it, encouraging her. "I think they must be using demons in the community to work with the technology, and possibly other non-human entities. I'll check in with my contacts and see what I can find out."

"Excellent." Trinity turned back to the twins. "What else do you have for us?"

Roice frowned. "That wasn't enough?"

Before Trinity could lose her shit, Boice chimed in. "He's kidding. We think the key to solving this is tracing the collected energy back to its source. But we have no idea how the energy flows from the phones to the storage units. It could be by magical or mundane means, or some combination of the two."

"And the only way to figure it out is to run tests during an energy collection," Roice said, grabbing the phone. "Which means we need a volunteer."

CHAPTER NINETEEN

I flew out of the chair and screamed, "No!"

My teammates stared at me in stunned silence, except for the twins, who looked at me with a mixture of sympathy and wariness and said, "It's the only way."

"You don't know what it's like to be trapped," I said, hands shaking, breath coming in gasps and wheezes. "It's like pure bliss and everything you've ever wanted and needed rolled into colors and lights and peace, and...and..."

This was the hard part. "When it's gone, it's worse than hurting. It's despair, and hopelessness, and agony, and if you can't get it back, all you want to do is die."

A horrifying thought occurred to me then.

"Are we tracking the people from the explosion? The ones who were trapped?"

The phone zombies had been the tip of the iceberg. ZenMax had probably sent out thousands of copies of their "game" under the guise of beta testing. When they went global—assuming the tech and magic could breach whatever barrier was holding demons and celestials in Nashville —billions would be trapped. And due to its addictive nature, humans would choose the game over life, work, caring for their families and themselves. I could see it. An apocalyptic landscape serving as a battlefield for demon or celestial annihilation.

Before that, when the celestials had enough magic to power their weapon, they'd destroy the game and feast on the misery of humans in withdrawal until they went mad or killed themselves to escape the utter desolation. I'd been trapped for less than an hour, and for a brief moment I had considered using my knife to end the suffering.

How much worse would it be after days? Weeks? A year?

Strong arms wrapped me in a warm embrace and kept me from falling. D kept me on my feet and gave me his strength and resilience, his warmth, his compassion, and his understanding. He'd endured darkness and had succumbed to it during his brutal training in his father's legion. Instead of giving in to despair, he'd held onto hope. Hope he could escape. Hope he would someday find me again. I had been his shelter, his beacon, and his hope. Me, the demon girl, the bad seed, the loneliest kid on the block. I'd done that.

If I could do that, I could pull myself out of the pit of despair and fight. I didn't have to do it alone. I had D.

Leaning on those you love and who love you worked. Who knew?

"We finally hacked into their computer system. They're monitoring all "test subjects," who are currently alive and as well as can be expected. We can find a way to save them," D said. "We *will* find a way to save them."

D's words gave me a spark of hope.

Reluctantly, I pulled away, out of his embrace and back to reality. Not so very long ago, I would have been mortified by my display of emotion in full view of my team. But when I looked around the room, instead of eyes averted in discomfort, second-hand embarrassment, disappointment, or judgement, I found understanding, empathy, camaraderie, and unwavering support. They got it because they'd been through it, too.

And seeing Mara's hand locked tight with Lacey's, Sam's hands on Trinity's shoulders, the twins standing shoulder-to-shoulder at the ready with brotherly trust, Mom's arms wrapped around Megan on one side and Alexi on the other—no idea what had happened to Brad—I knew that this team was operating on a different wavelength than we had before. We'd been a rag-tag band of misfits thrown together by association with the demon world, working under the iron fist of our former boss. Now, we worked for ourselves and for the common goal of saving the world and fear was not our primary motivation.

It was love. The love for our world and the humans, demons, and other preternatural entities who called earth home. The love of this found family, twisted and still dysfunctional, but not broken. This was worth fighting for and risking everything to save.

I took a deep breath for courage and said, "I'll do it. Have Dr. Khatri ready to pull me out.." Turning back to D, I gulped. "I'll need you to be my anchor. Make sure I don't lose myself."

He looked deep into my eyes, his sparking with unearthly intensity. Fumbling in his jeans pocket, he pulled out a tarnished chain with a pendant attached. No. It couldn't be.

I took the chain when he offered it and examined it, still familiar and comforting in my hand as it had the day I'd given it to D. It was cheap, the chain the kind that turned green after a few months of wear, all I could afford by skimping on school lunches to save up for a token of my affection for D. At ten years old, he was a friend. No physical attraction then. We'd been so very young, clinging to each other through life's cruelties great and small and finding small joys in each other and in the simple things we shared—a snail shell, the feather of a blue jay, pressed flowers and clover necklaces and crowns woven during long summer days.

And the locket.

Objectively, the heart locket was cheesy, but through the lens of an outcast child who treasured her only friend, a secret friend who understood her and shared her oddities and was as lost as she, it encompassed all she felt, all I felt, about D.

I put the locket around my neck, tucking it beneath my shirt to rest near my heart.

"I've got you," he said, giving me a gentle kiss for luck.

I stood in one of the twins' laboratory chambers. The reinforced steel and concrete walls were with demon glass to contain any explosion my volatile energy might cause. Sam and D used their magic to create a protective spell to protect my body in the event of an explosion, as well as the small furry body of my demon cat. Sully perched on my shoulder, her warm weight reassuring. Dr. Khatri had put me through my paces with deep breathing exercises to clear my mind, relax my body, and mentally rehearse getting in and out of the trap with my sanity intact. My time limit was fifteen minutes.

If the twins weren't able to trace the energy's mode of travel in that timeframe, D would get fifteen minutes, followed by Alexi, Lacey, Mara, and Sam. Trinity reluctantly agreed with our decision to exclude her from participation. We needed her sharp and at the ready to lead the team and couldn't afford for her to become incapacitated.

Mom looked grim but didn't voice any objection, for which I was grateful. I understood her fear, but beneath it I also saw the pride and respect she carried. She and Megan were my other anchors. I'd tucked locks of their hair into the locket, as the twins assured me that family attachments carried powerful protective magic and would boost the power of D's locket, helping me stay grounded rather than losing myself to the magic of the celestial trap.

The twins set up their mundane and magical tracking equipment in preparation. They'd both come to me and apologized for their behavior and how they'd used my soul energy, but I waved it off. It was their nature and in spite of what I considered reckless stupidity, it made them excellent at their jobs. I apologized for disrupting the meeting by playing keep away with the storage container.

They conceded it was my nature and in spite of what they considered reckless stupidity, it made me good at my job.

Man, I loved those two pains in my ass.

Once all was at the ready, I completed my mental preparation went on autopilot so I could let myself fall into the trap instead of fighting it, thus allowing smooth flow of my drained energy through magical or mundane means, or perhaps some combination of the two. I tried to put Sully down, but she swatted my hand with a tiny paw and kept her rump firmly planted on my shoulder.

"The trap most likely won't work on her," Roice said, handing me the phone. "Let her stay. I hope...I hope she helps. And I'm sorry for asking you to do this."

I offered him my best wry smirk. "Always happy to take one for the team."

My stomach clenched with dread and a fine sheen of sweat broke out on my forehead, but I did my best to ignore it. I survived the trap the first time. I would survive it again.

The twins cleared the room and sealed themselves in with me, D, and Sully. The rest of the team would observe us through the office windows during our experiment and keep an eye on the small breach the twins had created in the room's protective layers, designed to give the energy an escape route.

I took the phone from Roice and forced myself to look at the screen.

The colors and shapes beckoned me, calling to me with their beauty and peace. The shimmering red diamond flew out of the phone and caressed my skin, sending delicious tingles all over my body and inundating my senses with the scents of cinnamon and apples—my favorite—and singing a lullaby to soothe my aching soul.

Sully growled and swatted at the diamond, distracting me from its enchanted call.

I pushed it away with effort, struggling to stay grounded. Pain and an overwhelming sense of loss washed over me before a blue pyramid emerged and washed me in cool ocean waves full of playful dolphins that circled me. My first memory was of the vast, mysterious ocean as far as my child's eyes could see, of a sea breeze tickling my skin and giving me goosebumps and sand squishing beneath my toes.

Yeah, the trap had brought out the big guns to pull me in. My anchors didn't stop the pain of withdrawal or despair, but they gave me more strength and clarity so I could manage it.

For now. Wasn't sure how much longer I would last.

If the magic thought water would be a deterrent to a demon cat, it was sorely mistaken. She flew above the water's surface, grazing her paws against the surf, and then dove beneath the waves. When she came back out in a flurry of wet fur, wings, and seaweed, she had fat, shimmering fish in her mouth. Kitty floated on the water like a freakin' duck, wings tucked tight against her flank. Uh oh. Happy cat with a tasty fish? Maybe the trap was working on her, too.

I couldn't resist the urge to reach out and touch a dorsal fin and was carried through the surf with dizzying and delightful speed. We plunged beneath the waves to join with schools of brightly colored fish as they emerged from a thick forest of coral like a scene out of one of those animated movies I used to watch with D.

D. Demoriel. He was my anchor. Focusing on an image of D's face in my mind and gripping the locket, I let go of the fin and surfaced, only sunshine and marshmallow clouds had been replaced with wickedly dark and brooding storm clouds. Sully latched onto my hair, growling and hissing at the sky. The silver fish she'd caught swam around us and snapped with jaws filled with needle-like teeth. Like me, the demon cat recognized and resisted the trap, and the celestial magic within wasn't best pleased.

Lightning flashed and a tidal wave covered me and pushed me beneath the surface once more, this time with Sully in tow. The enchanted sea life waited, so much more appealing than the violent weather above. Swimming among iridescent angel fish and pufferfish that swelled and swirled as we passed, I stopped fighting the pull of the magic but was careful to engage with it as little as possible. Each time I smiled at a colorful moray or pet a multi-colored parrot fish, my body relaxed, and it became a little more difficult to swim.

I took it as a sign I was losing energy to the trap, giving the twins a trail they could trace.

A small cluster of hermit crabs frolicked in the sand beneath after I reached the reef's outer border. Cute. I wasn't a fan of spiders, centipedes, or other creatures with too many legs, but I'd always enjoyed catching and examining hermit crabs when we took a driving vacation to the beach. Those trips had been less frequent once my deadbeat dad left, but Mom managed to scrape together enough money to take us a couple of times as a single mom.

A beautiful sand dollar, perfectly proportioned, beckoned to me. Unlike the kind Megan and I had found on our beach trips, it gleamed brilliant white and was as pristine as the souvenir sand dollars in every beach shop we'd visited to look but not buy. I'd loved those sea creatures when I was young, but I'd been sad when I learned the bleaching process that made the sand dollars in the store so pretty actually killed them. The beauty was an illusion, just like this place.

This game was insidious. I focused on mom and Megan, my other anchors, and used anger to keep moving.

I turned away from the hermit crabs and fake sand dollar and swam away from the sea kingdom and into the current. In the logic of the game's simulated reality, the current had to represent the pathway my soul energy flowed. If I followed it, maybe I could help Boice, and Roice figure out how it traveled and where it went for collection and storage. The water grew darker, and I knew instinctively that other, less friendly sea creatures were watching me. Sully growled low.

"Yeah, girl, I sense them, too. I think the game wants us to turn around and go back, so I figure we're on the right track."

The beauty and peace of the trap beckoned when I risked a glance back. Something darted in front of me in the water after I take me when the sea floor rumbled, and a large crack split the coral forest, opening an enormous trench. From its depths emerged a brilliant orange sea serpent with a large head, long, sinuous body, and a deafening roar.

It locked its predatory gaze on me and shot through the water.

CHAPTER TWENTY

Nope. Now wasn't the time to give up or give in. I could flee, but instinct told me the game would change the rules and send an even nastier monster after me.

I'd have to fight the damned thing. If I got injured or killed in confines of the game, I figured I'd be toast in the real world.

Luckily, I could fight dirty.

Steeped as I was in celestial magic, my own celestial power came to my call. Conjuring a spear—this time on purpose—I pointed it at the beast of a water dragon flashing its spikes and sharp teeth and unleashed a wave of magic worthy of Poseidon. Magic flowed from my spear and hit the dragon surface. For a split second, the creature transformed into colorful pixels that lacked the brightness of the high-resolution graphics from the game.

Without celestial magic, they were strictly digital constructs, not real. None of this was real. The illusions created by the trap had taken the form of things I loved and were drawn to, like the ocean and its wonders. While I fought, my mind and most of my energy remained intact. That was it! I could destroy the illusion by fighting magic with magic until only the digital technology was left.

Crap. It wouldn't help the twins with their energy tracing efforts. I kept the magic flowing so I could immobilize the dragon, giving me a small window of time to think and strategize. Sully growled and darted toward the trench that had unleashed the dragon.

"Sully! Don't go down there!"

She disappeared into the darkness, filling me with more despair than the game's trap inspired. I had to go after her. I withdrew my magic and swam as fast as I could toward the trench. The current grew stronger and pulled me faster and faster to the dark depths.

Not fast enough. The dragon swatted me with its tail, knocking me out of the current. I slumped in the water, dazed. When I came to my senses, I faced an open maw filled with teeth as long as my body and a deafening roar. I shot a bolt of magic down the dragon's throat and swam out of the way as it closed its jaws, making for the trench with all the speed I could muster.

The dragon circled my body and blocked my path with its enormous head. What was up with this thing? You'd think after being nearly blasted out of existence that the stupid thing would go somewhere else or maybe turn into the thing I desired most in the world. Sully chose that moment to reappear, thank the fates.

"Don't do that again," I said, swimming backward with the cat in tow. The dragon stayed where it was. Weird.

Wait a minute...

"Sully, is the dragon trying to keep me out of the trench?"

I didn't expect an answer, but the cat nodded her tiny head up and down. Damn, the dragon must have knocked a few of my screws loose. Assuming demon cats were like their earth realm counterparts, Sully could in theory learn several words, including her name—which she knew—and a few tricks given training with positive reinforcement.

I grabbed the kitty and held her in front of my face. "Sully?"

She meowed and squirmed, trying to wiggle out of my hold.

"Stop. I need you to focus. Is the dragon trying to keep me out of the trench?"

Sully hissed and then nodded her head up and down again. Then she stared at me, tail flicking back and forth in irritation. "Okay...what's in the trench?"

Sully cocked her head and growled, presumably in frustration. "Right. Guess I'll have to go with you to find out. But I'm going to have to get past the dragon."

Sully wiggled again and I let her go. She swam toward the dragon at supernatural speed and swatted it on the nose. The dragon howled and backed up. Seriously? The cat was less than a hundredth of its size, and her claws were tiny. She went in again, this time scratching the dragon below one eye before darting away from the trench.

The dragon roared and turned away from the trench to give chase.

Trusting Sully to be quicker than the dragon, I swam back to the current and let it carry me into the trench. Just before light faded from the abyss, Sully's claws latched onto my hair, and we dove into darkness.

CHAPTER TWENTY-ONE

If the trench was part of the trap, it wasn't very good. Between the stygian darkness, complete silence, and overall sensory deprivation, all I wanted was to escape. The current pulled us down at a steady rate, but I couldn't hear it. I reached up and pulled Sully out of my hair and cradled her in my arms against my chest.

She clung to my chest with all her might and burrowed her tiny head against me. The vibrations of her purr centered me and kept me sane. How long had we been sinking into the trench? I couldn't take much more.

But this was an illusion, right?

I pulled on my celestial magic—why couldn't it be this easy in the real world? The magic illuminated the space around us, revealing a pixelated...landscape. Holy guacamole, it was like I was inside what looked like an old-fashioned computer screen, one of those early prototypes from the 80s. Even weirder, *Matrix*-style binary code ran down from the top of the trench in waterfalls. We were definitely in the digital bowels of the game.

And I was getting a boost of energy better than any energy bar or caffeinated beverage I'd ever tried.

"We're following the energy," I whispered. "This must lead to the source."

Sully and I kept traveling down, down, and down. Suddenly, we started picking up speed. We were likely getting close to the point of collection. I braced for...something. I wasn't in the game as a physical entity, but as something like an avatar. I wasn't sure how far my avatar could travel, but I didn't think it would be beyond the bounds of whatever magical or digital pathway Sully and were currently following.

But it was too late to turn back now. We'd find the end or the twins would pull our consciousnesses out when our time was up. Time seemed to pass differently in the game, since it felt like we'd been in the trench for hours. We were supposed to get out after fifteen minutes.

The muffled sound of voices pulled me out of my musings. Did that mean we were getting close? The current picked up speed and we rushed toward a split in the trench leading to two different pathways that looked like tunnels. *Which way, which way?* The voices seemed to be coming from the from the tunnel on the left, and I could feel the tug of the energy pulling to the right. I steered us to the left, figuring it was a better bet than storage. Taking a dip into so much soul energy—energy the celestials were going to weaponize—didn't seem like a good idea.

After a dizzying ride through the tunnel, Sully and I were dumped into another void. Crap. This was getting old. A small speck of light shone in the distance. With no other options, we swam toward the light, the voices getting louder as we got closer. The light source was shaped like a screen, and through it I saw what looked like a warehouse filled with stacks of storage containers like the one I'd swiped from the celestials. There were stacks of them from floor to ceiling. Oh my God, they'd drained all that energy from innocent humans, demons, and possibly other sentient creatures?

A familiar voice sent a jolt of excitement through my avatar. It was Labrador, the powerful winged eyeball-covered celestial. Much as she had been when I woke up from being trapped at her office, she was arguing with Pinstripe, a.k.a. the Cthulhu-like eyeball covered tentacle celestial.

"We need all the energy for the prototype. There's nothing to spare for your little side project." Pinstripe said, her voice dripping with disdain.

"Please," Labrador said. Something told me "please" wasn't a normal part of her vocabulary. The righteous anger beneath the pleading was proof enough.

The celestials came into the screen's frame. They wore their human glamour, but it flickered. Did that mean they were getting ready for a celestial smackdown? Not a good idea in a warehouse full of powerful and potentially volatile soul energy. While they argued, I focused on the warehouse, looking for any distinguishing feature that might help the team identify it. If we could figure out where this storage facility was, we could raid it, put an end to the operation, and use the Sigillum Dei to send the celestials away from earth and back to their own realm.

No windows were in frame to give me any clues to the surrounding area, and there weren't any signs other than a generic neon red "Exit" off to the right. Just metal shelving with neat, organized rows of storage containers and a table with laboratory equipment similar to what the twins had in their lab. Ugh, why couldn't we catch a break on this case?

I focused on the celestial argument again.

"Bella doesn't need much. Just enough to keep her alive in this realm until we can collect more," Labrador said. "Belial should never have sent her to earth. A realm with so little magic cannot sustain her."

Belial sent Bella to earth? Did that mean Bella was a demon? If so, why would a powerful celestial like Labrador be interested in keeping her alive?

A door opened somewhere out of frame. Both celestials turned their attention in the direction of the sound, and I strained to hear what they did. What sounded like a motor came closer until a wheelchair came into frame, piloted by a painfully thin woman swallowed by oversized clothing. Her skin was pale and mottled, and her scalp was visible in patches where clumps of dull blond hair had fallen out. With a that looked like skin stretched over a skull with no layers of muscle in between, she looked to be starving.

But her eyes, blue and unblinking, burned with the life and intensity her body lacked.

Those eyes. They were like Labrador's.

"You brought her here?" Pinstripe said, incredulous. "You brought a master demon into the heart of our power?"

Pinstripe transformed into her Cthulhu monster celestial form, tentacles quivering with rage. Labrador transformed into her creepy winged form and flew between the woman in the wheelchair and Pinstripe. The woman in the wheelchair grinned, reaching out to stroke the feathers of one wing.

"Sister," she said, her voice a dry rasp. "Feed me."

Sister? Hold the phone, the woman in the wheelchair—allegedly a master demon—and Labrador the psycho angel were *sisters*? How? Demons and celestials were two distinct species. Every demon hunter knew that, learned it on our first day of training. They despised one another and waged war through the ages. Then again, according to earth's religious mythology, demons were fallen angels—celestials. A lot of that mythology was propaganda, and much of it had been misinterpreted by humans, stories changing over millennia of oral tradition, but maybe there was a grain of truth.

Both species were magic-using entities. The celestials I'd encountered could use glamour as well as any demon. Celestials and demons were power hungry and not above using humans as metaphysical food sources—feeding through temptation or harvesting misery and, apparently, soul energy.

Sameal, our team's old boss was a demon, or we'd thought. But one of his titles was Angel of Death.

Once again, we we'd been misinformed. If demons and celestials could be related to one another, they were the same species. Had to be.

We were totally going to have to rewrite our team training manuals.

Pinstripe sent a bolt of magic at Labrador, who conjured a shield like the one Cassie had used to deflect my spear. Crap, if they weren't careful, they'd hit the storage containers and blow up a few city blocks if not the entire city. And there was nothing I could do to stop them.

Not while trapped as an avatar in their freakin' otherworldly video game.

Then again, if magic let me operate as an avatar in this hybrid digital-magical construct, surely, I could do the same thing in the real world. Was that astral projection, or was that only a witch thing?

Sully didn't hesitate. She leapt through the screen, and I watched in wonder as she flitted about the warehouse, swooping at unnatural speed to avoid burst of magic coming from the monstrous celestials duking it out while the cadaverous demon sat back and watched.

Smiling.

Oh shit.

Without thinking, I burst through the screen, residual celestial magic clinging to me, and I sent a bolt of magic in the direction of the demon who suddenly looked much more vital and healthier than she had a few seconds ago. With a flick of her wrist, she deflected my magic as she rose from her wheelchair, the façade of a sickly woman melting away as she donned a new glamour, or possibly her true form.

A balding scalp gave way to luxurious blond locks that cascaded down past her waist, and her face filled, becoming a younger version of Judy Labrador in her human guise complete with wide, unblinking blue eyes and an eerie, intense gaze. Heavy curved horns emerged from her scalp and a ring pierced her nose at its base.

She was all curves and softness, though, pleasantly rounded where Labrador, her sister, was angles and sharp edges. Dressed in finery I'd come to associate with demon nobility, silky material embroidered and shining, and accented with bits of metal in a mixture of medieval armor meets a goth BDSM club, Bella gave me a mocking smirk as I approached her, knife at the ready.

The celestials were still too wrapped up in their own battle and hadn't noticed my appearance or the transformation of Bella, who I'd just worked out was the Master Demon of Sloth. Bella Gore. Belphegor, patron demon of the belphs who tempted humans to abandon their labors, their passions, and their dreams for idleness, wasting their potential and their lives.

With a lazy grin, she said, *"You're* the warrior? But you're just a little thing. Belial told me you were small and insignificant, but it seems you have spirit. Let's see how you stand up to my warriors."

Out of nowhere, three dragon demons like the one D and I encountered in the burning downtown building materialized, surrounding me.

It got the attention of the celestials, who stopped fighting each other and came after Bella—Pinstripe to fight her and Labrador to protect her. Not that I had time to dwell on their battle. I had my own to fight. At first, I used my knife and martial arts training to deflect claws and sharp teeth. They weren't using magic. Not yet. They were toying with me, like cats tormenting a defenseless mouse.

I was no mouse. I was a warrior, damn it, a demon hunter.

Fuck celestial powers. These were demons. I'd fight them like demons.

Yes. We will crush them beneath our fangs.

Zer spoke to me, letting me know she was hungry for battle. On that, we agreed.

I let the demon wolf take me over, sprouting a phantom lupine-humanoid body with claws, muscle, and fangs guided by the wolf's innate cunning and instincts. This was so different than when I'd let Hannah out to play. Never in a million years would I have given her as much control, too afraid she'd unleash hell fury on earth.

She would have, crazy as she'd been.

Zer shared. We'd made a pact, and as her partner we'd sworn allegiance to Trinity as our alpha. Trinity would approve of this battle in the warehouse, because unlike my other demon and celestial powers, my connection with the demon wolf spirit was stable and we were in perfect accord.

The dragon demons took a step back when I growled. Using their surprise to my advantage, I lunged at the one on the right and knocked it into its companion in the middle. They writhed in a pile at my feet as I reveled in tearing a hunk of flesh from their limbs—an arm here, a leg there. I let Zer relish the taste of blood, so I didn't have to. I enjoyed hot chicken, pulled pork BBQ, and medium rare steaks, but not demon flesh.

Ick.

The third dragon demon leapt onto my back, digging its claws into the phantom wolf flesh on my flank. Zer shielded me from pain so I could take over and flip the dragon demon over my shoulder and slash it with my claws. One of the former floor demons lunged at me from the right as the other came from the left. I ducked and slashed at the colliding dragon demons, hitting one in the femoral artery, which covered me in demon blood.

The demon fell and I roared in triumph as Zer attacked the other demon, ripping at its throat.

The third demon grabbed me with its wicked taloned hands and hauled me into the air, its great wings flapping. Damn it, the warehouse was huge with high ceilings well suited for flight. Zer assured me we'd land on our feet if the demon dropped us, but there were plenty of sharp corners and edges of shelves. They could do real damage to her semi-corporeal body.

And there was all that energy just waiting for a spark to ignite it.

Shit. The energy.

I'd been so occupied with her demons I hadn't been keeping a close enough eye on their master. Bella had Pinstripe pinned against a wall in some sort of magical trap. Labrador had reverted to her human guise and sat on the ground, staring at the scene in wonder and reverence.

"You fed upon my gift, Bella," Labrador said, her voice fever-pitched with triumph. "You are restored, my sister. Let us leave this cursed realm and travel to another."

Bella smiled at her sister, the gentleness so wrong on that cruel face. "You think I'll join you in the celestial realm? I would be no more welcome there than you would be in the demon realm. We are at war."

Pinstripe's monstrous celestial form struggled against Labrador's trap, tentacles writhing and tearing at streams of magic that burned her eyeball-covered appendages. Bella cast out her hand and a surge of red demon magic flashed out and hit the trap.

Pinstripe stopped moving.

"It's not our war," Labrador said, standing and facing Bella and apparently not at all concerned that her fellow celestial might no longer be alive. "It was never our war. Let the others fight and destroy one another. You and me—we are survivors. You are the cleverest creature I know. You inspired this." Labrador waved her hands around the warehouse of evil, filled with storage containers of ill-gotten soul energy, laboratory equipment, and something in the corner I hadn't noticed before.

I wasn't large, but I presumed the golden, spike-covered ball was the celestial weapon.

"Yes," Bella crooned. "You've done well. Have you tested the weapon?"

Labrador's eyebrows furrowed in puzzlement. "No, the weapon was a ruse. I don't care about the war effort. I only built it so I could keep capturing the energy you need to live here, on earth. You were so ill, so fragile. But now, you are restored."

"I am, my dearest, I am. But you've worked so hard, with such diligence. You should see if your efforts have borne fruit. Show me the weapon. Fill it. We'll find a place to test it before we find a portal and go to another realm. Wherever you like."

Bullshit. Bella was playing Labrador. Whatever her game, it couldn't be good.

I was getting dizzy from being flown over the warehouse and repeatedly slammed against walls rafters. I needed to get this dragon demon off my back and get down there after the Master Demon of Sloth, the first of my seven targets.

Zer and I twisted, turned, and even managed to slam the demon into obstacles as often as it slammed us, but the wicked creature wouldn't let us go. And I feared I'd be worn out before the demon. I couldn't tap into my celestial power, and the other demon powers I had at my disposal wouldn't do me any good against this enemy. Glamour, tech skills, and investigative prowess versus brute force wouldn't do.

Zer and I weren't exactly outmatched so much as evenly matched. And that was all Bella needed—keep us occupied while she completed her nefarious schemes.

Like stealing a celestial weapon of mass destruction.

CHAPTER TWENTY-TWO

Desperate, I hoisted my body complete with phantom lupine back legs, using them to claw at the dragon demon's face. It roared and bit my foot hard enough to penetrate the demon's limb and nearly crush my own foot. Pain wasn't the issue. We were old friends, me and pain. But the damage could seriously interfere with my ability to fight once back on the ground.

This aerial battle had to end, but I was fresh out of options.

Suddenly, the dragon and I were hit by what felt like a truck at high speed—I actually knew what the felt like, hazard of the field—and we slammed into the wall. Sliding down the wall, I stared in wide-eyed wonder, or possibly horror, as my precious little demon cat Sully morphed into something out of a horror movie with a dash of anime. She'd grown to the size of the dragon demon, her wingspan massive and her lithe body muscled and built for speed and power.

Claws and fangs, not unlike the phantom versions of my wolf demon, flashed as she zeroed in on the fallen dragon demon. She landed, placing her large, panther like body between me and the dragon demon, growling and moving toward the demon slowly. Sully was stalking, and the dragon demon was her prey.

If we lived through this, I'd have to tell Boice and Roice that their mom wasn't lying about the species. I only hoped I wouldn't be on the menu after.

Speaking of menus, Sully had made it to the dragon demon and loomed over it, mouth open to take in the scents of blood and fear. The dragon demon roared and lashed out with a taloned hand. Sully batted it away and a sickening crunch echoed through the cavernous warehouse. The demon screamed in pain and Sully pounced.

Ick.

I looked away, not because I was squeamish. I'd seen my share of gore during my previous investigation that led to the great demon escape. But I couldn't reconcile my precious little kitty girl with double ears, bitty wings, and a button nose with the creature tearing hunks of meat from the dragon demon and swallowing them whole.

My wolf demon, however, was very interested in the process. She was in the mood to kill, to rend flesh and taste the blood of her enemy-turned-prey.

Before I could stop her, she turned her gaze on the injured dragon demons we'd dispatched, still writhing on the ground. I so did not want to be a part of this. It had been bad enough when Hannah had feasted on the essences of demons, but blood and guts and raw meat?

No meat. Just essence. Let me take over. Just for a short while.

She made a fair point, the sneaky wolf. I let Zer take over the driver's seat. When she relinquished control, the demons were gone. What the hell?

I rendered them immaterial. What's to be done with the Motiaummerr?

Oh shit! Sully!

A low growl sounded from nearby followed by a horrifying screech that reminded me of a mountain lion, but more intense. Sully crouched in a dark corner with what was left of the dragon demon, green eyes glowing with red sparks. Zer held our ground and tamped down on my fear and sadness at the prospect of losing my sweet Sully girl. If she became a danger...

No, I wouldn't put her down. Never. I'd capture her and hand her over to Cooper for safe passage back to the demon realm.

Zer's phantom ears perked up and she raised her tail. With my permission, she took a step toward Sully's corner. I wasn't sure it was such a good idea, but we had to try. Plus the novelty of having a demon partner sharing my body *and* asking permission to act was thrilling and refreshing. Sully hissed again.

"Hey there, Sully," I said, voice soft and gentle. "Remember me?"

She stopped snarling and all four ears perked up as she sniffed the air, catching my scent. Zer took another step and she backed further into the corner, hackles rising.

"It's okay. You saved us. Good girl. It's okay. It's me. It's Jinx."

Sully responded to my voice but continued to snarl and growl when I moved—when Zer moved.

Oh. Right. Cats and dogs didn't mix, so demon cats and wolf demons probably didn't, either.

I thanked Zer for her service and promised to let her out to play again soon but asked that she go back into my subconscious or wherever she went to rest so I could sooth Sully. In an instant, the phantom claws, fangs, and other lupine features were gone leaving me.

"Sully, we need to stop the celestials and the Master Demon of Sloth before they blow up the city." I held out my hand and waited for Sully to give it a sniff.

We didn't have much time, but I couldn't afford to rush her, either. Considering this was her first shift—or growth spurt—she might be disoriented or scared. What she needed was reassurance and patience.

A head larger than my own emerged from the shadows and the big cat sniffed my fingers. I hoped there wasn't residual demon essence or gore on my hand. I didn't want kitty to mistake me for an enemy or dinner. A forked tongue like a snake's flicked out to taste my skin. That was new, and a little disturbing, but the way the big cat cocked her head and slow blinked was just like little Sully. The headbutt against my hand gave me hope, and I stroked her from her ears down along her thick neck and moved to scratch under her chin.

The big cat's purr rumbled and vibrated through the floor.

"That's my girl," I said, booping her nose. "Zer is a nice wolf demon, but I guess it's going to take some time for you to get used to her. I get it. It's taking me time, too."

I gave her a few more chin scratches and said, "Want to play with some celestials and the big, bad demon?"

Sully growled and wiggled her giant ass in anticipation. That behavior had been cute when she was stalking a feather toy in her kitten form, but it was hella scary in her big cat form as powerful muscles undulated and her gaze widened, pupils dilatated and filled with red demonic sparks of power.

She stalked out of the corner, and I followed, limping from the injury I'd earned from the dragon demon's bite. I could call Zer back out as backup or I could try to call my unreliable celestial magic, but our best bet was Sully.

In the time it had taken to defeat the dragon demon squad, Labrador and Bella had been busy filling the golden orb with soul energy using about a quarter of the storage units by my estimate. They were engrossed in the task and took no note of Sully and I as we observed from the shadows of the warehouse shelves.

Pinstripe hadn't moved, and most of her tentacles were burned to a crisp or blistered.

"Sully," I whispered. "We need a distraction. Do a hit and run on the celestials but don't hit the golden orb."

I hoped she understood. She bobbed her giant head up and down in what looked to be an affirmative, like she'd done before while tracking the energy source to this warehouse.

"See if you can get them to chase you, but don't risk your life. I'll get the weapon and you can fly us out of here and back to HQ so we can get some backup."

Sully leapt into the air and flew toward the celestial and her demonic sister. Labrador shrieked in surprise and Bella cried out in rage, casting bolts of demon energy at my warrior demon cat. Sully dodged and did a series of loops, stalls, and banking maneuvers that rivaled anything I'd seen from Naval aviators. Then she swooped down and took a swipe at Bella with murder mittens on steroids, leaving an ugly gash across her cheek and cutting off a sizable chunk of her right horn.

"No!" Labrador transformed into her winged celestial form and flew at Sully with murder in the gaze of the hundreds of creepy eyeballs lining her wings.

This was the best chance I'd get, so I breathed through the pain in my foot, drew my knife, and rushed toward Bella.

The demon grabbed the orb and dematerialized, reappearing on one of the high shelves. Damn it! So much for the element of surprise. I couldn't get up there without Sully, but she was busy fighting a pissed off celestial. I let anger fill me, body and soul, calling to the celestial power within. Magic erupted from within me and shot out, filling the room with light and heat threatened to spill out from the magic.

Crap. That was the last thing we needed. I tamped down on the magic and tried to redirect it to do something useful, like making a Wonder Woman-style lasso to wrangle the Master demon or allowing me to sprout wings like a bona fide angel—hopefully without a gazillion eyeballs.

Labrador stopped fighting Sully and cried out to her sister.

"Bella! What are you doing?"

Bella smiled wickedly. "Thank you, my sister, for this glorious weapon. I shall deliver it to Lord Belial. If you come with me, you'll be spared the horrors of the war and will be granted sanctuary."

"No," Labrador said. "I didn't make the weapon for demons. I only made the weapon so I could keep harvesting energy for you. To save you. But..."

Looked like Labrador finally caught on. Bella wasn't sick and didn't need to consume the soul energy she'd tricked her sister into harvesting. No, in true master demon fashion, she'd double-crossed her celestial sister so she could steal the weapon Labrador had built for the celestials.

"Last chance," Bella said, holding out her hand. Labrador fell to the ground, transforming back into her human guise on the way down, and began shaking.

"You *lied*. To *me*."

Bella's smile faded and her expression turned to stone.

"It's not personal. This is war. I hope we do not meet on the battle-field. Goodbye, Judaliel," she said before disappearing with the weapon.

CHAPTER TWENTY-THREE

"What do we do with these two?" Trinity asked, eyeing a groaning Pinstripe and Judaliel, a.k.a. the universe's stupidest celestial inside the magically reinforced cage. It was good to see Trinity in the field, back in combat gear and armed with demon steel and a variety of specialized weapons Sam had given her. Even geniuses needed to kick ass every now and again.

The team arrived at the warehouse shortly after Bella took off with the weapon. When Sully and I disappeared from the twins' lab, they'd set about tracing our whereabouts via our digital and magical signatures. I had no idea what that involved, but I was grateful they'd found us.

Too bad they didn't show up in time to stop Bella the Sloth Demon from taking the celestial weapon.

No, that was my fault. I shouldn't have let her get away. Trinity was right. I wasn't ready to face off with a demon of her class. I'd failed, and the entire city was at risk.

If she broke loose with the weapon, the entire world was at risk.

Boice and Roice were securing the remaining containers full of soul energy and decommissioning the lab while Alexi and D took care of what remained of the dragon demon bodies. Pinstripe was still trapped inside Judaliel's magical cage, too injured or weary to mount an escape attempt.

Judaliel was still on the ground where she'd fallen and hadn't stopped sobbing since her sister abandoned her. I'd tried to conjure a cage for her, but my fickle celestial magic failed me once more. Luckily, Sully had taken it upon herself to guard the celestial.

"Good question," I said to Trinity. "Ouch! Sam, you are a terrible nurse."

Sam frowned at me as he poked and prodded my injured leg and foot. He'd traded royal demon robes for combat gear, too. Probably Trinity's idea since he looked so good in it. "Hold still. I must immobilize the limb before we transport you back to headquarters for a proper healing."

"We could send them back to the celestial realm," Trinity mused. "Or we could hold them hostage and negotiate with the other celestial leaders for their release."

I snorted. "After their monumental FUBAR, I don't think the celestials will be too eager to rescue them, especially that one." I pointed at Judaliel. "We need to interrogate them. Get them to tell us how to restore the soul energy they stole to the rightful owners and get them to dismantle their operation."

"Agreed." D, who'd used some magic to dispatch the demon dragon remains, had joined us. He was wearing combat gear, too. Jeez, had they all decided on a wardrobe change before coming to my rescue? I wanted to ask if he'd turn around so I could ogle his ass, but he started talking again. "They can help us track down Belphegor and the weapon. She'll need a portal to get it to Belial, and we're guarding the known portals in the city. She'll be looking for a summoner."

Which she wouldn't find. The remaining summoners in the city were vetted and reliable. Belial had killed the summoner who'd allowed his henchman to travel to earth through a portal he'd highjacked. Our team wouldn't let anything like that happen again. Lesson learned.

"Simon contacted our summoners. They'll tell us if she reaches out," Lacey said.

"If they can," I muttered. "A demon as powerful and devious as

Belphegor could coerce a summoner to do her bidding by threats, torture, or using some variation of the mind control magic she'd "inspired" her sister to create."

"Then we'd better get busy investigating," Megan said. I looked up at my sister, grateful she was trustworthy and had my back unlike the celestial's sister. She looked good in her field gear, and she'd been using her demon steel knife to sweep the room for any residual demon or celestial magic.

"Right, once I get healed up, I can go talk to some of my informants in the demon community, though I may not be welcome at The Hellbound." During our last investigation, I'd been trailing a rogue summoner and caught up with him at one of Nashville's secret watering holes for the supernatural community. Though justified, the bouncer I'd knocked unconscious and the resulting property damage I'd facilitated during the chase hadn't endeared me to the establishment's owner. His exact words were, "Don't show your face again here for a thousand years or I'll break it."

Glancing over at Trinity, I said, "With your permission, that is. You were right. I'm not battle ready, not against demons and celestials like these. It's my fault Belphegor escaped."

Trinity cocked her head at me, brow furrowed. "How do you figure? This wasn't supposed to be a combat mission."

"No," I said, dropping my gaze. "But I made it into one when I engaged with Belphegor instead of observing or alerting the team."

Trinity rolled her eyes. "Seriously, you may be the 'chosen one,' but not everything is about you or caused by you. You managed to track the soul energy and secure a good portion of it, and you captured these two celestials. That's progress in my book."

Wowzers. She wasn't mad at me? I looked around at my team, realizing I'd been avoiding their gazes, which I imagined would be filled with anger or frustration or judgement. I figured I'd see disapproval written all over their faces—Jinx the Screw-Up at it again, creating more problems than she solves.

Instead, they were all nodding, and a few were smiling. Not Lacey, though. She preferred smirks and giving me shit was her love language. But the rest of the team from Alexi to Sam, D to Megan, and Mara seemed to agree with Trinity's assessment. They didn't think this was a huge clusterfuck.

I ducked my head again and blinked hard. There was no crying in the field.

"I'll cover The Hellbound. They like my vodka there." Alexi grinned at me when I looked up. "I see your wolf came out to play." Pointing the claw marks on the ground and shelves, he asked, "Zer fought well?"

"She did," I said, perking up. "We were in sync, and she saved my ass from a date with gravity and the floor when one of those dragon demons picked me up and flew to the ceiling. It was so cool. Sully saved me from the others."

I blurted it out before I had the chance to consider that calling attention to my monstrous and much larger demon cat might not be the smartest idea.

Too late. Sully, who'd heard her name and was an unabashed attention ho-bag sauntered out of the dark corner I'd shoved her into and displayed her fearsome, big cat form. She stretched bowing to the front with her rump in the air and then stretching her back legs and wings as my team stood frozen and stared.

Unperturbed, Sully trotted up to D and flopped at his feet, rolling over to expose her belly. I held my breath and glances surreptitiously at the twins. After all, they'd been terrified my demon kitty would turn into a dangerous, murderous beast that would kill us all. Hell, I'd had that fear when I'd first seen Sully in this form. But I knew, *I knew*, she was still my Sully. She was my companion, my friend, my emotional support demon kitty, and an ally.

The twins wore identical expressions, but I couldn't for the life of me guess what they were thinking.

I turned my attention to D, my heart no doubt in my eyes, and waited.

D leaned down on his haunches and crooned to Sully. "Hey, girl. You got big, huh." He ran his hand down her neck and moved it up to rub her chin, which made her close her eyes, wiggle, and start purring while making air biscuits.

D chuckled. "Big baby."

The tension broke and I breathed a sigh of relief. "You should have seen her," I said, hobbling over to my cat and my demon man. "She was the one who figured out where the energy was going in the game, and she told me—well, she didn't tell me so much since she can't talk, but it was like Lassie leading the rescuer to Timmy in the well—and she fought even before she got big, and then she saved me from the dragon demons because she's so smart and loyal, but she doesn't like Zer. She kept growling until my wolf demon went away and...and I'm babbling."

"What else is new?" Boice said, cautiously approaching Sully.

Not to be outdone, Roice said, "If you started making sense, we'd have to check you for a concussion."

I laughed. "You're okay with having a Motiaummerr on the team?"

The twins gave me the thumbs up, but I could see the wheels turning as their devious little minds concocted something outrageous that involved my cat. No way would I let them experiment on her. Come to think of it, Sully wouldn't let them either. But they were sneaky.

"Okay," Trinity said. "Alexi's hitting The Hellhound and other supernatural hangouts. Lacey, you and Simon monitor the portals while Demoriel works with the twins to track down all our summoners. Mara, report?"

Mara stood a little taller and said, "Some of the demons in my network are working to locate Belphegor. They were already working with me to track powerful demons in hiding, so it'll be an extension of their work."

"Excellent." Trinity turned to me. "Jinx, get patched up and take Megan with you to check in with your informants. We'll meet back at HQ in three hours."

I loved it when a plan came together, especially when it gave me hope that we could actually find Belphegor. But first, we'd have to figure out how to capture or destroy her when we did. I looked at Trinity and mouthed, "Sigillum Dei?"

She nodded. Good. If we sent her back to the hell realm, she'd have a hard time getting back on earth with our portals secured. Plus, Sam told us he could "program" the artefact to restrict her return through any other portals on earth. Nifty trick, but we'd still have to find and outwit her.

"Are you guarding the celestials?" I asked.

Trinity smirked. "Nope."

She pulled out her cell phone and dialed someone. "We have a situation. Get over here pronto."

Who was she calling? Dr. Khatri wasn't authorized for field work, and as far as I was aware, we hadn't hired or requisitioned any other team members. I hoped she wasn't calling in more favors from the demons she'd bargained with. Their price tag would be way to steep.

Before I could ask, a brilliant light burst through the room. As the light faded, a tall, imposing figure dressed in white and sporting wings stood in our midst. They—couldn't tell if the entity was male, female, non-binary, or gender fluid, so I went with the safe pronoun—had long brown hair, glowing silver eyes, and wore an ugly frown on their face.

At least they weren't covered with eyeballs.

"Time to start acting like an ally," Trinity said, glowering at the celestial. "Keep these two out of trouble and see if you can get some intel out of them while you're at it."

The celestial's lips thinned, and their frown deepened. Somebody obviously didn't like taking orders. That fit the MO for the celestials I'd met.

Wait a minute...

"Cassie?"

"Yes, it is I, Cassiel, and I don't appreciate being kept out of the loop."

Oh, the unreliable angel was learning the lingo. I might have told her I was proud of her—them—if they were nicer.

"How come you have the angel's number and I don't," I whined.

"I asked," Trinity said with a hint of smugness.

CHAPTER TWENTY-FOUR

After getting treated with demon healing mojo Megan and I pounded the pavement in downtown Nashville. In spite of the recent explosion, the streets were bustling with tourists and locals alike out looking for a good time. Man, I loved this town. Music poured out of honkytonks, dive bars, and upscale venues tucked away off Printer's Alley, mixing with the miasma of fried delicacies, BBQ, and food truck kebabs. My mouth watered and my stomach rumbled.

At least it rumbled until I caught a whiff of stale cigarettes, sewage, and a dude who'd apparently bathed in cologne. Seriously, dude. Spray, delay, and walk away.

Megan wrinkled her nose and shared a grimace of solidarity with me. Like me, she'd traded combat gear for street wear. For her it meant a trendy tunic, elegant slacks, and peep toe sandals. So classy. Since I had neither her sense of style nor the good sense to care about it, I'd opted for tight-fitting jeans and a T-shirt that read, "I stopped fighting my inner demons. We're on the same side now." My black leather cowgirl boots had cost a small fortune and were embroidered with roses and vines surrounding a skull. I loved them almost as much as I loved my Doc Martens and they did a good job of helping me blend in with tourists.

Tennessee had a rich and sordid history that included colonialism, slavery and plantations—many of which were still open for business and celebrating a whitewashed version of history—and prouder moments like the founding of the Grand Old Opry, the invention of Goo Goo Clusters and Moon Pies, and good whisky. The state's history did not, however, include cowboys, outside of men who went west after the Civil War, though folks in the state did their part to keep cowboy culture alive.

That meant lots of boots and hats, the latter of which I skipped. Figured it was overkill.

We waved at a tour bus full of co-eds in full party mode, having the time of their lives without any men in sight. Good for them. Sometimes a night out with the girls was just what the doctor ordered.

I turned to Megan. "Did you ever do anything like that back in the day?"

She laughed. "Back in the day? It wasn't so long ago, but I know what you mean. I always wanted to, but I couldn't afford it."

My heart ached. Of course. It was easy to forget that Meg and I came from the same roots of poverty. She'd eased into the upper echelons of Nashville society after dating and marrying Brad with his healthy bank account and connections. But back in college, she was scraping by on scholarship funds and a work-study program that didn't include a budget for recreation.

I'd been too wrapped up in my own angst at the time to consider what Megan was going through, and I'd always had a bit of a chip on my shoulder and case of envy when it came to my big sister. She'd been the golden child, the good kid, the one destined for success and who did all things with poise and grace. Very unlike me.

Then again, at the time, I was knee-deep in demon hunter training, which didn't leave me any free time to party. Not until later. But by then, I was spending most of my time scoping out the social scene for demons through undercover work and squeezing in the occasional hook up with pretty men I appreciated at the time but who held no real appeal on a deeper level.

"What about when you met Brad? Did you ever cut loose and do some partying when he wasn't climbing the corporate ladder and making tons of money?" I asked, teasing.

Megan looked away. Oh dear. There was definitely something going on with my sister and her hubby. Was I going to have to beat his ass? I would if I had to—it was the least a sister could do. The fact that I would enjoy it was just a bonus.

"Brad is having some trouble...adjusting to our new reality. He's seen more in the past two months than any mundane could be expected to handle."

Whatever "trouble" he was having hadn't slowed him down when it came to his work as a money man, but I knew better than to say anything about it. "You and Mom seem to be adjusting just fine and dandy, and Mom is purely mundane. Sounds like a Brad problem to me. Maybe Brad is having issues with you doing your own thing instead of catering to him."

Megan frowned but didn't say anything. I must have guessed right since she didn't rush to his defense. "You're really doing with great with all this," I said. "I wish...I wish we could have started working together sooner."

Megan laughed. "Yeah. We can blame dad for that." Shifting the topic, she asked, "You didn't do much partying between cases?"

I shook my head. "Nope. Pathetic, aren't we? Reckon we're still young enough to hitch a ride on one of those things?" I pointed at the next party bus boogeying down the street. My voice held more longing than I'd meant to show.

Megan must have picked up on it since she put an arm around my shoulder and said, "We're totally going to do this after we wrap up this case. Even demon hunters need a break."

I agreed. Assuming we lived long enough, Megan and I would be downing shots and getting our "Woo Hoo" girl game on in the near future.

I pulled out my knife, glamoured to look like a cell phone, and caught a flash of red. Demons were nearby, and judging from the guitar riffs and rough voices, I knew who they were.

Imps. Just the demons I'd been hoping to find.

These little scamps weren't on my authorized bag and tag list, but I'd been tempted to do a little rule breaking after they'd set me on the trail of a Cauchemar, a supposedly minor demon who disrupted sleep. The rat bastard cursed me with a scorching case of temporary sleep apnea. I'd had to wear a CPAP to bed for over a month and deal with messed up sinuses for three months. They could have warned me, but being imps, it was in their nature to sow chaos and mischief wherever and whenever they could.

Otherwise, they were pretty good informants.

Glamoured to look like street musicians complete with torn jeans, western shirts, cowboy boots and hats, in reality the pair of corporeal demons looked like the unholy offspring of a dragon and an oriental shorthair cat.

"Hey there, pretty ladies. Save a horse, ride a demon?" The imp smirked and looked me and Megan up and down in a deliberately skeevy way.

"Shut up, Abe, or I'll slice you into the next life faster than you can write a whiny ass country song about it," I said, looking bored. All conversations with these guys started like this. It was kind of our thing. I hadn't clued Megan in, though, and the look on her face was priceless.

Abe, short for Abezethibou, had come over to earth in the early 60s, done waaaaay too many drugs, and fallen in love with human music. His buddy Brax, a.k.a. Abraxas, had joined him in the 80s. It had taken a while to blend folk country with synth pop, but the two weren't bad. If they hung around a few more decades, they might even make it into the music biz. Until then, the pair were my best informants when they weren't being pains in my backside. Abe was holding a smart phone. No video games, but a video of me getting bitten in the ass by an escaped demon weasel from a few months back flashed across the screen.

Someone got the whole embarrassing scene on vid. Great.

"That better not go on the Internet," I said, salvaging as much dignity as I could.

Brax grinned. "You aren't going to off my partner, right?"

I sighed. "I'll let it slide this time, but only if you delete the vid."

Both Imps arched their brows and looked pointedly at the guitar case on the sidewalk below them. I reached into my pants pocket and tossed a fifty in. I'd put it on my expense account. With a slow, wide, lazy smile, Abe handed the phone to his buddy and began strumming a sweet little blues number, singing about a short girl with a nice badonkadonk and a mean-ass temper.

Aw, he wrote a song about me. How sweet.

Brax's fingers flew across the phone, demon fast, and then he held it out so I could see the vid was gone. Unless he'd saved it to the cloud. Damn it, I didn't have time for this. I'd have to beat or bribe them later. Right now, I had a job to do.

"Who's your friend," Abe asked, eyeing Megan with interest.

"This is the newest member of our demon hunting team and my sister. She's married and she's not interested in cross-species dating, so don't bother flirting. Or stalking. We're looking for information."

Abe grinned. "I'm sure you are. Life in the city's gotten more interesting in the past couple of months. Rumor has it you and your team let a bunch of power brokers from our realm and the other side loose on earth."

I shrugged. "I heard the same rumor. Sorry to disappoint, but it wasn't me. It was Lord Belial and his consort, Haniel, a celestial. That's something new and interesting. Didn't think your kind associated with celestials, but I recently ran into a pair of sisters—one from the demon realm and one from the celestial realm."

Brax stopped typing and Abe's face froze. Ah ha. This was new and interesting to them, too. Good. They accepted cash, but preferred intel and knowing more about the goings on in the Nashville demon community than their fellow demons living in the city was its own kind of currency.

"That is interesting," Abe said. "What's it got to do with us?"

Megan opened her mouth to respond but I held up a hand. "Maybe nothing, but rumor also has it that high ranking celestials and master demons are colluding, and they aren't above using lesser demons as cannon fodder or test monkeys."

The imps shrieked and for a split second the demons showed their true form beneath the glamour. Maybe it was shock, anger, fear, or some combination, but they had good reason to be afraid. Lesser demons had found a safe haven on earth, most of them fleeing more powerful demons in their home realm. The idea of powerful demons invading their refuge and bringing celestials along for the party would be terrifying.

And infuriating. Unlike lesser demons seeking protection or power by working with the invaders, Abe and Brax were smart enough to steer clear of them. They'd want the powerful demons off earth as much as my team did.

"Some of the less intelligent members of our community have been hanging around an escape room—"

"An escape room downtown?" Megan blurted. "Which one? Where—"

Abe grinned at her. "You are a noob, aren't you?"

Megan blushed. Poor thing. I remembered my first years making contacts in the demon community. The demons had had a lot of fun at my expense and had sent me on more than one wild goose chase. I didn't have anyone looking out for me. Glad I could look out for Megan.

"I may be new, but I've seen some shit tonight that would scare the horns right off your head, or wherever you keep them," Megan said. "How'd you feel about getting your demon essence sucked out of you—not in the fun way, but in a slow, agonizing, excruciating way that'll turn you into a mindless, writhing mass of ectoplasm."

Nice! I'd have to tell her not all demons had horns and that ectoplasm was a ghost thing, but she'd put enough menace into it with a splash of inuendo as the cherry on top. Megan was a natural.

Abe blinked and looked at Brax, who shook his head and grimaced. "You two are totally related."

I fist bumped my sister. "You were telling us about an escape room."

"Off Powell South of 100 Oaks. Lots of demons hanging around there and in the vicinity."

Megan arched a brow. "Not much out there aside from a couple of shops, a Southern chain restaurant and outdoor furniture store. Seems unlikely."

Abe rolled his eyes. "Have you even made it past basic training? Demon lairs are everywhere, hiding in plain sight. Above ground and below."

Bingo. We had a place to start. I put a hand on Megan's shoulder before she could think about smacking the imp and said, "Thanks boys. We'll keep you posted of any interesting developments. Let's go, Meg."

I dragged her down the street and spoke in a low whisper. "You did good for a noob. Got their attention and got them to give us a specific area to concentrate our search. They weren't lying about demon lairs. You can find plenty underground, like the demon bar D's checking out. That one's underneath the Parthenon and you can reach it if you know the sigils to use to open the secret entrance. It's probably something similar."

"Under the escape room?" Megan asked.

"Too obvious. But maybe not too far from there. We can send Simon out to scout and get Boice and Roice on electronic surveillance." I pulled out my phone and fired off a text to Lacey, the twins, and Trinity.

"Okay," she said. "What now?"

"Now," I said with a sigh and a frisson of dread. "We go to see a reaper and a soul broker about returning some soul energy."

The reaper responded to my text and invited us to meet at an address in the heart of Belle Meade. Figured. He was a total snob with a taste for the finer things earth had to offer and enjoyed hobnobbing with—and tormenting—the rich and famous in the city.

I had only met the reaper and his human henchwoman once, but once had been enough. Neither were demons. They had friends on the "other side" and sometimes worked with demons, but afterlife management wasn't our jurisdiction.

Soul energy, life force, was right up their alley. The henchwoman, a scary redhead who worked with a branch of celestials in charge of channeling souls to other realms, had supernatural powers no human had a right to possess, and she knew how to use them. She worked with the reaper on the downlow.

The reaper was in a whole other class of scary. I'd faced my scary former demon boss, Barbatos the powerful and traitorous demon, Mephisto the murderous messenger, Lord Belial and Haniel, and Belphegor, and the reaper still made me want to run screaming whenever I had the misfortune to spend time in his presence.

I hadn't shared information about the pair with the rest of my team, and in exchange I got to call upon the pair for information from time to time.

Not sure if the deal extended to favors, but I was prepared to negotiate. I hoped.

The address turned out to be an upscale, genteel mansion that screamed old money Nashville, all antebellum columns and mature trees illuminated by carefully placed outdoor lighting. Every light in the house was on and we saw people in elegant dress bustling through large windows. What kind of game was the reaper playing?

"Looks like a party, and we're under-dressed," Megan said. She followed the circular driveway and stopped in front of a valet stand. A gentleman dressed in red velvet and wearing a top hat opened my door and offered a hand, which I took. He helped me out and walked quickly to the driver's side to offer the same service to Megan and handing her a ticket.

We stood on the steps as the valet drove off into the night with Meg's car.

"What now?" she asked.

"I guess we go upstairs and tell the big guy by the door we have an appointment with Mr. Darkmore."

Megan and I ascended the stairs—these were the type of fancy stairs one ascended rather than climbed—and approached the doorman? Butler? He looked more like a bouncer, but that was to be expected in a place like this. Anyone associating with the reaper would need protection from his enemies and their own. Nice people didn't general keep company with Lazarus Darkmore.

"Good evening, ladies," the bouncer said. He had good manners for a guy who looked like a Mafia enforcer.

"We have an appointment with Mr. Darkmore."

The bouncer went very still before nodding gravely. "Follow me."

We followed the man through the door and down a corridor off the main living space filled with partygoers, leaving them behind for the darkness.

CHAPTER TWENTY-FIVE

The bouncer led us to a room at the end of the corridor. He stopped in front of it but didn't knock and made no move to enter and announce us. Weird, and not very mannerly. I stepped to the side and raised my hand to knock, half expecting to be attacked by the bouncer.

"Reginald would never do such a thing," said a deep, cold, and oddly seductive voice from the other side of the door. "Please, do come in, Jane and Megan McGee."

Megan's gaze went wide. I shrugged. The reaper liked to do creepy shit like that.

I opened the door to a room filled with the soft glow of candles and recessed lighting, decorated in a deceptive style that managed to show-case both classic and modern features. Upholstered antique chairs and Persian rugs—authentic by my reckoning—blended with dark woods shaped with modern sensibilities in mind.

The reaper sat in one of the antique chairs next to his henchwoman. She wore jeans and a hunter-green T-shirt that complemented her coloring and red hair underneath a leather jacket. It was a great jacket, and it was nice to not feel so underdressed. The reaper wore his usual white suit, though he'd removed his white Stetson hat and placed it on the low table in front of them where it contrasted with the burgundy velvet runner.

"Are we having a séance?" I asked. Yeah, he was scary, but it didn't mean I had to show fear. And I didn't want him paying too much attention to Megan.

Vivian smirked, which made me like her more. I couldn't afford to like someone that dangerous, but it was hard to ignore a kindred spirit and fellow smartass.

Darkmore smiled showing lots of white teeth. "Is there someone you'd like to contact? Dear old daddy, perhaps?"

Megan stiffened. I rolled my eyes and said, "Last I heard he was still in the land of the living. For now. I'll deal with him later."

"I've no doubt," the reaper said, smile widening. Was he doing his best impression of a shark? "Please, have a seat. Wine?"

The reaper gestured to the chairs opposite him and his companion and then to a tray with a bottle of something red and likely expensive surrounded by four glasses. Megan and sat and the reaper began filling the glasses with wine worthy of the fine crystal. I accepted a glass when offered and glanced at Megan in an unspoken request to do the same.

Once served, the reaper said, "A toast. To good health and peaceful souls."

We raised our glasses and drank. It was really nice wine. I didn't have a refined pallet, but even I knew this stuff wouldn't give me a headache tomorrow.

"So," I said, setting my glass down. "We have an issue related to souls and we think you might be able to help."

The reaper stared at us with hooded eyes. Going silent. Nice negotiating tactic. Fortunately, Vivian the henchwoman was ready to get down to business. "What's the issue? Protecting souls from demons is your department. We're in charge of helping souls cross."

I took a deep breath. This next part was tricky. I had intel that might make me a target or get me killed if they thought I was making threats. "It's about protecting souls. A pair of celestials devised a method to harvest soul energy from humans and other sentient entities on earth and have been using it to drain the citizens of Nashville. We've recovered a good bit of the stored energy. We'd like you to get it back where it belongs. I hear that's your department," I said, looking at Vivian.

She went very still and the temperature in the room dropped. Shit. Time for damage control.

"Look," I said, speaking through chattering teeth. "What you do is your business. It doesn't concern my team or my supervisors. They don't need to know about it. All they need to know is we're turning over energy we recovered to interested parties who are willing to re-distribute it back to the rightful owners."

"Did you come here in good faith or to blackmail us?" Vivian asked. An aura of red surrounded her. I was sorely tempted to pull out my demon steel knife to get a read on what looked very much like demon essence, but that would send the wrong message.

"No blackmail," Megan said. "We all want the same thing, and we have our secrets, too."

I stared at her and widened my gaze, telegraphing, "Don't help," as clearly as I could without actually saying it.

The temperature rose as quickly as it dropped and the tension in the room dissipated. Whew. Megan had a knack for improvisation, but she had no idea what kind of dangerous game she was playing.

Darkmore sat back and said, "Secrets. I'm always interested in secrets, especially when it comes to Sameal. The Angel of Death is a fascinating subject. Tell me, has he resurfaced?"

"Nope," I said, sitting back and crossing my legs. See, I was relaxed and not about to pee my pants from fear. We were just having a nice chat. "He went AWOL when seven Master Demons and seven Archangels escaped through a portal opened by Lord Belial. My team is hunting down the escapees. We have two of the angels in custody and we'll capture Belphegor."

Darkmore smiled. "I was aware of the demons who escaped through portal, but not angels. Is that a secret?"

"It's not common knowledge. Nor is the fact that Belphegor stole a weapon fueled by the rest of the soul energy from her *sister*, Judaliel. She built the weapon for the celestials so they could use it on the demons, but Belphegor tricked her out of it."

Vivian scowled and muttered something about, "guardians" under her breath. Right. They called celestials guardian spirits. So many names for greedy, selfish, arrogant, meddlesome creatures from another dimension.

Darkmore took another sip of wine before he spoke. "The Archangel of Diligence has been busy, which isn't surprising given her nature. Did she do it for the love of Bella?"

Damned reaper knew more than I realized, the bastard. But it was good to know we had one of the escaped Archangels in our custody. "She did. Are demons and celestials the same species?"

The reaper's laughter was rich and deep. "Of course they're related. Two sides of the same coin—sloth and diligence, gluttony and temperance, wrath and contentment—but they're rarely in balance, and not all of them work against one another or share blood ties."

No. That would be too easy.

"What you want to know is what to do with the celestials and the demon Belphegor, assuming you manage to capture her."

He was fishing. I was sure of it. I couldn't tell him about the Sigillum Dei. No one outside of our team could know, besides Cassiel who'd tried to bargain for it.

"What I want to know is will you take the soul energy and return it?"

"We will." Vivian didn't speak loudly or often, but when she did, she made it count. "We will distribute what you have in your possession to all affected individuals in exchange for the soul energy within the weapon."

Now that was interesting. I knew she and the reaper were doing something with soul energy, but I had no idea if it was for good or ill, and I didn't think asking them what they intended was a good idea. I'd made bad deals in the past for the greater good, but not on this scale. Putting my soul and the souls of my family on the line was one thing. Putting the souls of the larger mortal and supernatural community in my city on the line was another matter.

"Do you promise to do no harm?" I asked. "With the soul energy. No harm, and you'll make sure the people to whom you return the soul energy will be healthy and whole when you're done?"

Vivian nodded. "I will not use the energy for harm, and I will restore the innocent to their former state. The reaper will help."

It was the best I could do. Maybe Boice and Roice knew what they were up to. They'd worked with the reaper on occasion. Our old boss Sameal loaned them out from time to time, and it made sense that he'd work closely with a reaper and a soul broker. In the end, I had to ask myself if I believed Vivian and could take her at her word.

"Give me your hand," she said. The reaper opened his mouth, but she shook her head at him. "She asked the right question, and I need to show her my word is good."

I slid to the edge of my seat and took the hand she offered. Hers was warm, the skin smooth and...comforting. Then, she did something. My sigil tattoos lit up like a Christmas tree as I threw my head back in a mixture of pain and relief so incredible that I thought I'd melt. All the guilt, the terror, the anxiety of the past few months flashed through me with horrifying vividness before it left my body. I raised my head and stared at our linked hands in wonder as red light poured out of my hand and disappeared beneath her skin.

It was miraculous. And terrifying.

Megan had left her chair and come after Vivian, knife at the ready. Darkmore blocked her, manhandling my sister and holding her back. Megan's eyes glowed brilliant blue as she channeled powerful celestial energy. It gave the reaper pause. He let go, but he loosened his grip and his flesh reddened where it touched my sister's skin.

Holy shit. Megan was tapping into her celestial energy and fighting the reaper. For me. And she wasn't losing.

"It's okay, Meg," I said, breathing deeply and holding on to the peace Vivian had granted me. The respite was a gift, and I understood what it was this remarkable human could do.

It cost her, though. She'd gone pale and had a pained expression on her face. Holy shit. She'd taken my burdens into herself and was feeling them all. Wow. Empathy was great and all, but this much had to suck. But it did let me know that Vivian understood more about suffering its impact than anyone else on the planet and knowing what she did, she wasn't the type to cause harm.

Megan jerked out of the reaper's grip and rushed over to me as I let go of Vivian's hand. Darkmore went to Vivian and bent down on one knee, crooning to her with tenderness. I shouldn't be watching. It was too intimate, especially when he pressed his lips to hers and relieved her of my burdens, my energy.

She was feeding him. Weird, but so long as it was consensual, I wouldn't judge. We were good. Whatever they were planning to do with the extra soul energy, it wouldn't hurt the innocent. If they hurt anyone else, more than likely their targets deserved what they got.

I fell back against Megan and waited for the reaper to finish feeding. When he was done, I looked at Vivian and said, "We're good. I'll text you the address where we're keeping the energy we confiscated. After we retrieve the weapon and the rest of the soul energy, I'll be in touch."

Vivian nodded. The reaper eyed us with a little too much interest and speculation in his gaze. Right. Time to get the hell out of here. I stood and took Megan's hand, getting ready to quietly exit the room.

"Jane."

I turned back. Vivian looked at me, her gaze intense. "I have a message for you. When the time comes, use the ring. Soon."

Ring? What was she talking about?

Wait. The ring my father gave me. I'd seen it in the vision of the past Cassie showed me. My father had told me that it would help me when I needed it most. I'd never been one for signs, but that was before I'd become a demon hunter and found myself featured in a cryptic prophecy from the demon realm.

Prophecy.

Demons are red, angels are blue, and prophets wear green when they speak to you.

I wouldn't have pegged Vivian the Soul Broker as a prophet, but she was wearing green.

"I will," I said. Then I led Megan out of the room and shut the door behind me.

CHAPTER TWENTY-SIX

After debriefing the team and a good night's sleep, I woke up feeling better than I had in ages. Too bad I couldn't tell Dr. Khatri about Vivian's burden relieving abilities so she could try and duplicate them. It would make therapy and recovery much easier. But it wasn't my secret to tell.

I'd just have to be grateful for the one-time gift and do the rest of the work on my own.

"Prrrrp!"

"Oh, there you are," I said, smiling at Sully. She'd shrunk, not to her former size, but to a much more reasonable house cat size, and her tail had grown fluffier. I scratched her little head and pulled her onto my chest.

"You okay?" I asked.

Sully bobbed her head up and down and then head-butted my nose, demanding more affection.

"Good, because you're officially on the team now. Want a special collar?"

I expected her to hiss or snarl, but she cocked her head to the side and started purring. I'd take her to the pet store later and let her pick out a collar and a tag. It would help her pass for a regular cat so long as she kept her wings tight against her body and traveled at night. Darkness would conceal the double ears, too.

I'd have to make sure it was one of those snap off collars that wouldn't choke her if and when she grew again. I should probably stock up.

D hadn't joined me in bed last night. I wasn't sure how I felt about it, but I refused to let insecurity or doubt creep into my mind. We were in the middle of a mission, and he'd been out hitting supernatural bars for intel last night. I hope he'd had some luck narrowing down Belphegor's hideout. The element of surprise was key when we mounted our raid. The demon we were chasing was too powerful and could escape too easily if she figured out we knew where she hid.

I walked out of my quarters in my PJs and fuzzy slippers, searching for coffee and breakfast.

I wasn't alone. Trinity sat at the conference table nursing a cup of coffee and scrolling through her phone. She looked up and gave me a weary smile. "There's fresh coffee. Help yourself."

"Thanks," I said, heading to the kitchen. I found the coffee along with fresh bagels, a variety of cream cheeses, and a bowl full of fruit. Nice. Mom was keeping us well fed. I hoped she was getting some rest, too. I knew she worried about Megan and me when we went out in the field.

I needed to tell her about the ring and about Cassie's vision, though I had about as much desire to talk about dad as she was to hear about him. But I owed her the truth, including exactly how and when my father had saddled me with Hannah.

And the fact that we'd have to find him since he was supposedly the key to completing our mission to banish the celestials and demons from earth.

I filled plate and cup then headed out to the conference room, parking my ass next to my boss.

"How you holding up?" I asked. She was still busy on her phone, but she could multitask like nobody's business.

"Better now that your contacts retrieved the soul energy. Didn't like having that stuff sitting around, ready to explode."

"Right. What's the status on our celestial 'guests'?"

Trinity grimaced. "Pinstripe isn't talking. Won't even give us her name. And Judaliel hasn't stopped sobbing. It's going to be a chore cleaning up tears from all those eyes."

I laughed. "Good thing it's eyes instead of noses. Think we should go ahead and send them back to the celestial realm?"

Trinity sighed and put her phone down. "Pinstripe needs to go, but Judaliel may be a good hostage, assuming Belphegor cares about her. If she doesn't, the celestial may make a good distraction."

Fair enough. "We need to be careful. Cassie wants the Sigillum Dei. Can we hold Pinstripe without her?"

I popped a piece of fruit into my mouth. Peach. Yummo. Good thing it was Trinity's turn to talk so I could continue stuffing my face. I was ravenous.

"I doubt it," Trinity said. "That's why she's still here. But your ally seems content to stick around for guard duty, so there's no rush. In the meantime, we've got a lead on Belphegor's lair. You'll never guess where it is."

There was something about in her voice that gave me pause. She sounded bemused and a more than little irritated. Arching a brow, she stared at me. Ooooh, this had to be good.

"You said I'd never guess, so spill the tea."

Trinity pulled up Google Maps on her smartphone and put it on the table. It had an address, but it was zoomed out instead of showing the street view. I zoomed in and stared for a moment, puzzled. It was a scruffy patch of land with an area that had been recently seeded—rather unsuccessfully since there were bald patches. But the general outline of the new growth was a circle. The circle was flanked by flagpoles.

Flagpoles mounted with giant Confederate flags.

I almost choked on my coffee.

"No fucking way," I said, meeting Trinity's gaze. "Belphegor's hiding out in the spot formerly occupied by that eyesore of a racist Confederate monument?"

For years, a grotesque and poorly executed from an artistic standpoint statue of some best forgotten Civil War general from the wrong side of the conflict towered above this spot. It was huge, gaudy, and visible to anyone and everyone driving down I-65. They'd finally taken the damned thing down, but its memory lived on along with the stupid flags.

"Yup," Trinity said. "Think it's a personal message?"

"Dunno," I said. "If so, it could be for either of us, but I'm guessing it's more about being secluded, private property that isn't well-traveled or easily accessible. But we can totally burn all those Confederate flags on site when we raid the place if you like."

Trinity rolled her eyes. "No fires. Not until the weapon is secured. Anyway, staff meeting in an hour so we can come up with a plan of attack."

"Okay," I said, "I need to run to my condo and pick something up." Before Trinity could protest, I added, "It's for the mission. Got a tip from a prophet in green. Figured it couldn't hurt to follow her advice."

"Fine. Don't go alone. Take your cat and Demoriel."

I nodded, got up and grabbed my empty plate and mug and headed back toward the kitchen. Then I turned back and looked at Trinity. She was so controlled, her presence exuding confidence and benevolent authority. I believed it. But I believed the dark circles under her eyes and frown lines that spoke of sleepless nights and worry, too. We all had those, but hers were more prominent. She carried the weight of the mission and the well-being of the entire team on her shoulders.

And the burden of the deal she'd made to keep the players confined to the city.

"What kind of deal did you make, Trin?" I asked.

She blinked and stared up at me with a flash of abject terror in her gaze before putting on her I'm-in-charge-and-I've-got-this mask. "You don't need to worry about it."

"But I will," I said, holding her gaze. She dropped her eyes first. "And you know I'm not going to give up until I find out and find a way to fix it."

Her gaze darted back to mine, full of anger. "You know, you aren't some kind of all-powerful savior. Your job is to stay alive, train like hell, and then give hell to the demons and celestials until we can cast them off earth. Permanently. That's it. I don't need you to fix this."

Ouch. That stung. I was many things, but arrogant in my abilities wasn't one of them. I knew my limits, and I wasn't out to save her because I wanted to be some kind of goddamned hero.

"Someone is trying to play savior here, but it isn't me. You're my boss, but you're my friend, too. You don't have to carry the weight of the world on your shoulders while being some kind of human sacrifice. We need you and everyone else on the team." I was getting angry now, too. "So forgive me if I care about you and want to keep you safe. I'll stick my nose in your business or anyone else's when they're in trouble so I can help, and the rest of the team would do the same if you trusted them enough. No woman is an island. So suck it up and start dealing with this so we can all do our jobs and come out in one piece."

I stormed off before she could answer, passing Sam on my way to the kitchen. He gave me a reverent bow as I passed. Maybe he could talk some sense into Trinity. It hurt my heart that I couldn't, but I wasn't letting it go.

And I sure as hell wasn't giving up.

***

D picked me up in his Mustang, which I adored and wanted to drive so badly I'd almost stolen his keys. Twice. The clever demon always caught me and persuaded me to give them back by reminding me of the number of times I'd almost crashed the family car while learning to drive. Not fair. I was a much better driver now.

Then he reminded me that I forgot where I parked my car a couple of times a month on stakeouts, which ended the conversation.

I spent the drive to my house telling D about my rendezvous with the reaper and his soul broker companion with empathic abilities. The no-secrets clause in our relationship included work, and I knew he wouldn't spill the beans.

"She's the reason we're going to my place. Turns out she moonlights as a prophet."

D snorted. "I didn't think you'd be so enthusiastic about advice from your dad."

Sully, who'd settled on his lap for a snooze opened her eyes and stared at me inquisitively. Great. Even my cat was sticking her nose in my daddy issues.

D had a point, though. Maybe I should be wary of taking advice from a man—celestial—who'd saddled me with a demon and abandoned me. But it wasn't just him.

"Vivian told me I'd need the ring soon, and she's not in league with any celestials or demons involved in this mess. I don't think she'd sell us out."

D appeared to consider my argument. I liked that. He didn't automatically dismiss my gut instincts, call me an idiot or say I was being naïve. Then again, he'd just gotten back on my good side—and I'd gotten back on his.

"What do you think? If I'm doing something reckless or stupid, just tell me."

D didn't answer. Instead, he pulled into the parking lot of a strip mall and took an isolated space beneath a tree. Putting the car in park, he turned to look at me. "I don't think you're stupid. Reckless maybe, but I am, too. Do you trust the soul broker?"

I had to think about it for a minute.

"With this, yes? I don't know her well enough to trust her absolutely. She has her own agenda, and I'm still a little leery of handing over more soul energy to the reaper with no restrictions. But...if it was just my father or Cassie, I'd be suspicious. With Vivian? I think I should grab the ring."

D put his hand on my shoulder, the warm weight comforting as well as oddly sensual. Ugh, I was such a ho-bag. One touch and I was ready to crawl into his lap and engage in the kind of heavy petting that would get us arrested if caught.

D smirked, no doubt catching my thoughts. "Good enough for me," he said.

We exited the parking lot and drove to my condo. Troy smiled at me and gave D the evil eye. Fates save me from macho men.

"Troy, this is Dominic. He's an old friend. Dominic, meet Troy. He keeps this place running and knows all the best bars, restaurants, and hidden gems in Nashville and the surrounding counties."

D put on a charming smile, the one that showed his dimple and made him look less like the dangerous demon he was and more like a GQ model. Troy walked out from behind his desk and looked D up and down before a grin split his face. He offered his hand and D shook it.

"Well, Miss Jinx, glad to see you got someone looking out for you. I was worried. You and your roomies hadn't been home for a few days. Been out raising hell?"

I laughed. "Occupational hazard, and D does make a pretty decent bodyguard. Any messages?"

I held out a sliver of hope that our former boss, Sameal the Angel or Demon of Death, would contact me with some advice on what to do. Even better, the bastard could come back and help us sort out this mess instead of running off on some bullshit mission dealing with Archangels. If they were all like Pinstripe and Judaliel, they weren't going to be our allies and weren't worth the trouble.

"Nope. I'll be on the lookout. Where's your cat? You still gotta get your paperwork in." I'd left Sully in snoozing in the car, hoping Troy would forget about her. No such luck.

"Yeah, yeah," I said. "Send me an email."

Troy's laughter followed us as we walked toward the elevators. We were quiet on the ride up to the penthouse, standing on opposite sides of the elevator and ignoring the mounting tension.

We were alone. For the first time in months, it was just the two of us. No colleagues, no family, no kitty or Dr. Khatri. Just us. On our way up to my cozy condo that we'd have all to ourselves.

The possibilities were endless.

CHAPTER TWENTY-SEVEN

The ding of the elevator sent a jolt of excitement through my body. D and I entered the kitchen and all kinds of delicious memories of our first breakfast together filled my dirty little mind. I turned to D and said, "Can I get you something to drink?"

The look in D's eyes stopped me in my tracks.

I fell into his arms, and he grabbed me, picking me up and placing me on the counter as he kissed me and assaulted my senses with his mouth, his hands, his skin, his hair as I ran my fingers through his hair. I moaned as he pushed his body against the sweet spot between my legs. Oh, it was delicious and what I'd been longing for, been craving ever since he came back into my life.

When he lowered his mouth to my breast and sucked my nipple through the thin cotton of my T-shirt and bra, I arched my back and cried out, overwhelmed with sensation. He braced my back with one hand and put the other to good use, teasing my other nipple, which rose at his command as he lavished it with sensual pleasure.

My hand snaked down so I could return the favor, but he stopped me.

"No," he said. I was terrified he would stop all together, but he continued to lavish my breasts with kisses.

202 D. B. SIEDERS

I tried to free my hand, but he stopped me again. I cried out in pleasure and frustration. "Why?" I gasped.

D raised his head and looked at me, heat and sparks of demon power dancing in his gaze. He licked his lips and ran his hands up my thighs as my body cried out for more. For him.

"I promised you a date. Plenty of dates. Wherever you'd like to go and so we can make up for the time we missed. A proper courtship."

I threw my head back and groaned in agony. "We can still go on a date. We can go on a thousand dates. But I need you. Now."

I felt his head on my lap, heard him breathing hard, his breaths vibrating against the juncture between hip and thigh, so close to where I wanted him. He was right, of course. My head knew he was right, but my body and heart wanted and didn't much care for my head at that moment.

"I'm sorry," I said, patting his head. "We should slow down and wait. Do this the right way."

He looked up at me and cocked his head. "I said I'd take you on a date and give you a proper courtship. And I intend to do just that. But tonight," he said, rubbing his head against my thighs like a cat, "is about you. For you. You've spent your whole life fighting for the world and giving all of yourself. When we were kids, you took care of me, gave me shelter, food, companionship, and during my captivity, you gave me hope."

He slid his fingers to my waistband and slid his fingers beneath it, moving until he reached the button which he deftly undid and unzipped my jeans as he spoke. "You give. It's your nature. It's what you do. Let me give you this. Something special just for you. Let me taste you and give you pleasure, Jane."

There was power in his voice—not a command, but an irresistible invitation. I wanted so badly to accept that invitation. But I wanted to give him as much pleasure as he'd promised me. And, like Mara, I didn't want him to lavish me with pleasure, neglecting himself because he was afraid I'd leave him if he didn't worship me.

"What about you?" I asked, my body screaming at me in protest. "I want you with me, not serving me."

He grinned wickedly, "Oh, Jane, if I do this right, and I will, I'll be with you, and *you'll* be serving *me* when you come so hard you forget your own name."

He tugged at my jeans, and I lifted so he could slide them down. I busied myself removing my T-shirt and bra. Then he pulled off my panties and spread my legs, baring me to his hungry gaze. It was a heady and frightening experience, being so vulnerable, so exposed. I risked a glance at my demon and my breath caught as he stared at me like a starving man beholding a feast.

He was looking at *me* like that.

In the darkness of my home, safe—for the moment—from the weight of the world on my shoulders along with all the ordinary cares of life, I spread my legs wider, arching my back in invitation. His fingers tightened on my thighs, and he rubbed his stubbled cheek against the sensitive skin of my belly, his tongue running below my navel as I shivered in anticipation.

He teased me by trailing kisses down my belly before lavishing my thighs with the same attention. His magic enveloped me, and he channeled it to go where his hands couldn't reach, caressing my breasts as he drove me mad with wanting. I writhed and tried to move so his tongue would go where I needed it most.

He stilled along with the magic that had been caressing my body and driving me insane. I gasped in protest.

"Good things come to those who wait, and the reward will be so much sweeter."

"D, don't make me wait. Please."

He rose and kissed me hard, his lips and tongue claiming me, demanding I surrender to his command. This was his game of pleasure, and the pleasure would be mine if I submitted. I wanted to submit, but I wasn't used to being a passive lover. I gave as good as I got.

He released my mouth and met my gaze. "You always were a hard case. Can't stop fighting, huh?" he asked, not without sympathy.

I nodded. No more talk. I needed those kisses, those delicious magical caresses, and I needed them now.

"I can help, but we'll need a safe word."

A shiver of excitement traveled through my body and sent tingles to my core. D wanted to play, and I was so game. The thought of what he'd do to me...

"Mine's Chupacabra. What's yours?"

D laughed. "Let's hope we don't get interrupted by an actual Chupacabra. Mine is ralrach."

The demon word for safe. I wasn't fluent, but I'd heard the word often enough within the demon refugee community, especially from recently escaped demons who were able to let down their guards at last. For the first time in their lives, when they understood they were no longer prey, many demons broke into sobs, repeating the word over and over again.

Oh, D. You'll always be safe with me.

"Okay, now that we have that out of the way, what are you going to do to me?"

He muttered a few words in the demon language and moved his hands as if drawing sigils. Suddenly, I felt magic wrap around my wrists, binding them to the table and forcing me to recline.

"Okay?" he asked.

The magic held my hands immobile but caressed my skin softly. I tested the enchanted bindings and wiggled to get more comfortable. "Yes," I said. Are you going to bind my feet, too?"

His laughter was low and wicked. "No, I've got a better use for them."

Before I could ask him what he planned to do with my legs, he flung them over his shoulders and kissed my most sensitive flesh, flicking his tongue and sending a jolt of pleasure that reached my soul. Hot breath on my skin, light kisses and licks, D knew how to take his time, whipping me into a frenzy as he used my moans and sighs to guide him, learning my body and playing it like a fine instrument.

My demon was a virtuoso.

I braced my feet on his broad shoulders for leverage, demanding more. I was ready for a faster pace, more delicious pressure, and to reach the beautiful peak I'd been dying for, that he would give me.

But only when he was good and ready.

At last, he lavished my clit with his tongue as his magic caressed my breasts and the rest of my naked skin. So much sensation, it was too much and not nearly enough, and it trapped me at the precipice of release.

Then he backed off, the wicked creature, and gentled his kisses and caresses once more, making me beg for him to give me release. "Please," I whispered. "More."

"I'll give you more," he said, slapping my ass. "I'll give you more when I'm ready and you'll love every minute. And you won't come until I say so."

Fuuuuuuck. A hot demon dom held me at his mercy, and it was hotter than the fires of the hell realm. I could come just from his commanding voice. According to D, I would come from that commanding voice. If I was a good girl. If I was a bad girl...

I pushed against him in silent demand, and he slapped the other ass cheek. The sting set my body on fire and his soothing caress after made me feel safe, cherished, and worshipped. I could totally get used to this. I wrapped my legs around his shoulders and crossed my feet, pulling him closer and shivering as his tongue laved my center.

Then he grazed me with his teeth and sucked my clit hard. Oh, it was so good. I was so close. His tongue on my clit, his fingers caressing the sensitive skin around my core, his magic matching every flick of his tongue on my breasts. I gasped, unable to resist grinding against his face as his magic struck my ass again like a riding crop.

"D, please, I need this, I need to come," I cried.

"What's your name?" he asked. I remembered his promise to make me come so hard I'd forget my own name. It was my last conscious thought before he said, "Come for me. Now!"

His tongue pressed hard against my clit, and I exploded, stars flashing before my eyes and pleasure coursing through me in wave after wave. All the while, D rode me with this fingers and tongue, drawing out the orgasm until my legs shook and my pulse raced impossibly fast.

When I came back to my senses, D lifted and brought me over to my favorite couch, cradling my limp body against his chest and whispering softly in the demon language. I was too languid and limp to sit up, so I snuggled against him and wrapped him in my arms.

"I'm never letting you go," I said.

"Good," D whispered, "because I'm never letting you go, either."

After a long moment, I let go and started to disentangle myself from him. Not that I wanted to, I would have gladly stayed in his arms forever. But we needed to get back to HQ so we could prepare for the raid on Belphegor's lair.

D helped me up and grabbed a few towels from the linen closet for cleanup. He was so thoughtful. Then he brought me my clothes, which he helped me into with great reluctance. I put my arms around his shoulder and pulled him down for a kiss, tasting my essence on his lips and shivering at remembered ecstasy. "Next time," I said. "I get to tie you up and have my way with you. Fair's fair."

"Babe," he said, pressing his forehead hard against mine. "I'm counting on it. Now let's grab your ring and go complete this mission."

CHAPTER TWENTY-EIGHT

D and his demon companions—the ones who seemed to show up whenever we needed them and then disappeared before we could ask too many questions—teleported the team to the wooded area adjacent to Belphegor's lair. Simon had scoped it out and given us a strategy for entering undetected.

Unfortunately, that strategy involved crawling through a ventilation shaft. No magic. Belphegor would be expecting magic. No, we had to do it the mundane way, the hard way. Worse, the odors coming from the shaft were beyond revolting. No idea what the demon and her minions were up to down there, but it wasn't cleaning.

We all climbed in one by one, face to ass—except Trinity, who led the way by virtue of leadership—slowly making our way through the shaft. I was in the middle, flanked for my "protection," and in the perfect position to hear everyone and everything.

"How much further," Lacey whispered from behind me in the tunnel. "It smells worse than the twins' room."

"Hey," Boice said. "We're dating a bog hag. She likes old river water."

"Excuse me?" Alexi said what we'd what we were all thinking, only it wasn't his habit to swear. Demon bros were tight-lipped about their personal lives, though they were perfectly happy to get all up in mine and everyone else's.

"You heard him," Roice said after a grunt of effort. He must've reached the corner. Tight squeeze. "Don't talk smack about our girl. Chiara's no more evil than you are, wolfman."

I was about to come to Alexi's defense, but he beat me to it. "No smack talk. I'm just wondering how long it'll take her to eat your livers."

We all giggled, which earned us a stern warning from Trinity.

"She won't eat our livers," Roice said with enough inuendo to let us know exactly what he hoped she would eat. "Not as long as we keep her satisfied."

"And we do," Boice reassured us. "It's the perfect situation."

Well, I wasn't one to judge consensual relationships. I'd just hope for their continued safety.

We crawled for a bit longer. Damn, I should have stretched first since I was getting a cramp in my leg. Sully made it look so easy, maneuvering her tiny body up and down the tunnel, sniffing and giving each of us head butts and nose boops for encouragement. When Trinity reached the end of the shaft, she reverse rotated the screws that held the cover in place and carefully set it aside. Didn't take her long and she didn't use her demon steel knife or any other magical assistance. Our boss lady was always harping about how we needed to hone our mundane skills to the same level as our supernatural talents. Guess she practiced what she preached.

"Sully, you're up," Trinity whispered.

Sully belly crawled to the front and slithered out of the opening, sticking to the shadows as she crept around the room. We'd put her on scout duty since she was tiny, didn't have a magical aura we could detect, and was more likely to go unnoticed. Hopefully Belphegor wouldn't recognize her if she caught a glimpse. Considering kitty girl had taken out her dragon demon warriors with brutal efficiency, our cover would be blown if Belphegor paid her any mind.

Trinity sent a message down the line and we activated our coms devices. They would allow us to communicate with one another during the raid and had the added bonus of letting us hear what was going on in the underground lair.

"We need a portal. There are many here. Belial told me so." Belphegor's voice echoed through the cavernous underground space.

"They are all closed, my mistress," a male voice said. Most likely a lesser demon who'd decided serving the more powerful demon would keep him safe. Foolish, but understandable.

"Find one so we can unleash my legions and lead the army to victory. This fine weapon will ensure we escape this cursed city, and we will use this wonderous extraction system my sister devised to drain the masses and force them to fight the celestials alongside us."

Seriously? The Master Demon was giving a this-is-my-evil-plan monologue? Not very original, or smart. She clearly hadn't learned enough about earth technology to know about electronic surveillance or listening devices. Arrogant creature should have picked her sister's brain about technology. It was an advantage we could use.

I activated my com device and said, "Trinity, permission to release the mini drones. Copy?"

"Permission granted. And you don't have to say copy."

"But it's fun!"

I reached into my pack and activated the tiny devices that would serve as our eyes and ears. Pure tech equipped with audio, video, and small as a housefly, the twins had outdone themselves on these babies. James Bond level stuff.

The drones flew out just as Sully made her way back to our hiding spot.

"Lead the way," Trinity said, climbing out of the vent and crouching low. The rest of us followed. Sully led us along a narrow path between earthen walls and a series of shelves filled with mundane combat gear. Was that for the demons she'd called to her service or for the humans she planned to enslave?

Nope. It would be confiscated and distributed to the other demon hunting teams, because we weren't going to let Belphegor win.

Belphegor stood in the center of a large central space cleared of debris. Trinity gave us the signal to fan out. We had to find the weapon first, secure it if we could, then fight our way to the master demon and send her back to the hell realm where she belonged.

Trinity had the Sigillum Dei.

It was a risk to bring it, but what choice did we have? Belphegor was powerful. Our best course of action would be to open a portal with the artefact, shove her ass through, and close it before dealing with her minions. We'd left Cassie back at HQ, still guarding the two celestials, so she would be too preoccupied to swoop in and take the Sigillum. Probably.

"I've got a bad feeling about this mission," I whispered.

"Don't jinx us!"

I had to cover my mouth the stifle the giggles. "I have to, sis. It's all in the name."

Megan didn't respond and I tried my best to shake off the feeling of unease I'd been experiencing all night. Maybe it was residual withdrawal from the game, or your garden variety PTSD that came from the job, but this felt...different. I rubbed the ring I'd retrieved, hanging around my neck on the chain where I kept the piece of polished obsidian that served as a black mirror, the one I'd used to call and control Hannah. I had no use for it now, not since Hannah had escaped, but it had been a part of me for so long I couldn't bear to let it go.

The locket that D had given me rested against my heart. Three talismans to ground me, to keep me safe, and to help me defeat the master demon.

"We have a visual," Boice said. "Drones sent back an image of the weapon. It's behind demon glass—probably for safety—and under guard by three dragon demons armed to the teeth."

"Don't you mean armed with teeth?" Lacey said.

"That, too. The rest of the demons here are lower level, but they're still dangerous. Either Belphegor has convinced them their only chance for survival is by serving her or she's using mind control. They all have phones."

Great. The asshole demon was draining her own people.

Trinity's cool, commanding voice came over the coms. "Alexi, Sam, and Demoriel—secure the exits. Nobody gets out with the weapon. Sam's going to work a spell to block dematerialization before we attack, but it won't last long. Mara, you and Megan guard the ventilation shaft. Lacey and Jinx are with me, with the cat guarding our backs. As soon as the twins create a distraction, we'll go after Belphegor. Remember, time is our enemy. We grab her, send her back to the hell realm, and retrieve the weapon."

We all held our breath, waiting for each team member to get into position and confirm they were ready.

"Ready to unleash the spell on your command," Sam said.

"Boice, Roice?" Trinity asked.

"Ready, boss."

"Go!"

The twins killed the lights as a wave of magic washed over us. There were a few shouts of alarm and confusion, but not as many as I expected. It confirmed that Belphegor was indeed mind controlling most of the demons in the lair. Low lights from cell phones glowed in the room but didn't move.

Trinity, Lacey, and I ran toward Belphegor, who was busy flicking her hands to craft some sort of horrible magic. She'd screamed in outrage when she realized she couldn't just zap herself out of the lair. Good. After the evil she and her sister had unleashed, it was fitting for her to feel trapped. Sam came through, and all the exits were covered.

It was up to us.

Belphegor opened her mouth and unleashed a horde of wraiths. They flew at us, attacking from all sides and from above and below as I slashed at them with my knife, cutting off phantom limbs and heads as I spun, my demon graft sigils alight with the thrill of battle.

They kept coming. There were so many. Trinity, Lacey, and I should have made a dent by now, but they'd quadrupled in number and swarmed. It was so cold. The wraiths sucked the warmth from the air and from our bodies, making it difficult to move, difficult to breathe.

Holy shit. They were regenerating. Like the mythical hydra, every time we sliced a part of one wraith off, it formed into another hungry demon intent on consuming us.

"Stab, don't rend!" I screamed, hoping my teammates could hear me through coms. The wraiths screamed and hissed, their ear-splitting voices as much a weapon as their phantom talons and teeth.

I stabbed every wraith surrounding me, but it was an exercise in futility. The wraiths closed in. I couldn't extend my arm far enough to do any damage. They were going to suffocate me, swallow me whole.

Let me out. I'm hungry.

A jolt of shock coursed through me, the memory of Hannah speaking in my head, eager to feast on demon essence. But it wasn't Hannah. It was Zer. My sight and hearing went offline. I'd pass out from lack of oxygen soon. I couldn't control the wolf demon.

I didn't have to. I whispered, "Yes," and gave myself over to the wolf.

CHAPTER TWENTY-NINE

When I came to my senses, I found my fangs had slashed at the throat of the nearest wraith. It screamed and became a wisp of smoke-like essence. Zer drank it down and howled in triumph. Strength coursed through the body we shared as she consumed wraith after wraith.

Lacey flew through the air, carried by Simon, the immaterial demon screeching as he poured his magic into Lacey's knife. She zapped and he feasted, black wings rising and red hair flying like a freakin' Valkyrie. Not to be outdone, Trinity conjured a cage of fire and was busy blasting wraiths with magic from her knife, tossing the wraiths into the cage.

Sully had grown into her big cat form and was swatting wraiths out of the air.

"Zer," I said. "We need to get to Belphegor."

The wolf leapt over the bodies of dazed and disoriented demons, their phones on the floor as they awoke from their stupor. Had they survived the draining? How?

The twins. They must've disabled the game.

I rushed after Belphegor. She conjured a sword and took a fighting stance. My wolf froze and growled low, our minds and body in harmony.

All we had to do was dodge the master demon's weapon and lock our jaws on her throat.

We circled her just out of the sword's reach in a slow dance as she held it at the ready. She was a patient hunter, waiting for us to make the first move. Quick as lightening, we swiped at her feet with our claws and danced out of reach. The hit scored her boots but didn't draw blood. We tried again, aiming for a knee, then her back, then a thigh. She bled, and so did we as she sliced us with her blade.

We were at a stalemate. Trinity circled with us, the Sigillum Dei in her palm, but we couldn't disarm or disable her, and though Belphegor was the Master of Sloth, we would tire long before she did. All she had to do was outlast us and Sam's spell.

A low growl came from my left. Alexi's wolf had joined us in the hunt. Sully hissed as she landed between me and Alexi. Then she turned her attention to the demon, unleashing a roar to rival any lions.

We were pack. Alone, I didn't stand a chance. Together, we would prevail.

Belphegor opened her mouth to unleash a spell, another horde of wraiths, or some other horror, but Simon swooped down and clawed her throat.

She raised her sword and stabbed the mammon in the heart.

Lacey screamed. Simon fell.

"Trinity!" I screamed. "Now!"

Simon had given us this opportunity. We couldn't waste it. The Sigillum glowed as Trinity performed the incantation to activate it. She'd woven the sigils into a piece of demon leather to save time. The leather glowed as the sigils caught fire and rose. She held the artefact, which glowed white hot in her gloved hand.

Her face contorted as the Sigillum burned her flesh through the barrier of demon leather. At last, the portal opened. Alexi, Sully, and I closed in, taking hits from Belphegor's sword as she swung with unsteady strokes with one hand and clutched at her bleeding throat with the other. A battle raged in the background, presumably the rest of the team fighting dragon demons and the lesser demons guarding the celestial weapon.

Belphegor hit Alexi's head with the flat of the sword hard, knocking him aside. The fallen wolf demon didn't get up. Sully took a swipe at the demon and took a blow to the back. It was up to me and my wolf demon, and we were almost out of time.

"Jinx!" Trinity yelled. "Hurry!"

The unspoken, "I can't hold it much longer" came through loud and clear. The magic surrounding the lair began to fade. Sam was at his limit. The rest of the team were fighting for their lives or tending to fallen comrades.

Simon. Oh, dear God, Simon.

Now or never.

With a leap of faith, I released Zer and stood before Belphegor in my own skin, flesh, blood, and magic, bloody but not beaten. I had an idea. A wonderful, terrible idea.

"Boice, Roice! Hit me with the energy!"

"Jinx, don't do it!" Trinity yelled. "We can't afford to lose you."

"Trust me," I said. I put the ring on and waited for it to do something. My celestial magic came to life and surged through me like molten gold, veined with the silver of my demon magic, and I rose, letting it carry me into the air above Belphegor. Celestial energy and demonic energy, plus the energy of my human aspect that somehow ruled them both. I was the conduit. The ring was the focus.

"Now!" I screamed. My warped voice filled with unearthly power echoing through the room. The twins hit me with a beam of soul energy that lit the underground lair, filling it with light and power. I focused the power on Belphegor, blasting the volatile, explosive magic through the Master Demon as her mouth contorted in agony and rage she could not voice. She began to split apart, and I pushed, moving her closer to the portal, inch by inch, until at last she became caught in its pull.

"Go back to hell where you belong," I screamed. Then I gave myself over to the energy.

Belphegor fell into the portal. Dragon demons followed, tossed in by

Demoriel, Mara, and Sam as he staggered out of the shadows. Trinity dropped the Sigillum and collapsed as the portal closed and filled the lair with silence broken only by Lacey's sobs.

Had we lost Simon? Trinity? Sully? The thought filled me with rage and grief that fueled the energy coursing through me. The twin's had turned off the source, but I glowed and pulsed with unstable energy that could destroy everything around it. It wanted vengeance. It wanted war. It wanted to tear earth and the realms of celestials and demons apart. The power wouldn't stop there. It would tempt the beings once worshipped as gods with its allure and then feed off their destruction, growing stronger until it swallowed the universe.

Until there was nothing left.

"Jane!" D yelled. "You have to stop. You'll blow us all to kingdom come!"

I tried to pull back the power, to rein it in, but it had a will of its own and a singular purpose. The souls from which it was stolen cried out for justice. It pulled at my very soul. It had needed me as a conduit until it surged enough to exist on its own, a self-sustaining system of malevolence and oblivion.

It was tearing me apart.

"I can't," I screamed. "D, get everyone out!"

Mara and Megan were already evacuating the lair, gathering the freed demons and dragging our team out. The earthen walls rumbled with the force of the magic and energy and power I held. If it touched the weapon, it would be game over.

"Jane! Don't lose yourself. Don't let go. Fight!"

I tried. My body and soul were being consumed in the wake of power I was never meant to hold. Desperate and running on instinct. I yanked the ring off my finger and threw it on the ground. For an instant, I saw a vision. A creature so ancient and powerful that mortals trembled before him, built monoliths, temples, and entire cities in his honor, worshipped him and gave him power through their belief and sacrifices. Long of beard and tall of stature, his eyes filled with rage when his gaze met mine.

I knew those eyes.

I saw them in the mirror every day. I'd seen them in the old photograph I'd kept next to the ring and in the vision the angel Cassiel had shown me.

It was my father.

My father, but not as I'd known him. He may have worn a human guise, but he was no mortal, or celestial, or anything else I'd ever seen. Nothing of his kind had been seen on earth since the dawn of civilization. According to some ancient myths, he may have been responsible for humanity's organization into civilizations.

No, he had to be a celestial, because that's what I was. Demon steel glows bright blue in the presence of celestials. My signature was purple now because of demon grafts. Before the demon grafts, however, I was blue and so was Megan thanks to our father.

Was he an uber celestial? A primal emanation? I sure as hell wasn't calling him a god, even if others in the past had worshipped him. That would make me and Meg demigods. Nope. I had no delusions of grandeur. When I caught up with my dad, I'd kick his ass and prove he was no god.

My musings were one plug in the leak that was my soul. It barely made a dent in the flow of power. I couldn't control it.

I spotted Boice and Roice in my periphery. They were holding a series of collection tubes. What were they thinking? I couldn't control the power, let alone aim it. I'd be just as likely to hit my roomies.

"Trust us, Jinx!" Boice yelled. His brother pulled out something that looked like an enormous funnel. I could probably hit it.

"Okay," I yelled in a voice I didn't recognize. "Stand back."

I loosened the reins of my failing control and let the energy spill out of me. Most of it hit the funnel, but some spilled into the room, blasting anything solid it encountered to oblivion. Shelves, equipment, random furnishings—we'd be lucky if the team could retrieve anything from this site to analyze for future investigations.

The floor beneath the storage containers began to sink and chunks of sod and rock slid down the walls. I had to stop so we could get out of here, the twins and I, before the lair collapsed.

We were out of time.

CHAPTER THIRTY

With significant effort and the last of my strength, I pulled the remaining energy back. It hurt, but I could hold it for a little while longer. Boice and Roice caught me before I hit the ground, then they handed me to D who teleported me out of the lair and into fresh night air. The heat of the summer was fading. Not fall yet, but the dog days of summer were coming to an end.

"What was that?" D asked, holding me close.

I shook my head. I didn't know how to answer him even if I could speak. And I didn't want to scare him with the hunch I had about my father's true identity.

I was scared enough for us both.

"Is it too early...for a..." I coughed and spat chunks of the lair. Gross. I hoped I wouldn't get some form of black lung from it. Clearing my throat, I tried again, "Is it too early...for a pumpkin spice latte?"

D laughed and held me closer. His tears hit my face and blended with my own.

"Everyone make it out? Everyone okay?" I asked.

"Yes, everyone made it out, and the twins retrieved the storage containers."

My head ached and I knew as soon as I came out of the stupor and fatigue threatening to swallow me whole that my entire body would make me pay for the past few hours. We'd defeated Belphegor—barely.

D hadn't answered my last question.

"Simon?" I asked. I tried to move my head and find the little greed demon. Or Lacey, who would be by his side. But my head hurt too much to move.

D sighed. "He's hurt. Badly. The sword was infused with magic. It won't allow the metaphysical wound to close. That's why you and Trinity are in bad shape, too, but Sam is sure he can heal you. Simon..."

A sob escaped my throat. No. Simon was tough. Lacey couldn't lose him. The team couldn't lose him. Damn it all to hell, I couldn't lose him.

"Dr. Khatri's on her way with more supplies," D said, rocking me through my ugly cry. "Sam will keep him stable."

There was no hope in D's voice, though he tried to reassure me. If Sam couldn't heal Simon, a mostly human demon hunter wouldn't be able to either. Simon was immaterial. Human medicine was designed for beings with physical bodies. Just because Simon could manifest as a phantom in our world didn't mean our medical methods would affect him. I spared a thought for Zer and hoped my wolf demon wasn't as damaged. I couldn't do anything for her.

But maybe I could do something for Simon.

"D, how did I get my demon grafts?"

D stiffened. He didn't like thinking about or talking about how I almost died. It had taken the essences of every demon on our team to save me, including Simon. I needed to stop D from dwelling on my almost death so we could prevent Simon's impending departure from life.

"There was a ritual. Trust me, you don't want to know the ins and outs—"

"Actually, I do. I have a big chunk of Simon in me. I'd like to give it back to him."

D growled. "You're bleeding from more than a dozen slices to your flesh, on overload from carrying too much soul energy, concussed, and in danger of losing consciousness at any moment and you want me to perform a ritual that will take one of your *life-saving* grafts out of you. Now." His voice grew deeper and more growly as he spoke. He sounded like a grumpy bear.

I giggled. "You're kind of cute when you're mad," I said. "I'm not going to die. The other grafts will keep me alive long enough to heal, and Simon needs that part of himself back so he can heal. I'll be fine without his mad detective skills. I'm a pretty damned good detective on my own."

D was quiet for a long time. Then he kissed my forehead gently and said, "Fine. We have enough demons here to perform the ritual. But after we're done you're going straight to HQ so Sam and Dr. Khatri and put you to rights. Understood?"

"Sure," I said.

D carried me across the uneven ground, careful not to knock any part of me against stray shrubs and small trees. We reached a clearing where our team had set up a field clinic. Trinity's hands were bandaged where the Sigillum Dei had burned them, and she sat propped up against a tree, breathing hard. Someone had splinted her leg with a couple of sticks and some fabric torn from our field gear.

Sully was curled up next to Alexi. Alexi's wolf whined softly and licked her wounds as she panted. Megan sat next to them, exhausted, dirty, but with no obvious injuries aside from cuts and scrapes. D's demon companions stood guard as Sam crouched on the grass and drew sigils over the ragged form of Simon's phantom raven. Lacey sat next to them, holding Mara's hand in a death grip as she added her magic to Sam's sigils that fueled the healing spell.

Simon didn't move.

D said something in the demon language that had Sam and Mara jerking their heads up to stare at him in disbelief.

"Could work."

Boice's voice came from behind us. After a few seconds, he hobbled into my line of sight, leaning against his brother. They were badly burned —damn my aim—but grinning like a couple of fools.

"When you're done, maybe you can give us our essences back," Roice said, cheerfully. "You've gotten way too good at hacking into our accounts."

"This city isn't big enough for three tech demons," Boice added.

I laughed. "I'll put you both on the list. But first, we need to help Simon."

The twins took one look at the demon on the ground and dropped the snark. Boice gathered Alexi while Megan took over stroking Sully's big cat body. Mara kissed Lacey and handed her off to Trinity, who had hobbled over on her bum leg to see what was going on, the control freak.

With all demons present and accounted for, Sam started the ritual. I tried to focus, but dizziness made it hard, and my vision kept blurring. I think I feel asleep for a while since the activity going on around me seemed to fast forward between one blink and the next. There were hundreds of sigils floating in the air above us and the demons standing in the circle that surrounded Simon kept adding more until they swirled and coalesced into a ring above the dying greed demon.

"This is going to hurt," D whispered. "I'm sorry. With any luck, you'll pass out and I'll keep you sedated with my magic until we get back to HQ."

I nodded. Bad idea given the pounding in my skull. A flash of horror made me shudder as I remembered how my skull had caved in during the battle with Belial and Hannah. It had been a fatal blow—the fatal blow—that almost ended me.

But I wouldn't die tonight.

I could handle pain. And I might just save a life. Small price to pay.

A knife plunged into my arm, and I screamed.

Then, the world went black.

CHAPTER THIRTY-ONE

I was floating on a cloud made of cotton candy—a rainbow swirl of colors —and eating a ginormous chocolate ice cream cone. Below me, the ocean lapped in gentle waves as a pod of dolphins performed acrobatics around a pirate ship full of demons.

One had a pegleg, another stroked a parrot perched on his shoulder, and the captain wore a had made out of a block of cheese.

Okay, that cinched it. I wasn't dead. Cotton candy, dolphins, ice cream and cheese would feature prominently in my version of heaven, but demon pirates? That was ridiculous.

Nope. Clearly, I was on some really good drugs.

I sat up and immediately feel back against the gurney, its flimsy mattress doing little to cushion my fall.

"Easy there, champ."

D's voice was a balm to my body and soul. My lips curled into a smile that hurt. Crap. They were either chapped or I'd suffered a split lip some-time during my fight with Belphegor. A cool cloth pressed against my lips, soothing the sting.

"How are you feeling?" D asked.

"Great," I said. "Besides my lips, I'm not feeling any pain."

D laughed and I opened my eyes, smiling wider as his face came into focus. A small bundle of fluff and wings sat perched on his shoulder, green eyes slow blinking.

"Hey, cat," I said, lifting my hands to reach for Sully. I winced when the movement tugged the needle in my hand. Someone had put an IV in. An IV, when we had access to demon salves, balms, elixirs, and spells.

"Why the mundane crap?" I grumped. D adjusted the gurney so I could sit up and cuddle Sully in my lap, which improved my mood. She purred and rolled over showing me her belly, which I poked and then petted. Then I picked her squirmy little kitten body up and inspected her for damage.

All clear, and no shaved bald spots, scabs, scars, or IVs.

"We have to ration our demon realm treatments. Can't afford to open portals right now for trade and risk the legions of the Master Demons coming through. The six Master Demons."

He took my hand and kissed it, sending a frisson of delicious heat through my skin and to other more interesting places. "You defeated Belphegor."

"We did it," I said, shrugging. "One down, six to go. Think we'll get a break?"

"Oh, I think we'll be able to work in a couple of dates."

I grinned, wicked and wild thoughts running through my dirty mind. "Three date rule?"

He smiled and flashed his dimple. "As my lady wishes."

I was forgetting something important. What was it? Damn these mind-numbing drugs! I squirmed and huffed. I hope it was just the drugs and not the lingering effects of my head injury. Or possibly I'd fried my brain while being a living freakin' conduit for soul energy that had the power to wipe out a whole city. What was I thinking?

I stared at my arms and noticed something different. My demon tatts were still there, swirling and rolling with the demon grafts I'd been gifted to save my life, but a few branches were missing.

I grabbed D's hand, speaking past the giant lump in my throat as I said, "Simon?"

D grinned. "Giving back the graft worked like a charm. He's not back at one hundred percent, but a solid seventy-five."

"Tha's good," I said, eyelids fluttering. "Sleep, Jane. Rest. You've earned it."

Within a week, I'd healed up enough to venture out of sick bay at HQ and catch up on what I'd missed. Trinity got the magic healing mojo treatment on her hands, but only because mortal medicine wouldn't have been able to repair the damage. Same for cuts from Belphegor's sword, which I'd received as well.

Alexi and I met for a demon wolf sparring match slash play date in the gym. It was mostly play since he was still healing, and I wasn't up to my former fighting class yet. Sully joined in and we made her an official member of the pack, settling into a cuddle puddle after romping for an hour.

The twins let me know that the reaper and his companion picked up the weapon and drained it of soul energy. Every bit of tech and magic confiscated from the celestial warehouses, corporate office, and what had survived the demon lair's collapse were safely stored in HQ. The ZenMax game craze quickly faded from the public sphere like countless games before it. There were still hardcore fans scouring the Internet for bootleg copies. The twins put a stripped down, non-draining version out to satisfy the demand, but conspiracy theories abounded about the company's collapse and the sudden disappearance of the CEO and upper-level management.

We'd have to concoct a story to keep the mundanes from digging too deep, so the world of demons and celestials remained hidden. Fortunately, no one in human law enforcement had connected the downtown explosions to ZenMax, and nobody batted an eye when a giant sinkhole mysteriously opened up at the Confederate memorial site and swallowed the remaining flags.

Plenty of people saw that as karmic justice. I was inclined to agree.

Mom and Megan were still fussing over me, which I hated, but they kept bringing me my favorite foods, fuzzy socks, at-home spa packs filled with beauty masks and good smelling lotions, which I loved. All that was left to do was dispatch Pinstripe and Judaliel back to the celestial realm permanently. Trinity and Sam would take care of it on one of Cassie's breaks. Then we could call this case closed.

I hadn't told anyone about what my father's ring had showed me. I was still processing the vision, trying to convince myself it hadn't happened, or that it was a soul energy overload-induced hallucination. Maybe it had been.

Maybe...

I'd worry about it later. Right now, I was headed out to Lacey's condo to check in on Simon and my partner, best friend, and her girlfriend.

She and Mara had made it official. Mara moved in to help with Simon's healing, but she'd stayed when Lacey presented her with an emerald ring set in silver. Not an engagement ring. They weren't there yet. But a promise. A commitment. Mara wore it with pride.

My phone pinged when I arrived. I parked the car like a good citizen before I looked at the message.

It was from Cooper. Crap. My heart sank and I thought about ignoring the message, but I'd have to face the music sooner or later. I didn't want to give up Sully, and I didn't want to have to fight Cooper to keep her. My favorite summoner was a fighter with both mundane combat and magical skills.

He could also speak to animals—in their own language, be it growls, chirps, chitters, and other sounds no human should be able to make. A regular Tarzan, our Cooper. And bonus, he was hot enough to rock a loin cloth.

The only problem with Cooper was his mental health. All summoners were a little crazy. Anyone willing to summon a demon to earth was unstable. Other than paranoia, he was a good guy. Better than his late brother who'd worked for Lord Belial, and their father, who also worked for Lord Belial and had summoned D for him.

D knew it wasn't Cooper's fault, but he wasn't exactly on good terms with the summoner.

I stared at my phone. "Damn it, I saved your life," I said out loud, leaning my head back against the seat. He owed me, and I was cashing in on that debt by claiming my demon cat. I sat up straight and read the text message.

I'm not going to take Sully from you.

I exhaled in relief and read the next message in the chain.

The Motiaummerr has bonded with you and is your protector now. Bring her to me for a health check when you can.

That I could do. It would be fun! After her check-up, Sully could frolic in the woods, and I could see how Cooper was doing after his brush with death. I should have checked on him sooner, but I'd been busy healing, training, and battling demons and celestials.

I have information for you and for Demoriel about my father. Got a lead on where he might be hiding.

Wowzers. Wasn't expecting that. The twins had been busy trying to locate the elder Pendergrass, since none of us had wanted to put that burden on Cooper. I had no idea if Cooper had been close to his family. Was he grieving for his brother? Damn it, I really should have checked on the summoner sooner. When I'd told Cooper that his dad had summoned D for Lord Belial, he'd nodded and mumbled something about a family grimoire. I hadn't thought much about it at the time.

Apparently he'd been busy researching.

I texted him back.

Appreciate it, but I worry about how all this is affecting you. You okay, Coop?

It took him a while to text back, which gave me all kinds of time to worry. What if I'd set him off? We needed any information he had, but not at the expense of this fragile man's fractured mind. At last, his reply appeared on the screen.

Working with Dr. Khatri. My father's and evil bastard and I have no problem helping you and D find him. He did things to me and my brother. If D wants to kill him, he has my blessing. But I want answers first.

I totally got it. Looks like D and I weren't the only ones with daddy issues. Cooper was a gentle soul. Violence wasn't his natural tendency. He only used it to defend his portal and my team. D would be all too happy to take out the Pendergrass patriarch to spare Cooper more trauma, especially since the "things" Cooper's dad had done to him and his brother couldn't have been pleasant.

Okay—D and I will be in touch soon. Stay safe and take care of yourself.

· · ·

Cooper sent me a thumbs up emoji and I fired off a message to my roomies to let them know we had a lead before getting out of the car and making my way to Lacey's place.

Lacey and Mara's place.

I climbed the steps to her condo and was about to knock when the door flew open and a phantom raven latched onto me and dragged me inside, flew me to the couch, and landed on top of me, squawking and pecking at me gently. It was endearing and annoying at the same time, and I was tempted to turn him back into a chihuahua. Without his graft, I could no longer speak with him directly or understand him, but I got the message.

"You're welcome." I embraced his phantom form and then shooed him off to entertain Sully while I chatted with Lacey and Mara.

After they both attacked me and pulled me reluctantly into a group hug.

"Thank you, Jinx," Lacey whispered, holding me tight. "For everything."

Mara stroked my hair and rubbed my back, soothing and welcoming me. "Let me get us a drink," she said. "I have a bottle of three-hundred-year-old demon whisky. I've been saving it for a special occasion."

I sat with Lacey while Mara got our drinks. "How you feeling?" I asked.

"Good," she said. "I've been talking to Dr. Khatri a lot. I still wake up in a cold sweat most nights and I have to check on Simon and Mara. In my nightmares..."

I got that. I had nightmares of my own, and I'd been working through them with the doc. We all had. It was only a matter of time before the next Master Demon showed up with a plan to destroy the world while making war on celestials. Or the next Archangel. We needed to be ready.

"Yeah," I said. "Sully helps me with my rough nights."

"Not D?" Lacey asked, smirking.

"Nope," I said. "Not yet. We're taking it slow. He's taking me out tonight on a date, a real one, with food and a music performance down-town. I'm going to dress up and everything."

I had to hit the mall, first, since I didn't own any date night worthy clothes, but how hard could it be to find something?

"Well," she said. "If you don't want it to go too far, don't shave your hooha."

I fell back against the couch laughing. And remembering my last encounter with D. It didn't matter whether I lady scaped. D certainly hadn't minded the landscape when he'd explored that area.

Mara walked out of the kitchen with a tray holding a decanter and three glasses, each with a ball of ice. The liquid in the decanter was filled with a golden, glowing liquid. I'd never had demon realm booze before, let alone aged whisky, and my mouth watered at the prospect.

Mara poured the whisky and handed out glasses, the heady aroma of a faraway land and unfamiliar grains blended with a touch of magic.

Mara raised her glass. "To life, love, and freedom. May we treasure these gifts and fight to preserve them."

"I'll drink to that," Lacey said. I nodded and raised my glass before taking a sip of the smoothest, richest, most glorious whisky I'd ever tasted. Flavors of exotic wood and wild honey mixed with fruits I'd never tasted but couldn't wait to try someday when we could open the portals again.

We chatted about everything and nothing at all, sipping on whisky and enjoying each other's company, taking turns petting Sully as she jumped from lap to lap and listening to stories from Simon about his time in the demon realm, translated for us by Lacey.

"So," Lacey said. "What are you wearing for your date tonight?"

I looked at the time and got a jolt of panic. "Not sure," I said. "I need to motor so I can get to the mall and find something."

Lacey and Mara looked at each other and rolled their eyes.

"Uh huh," Lacey said. "What about hair and makeup?"

I rolled *my* eyes and said, "Makeup won't take long, and I don't care about my hair. Meg and I are going to ride on one of those woo hoo girl party buses before I meet D, so it's going to get all windblown anyway."

The got up from the couch and each took one of my hands, hauling me up and dragging me upstairs. There were four gorgeous outfits laid out on their bed ranging from a fancy schmancy cocktail purple number to a tailored pantsuit I could dress up or down with a T-shirt or a button down, a pair of dark jeans and a sexy blouse that would work well with my cowgirl boots, and a sundress and hat if I was feeling less badass honkytonk girl and more cottage core.

"Pick one and I'll do your makeup," Lacey said, heading off to the bathroom to get her giant ass bag of supplies.

Mara turned me around and stood me in front of a mirror. She eyed me for a moment and then used some magical succubus mojo. In a blink of an eye, she'd glamoured my hair in an elaborate updo that screamed bridesmaid.

She shook her head and my hair rearranged itself into a high ponytail with little wisps artfully falling out and curling around my face.

"I like it," I said.

"Okay, but what about this?"

Mara did something else magical to my hair. She had my dark locks cascading down my back and shoulders in loose waves that made me look flirty and feminine. Wowzers. This was going to be a tough choice. I loved this look, but the ponytail would work better for my downtown ride.

"I can fix it, so it bounces back in place no matter what the wind does," Mara said.

"Sold! You two are the *best!*"

An hour later I was dressed, pampered, and pretty. My two besties shoved me out the door, promising to bring Sully back to my place in the morning. I left them drinking more demon whisky and watching a commercial for some new hotshot real estate developer with big plans for Nashville. Real Wolf of Wallstreet type. Ugh, greedy bastard was going to drive already high housing prices through the freakin' roof. Oh, well, it was better than having the city destroyed by a celestial weapon. Compared to that, ordinary problems in the mundane world didn't seem all that bad.

I called Megan and let her know I was on our way downtown. Before my date with D, I had a long-overdue date with my favorite sister. When I disconnected, a text came through from HQ.

. . .

Getting new demon signs concentrated in Franklin. Nothing urgent. We'll keep you posted. Enjoy your date!

I sighed and shook off burgeoning panic and dread. It could be nothing, but if it wasn't, surely it would wait until tomorrow.

I hoped.

CHAPTER THIRTY-TWO

Megan and I downed one shot of tequila and joined the co-eds who'd joined us on the party bus in a great big, "Yee-haw!" in old-school Nashville style. As Mara promised, my hair fell back into place no matter how the wind blew and never blocked my vision. It made Megan all kinds of jealous and she made me promise to have Mara do her hair next time.

"We should do this again," Megan said as we climbed out of the bus.

The city lights had been spectacular, and it did my heart good to see my city's streets filled with locals and visitors enjoying all she had to offer, especially with the sounds of every type of music floating through the air chased by laughter. Music City had taken a beating downtown, but she was far from broken. My team and I would protect and defend her from the supernatural forces that sought to destroy her.

"We're totally doing this again," I said to Megan. "You off to hang out with Brad?"

Megan's shoulders tightened and she faked a smile. "Oh, he's busy working late tonight. Has to catch up at the office since he was out so long and stuck at HQ."

Before I could pry, she said, "I've got a date with my bathtub, a glass of wine, and a nice book. And you've got a date with your demon hottie."

Right on cue, D walked around the corner looking like a beautiful fallen angel with mischief on his mind. He looked me up and down and grinned before handing me a bouquet of flowers. So romantic.

I sniffed them and said, "Thanks. I don't have anywhere to put them."

D nodded to Megan, and I handed her the bouquet.

"Go," Megan said. "I'll be fine."

I was about to argue, but D said, "Wait. Alexi's on his way. He'll see you home safely. Until the demons and celestials who've invaded this realm are defeated, none of us travels alone."

"You traveled here alone," I said, putting my hands on my hips and staring at him in mock challenge.

"I teleported," D said. "But I'll stick close to you for the rest of the night so you can protect me."

We waited for Alexi, who showed up and offered his arm to Megan like a gentleman. I didn't miss the look of longing the Russian teddy bear gave my sister when he thought no one was watching. Neither did D.

"Poor guy," D said. "He's got it bad, but he won't act on it. He's honorable."

Too bad, I thought, and then chided myself. It wasn't fair to judge Alexi for respecting the sanctity of Megan's marriage, even if the marriage was on the rocks. And I only suspected it was on the rocks. I was biased. I never did like Brad and thought Meg could have done better. She deserved better, but she loved the guy and was trying to make things work.

"Yeah," I said. "Maybe the twins could set him up with someone in the Fae community."

D laughed. "I don't think a bog hag is his type, but rumor has it more of the old-world Fae are making their home in the area. A lot of them are shapeshifters. That could work."

The wheels started turning in my devious mind and D took me by the hand. "Nope. No matchmaking tonight. We have an evening to enjoy."

He was right, which is why I decided to hold off on sharing Cooper's intel. The night was ours. Work could wait. We walked side-by-side and made our way to Puckett's and enjoyed world-class BBQ, beer, and a decadent dessert that was rich, chocolatey, and tasted almost as good as D.

I held out my spoon, offering him the last bite. His gaze went molten, and he took my hand in his and guided the spoon to his mouth and closed his eyes as he enjoyed what he called one of the best things about the earth realm. I loved chocolate and normally didn't share, but for D, I'd give up my plate to make him happy. My demon had suffered so much. I couldn't take that away, but I could give him new memories and experiences filled with joy and, eventually, peace.

I could yank his chain, too, a pastime I was learning to enjoy.

Especially when he seemed to lose his way navigating downtown Nashville.

"You have no idea where you're going, do you?" I asked when he stopped and consulted his mobile phone.

He pretended to ignore me as his long, elegant fingers scrolled, but he couldn't hide the adorable dimple gracing his cheek as he fought not to grin.

"It's okay if you don't know where we are. I don't, either. Seriously, what is it with men not being able to admit they don't know something?"

D scoffed and looked up from his phone, arching a brow. "Oh, that statement isn't sexist at all."

"It wasn't a statement, it was a question, and a legitimate one. It's just dumb. This whole alpha male myth that doesn't allow men to be fully human and acknowledge their insecurities and character flaws and shit is wrong. Embrace your full humanity, babe!"

"I'm not human."

"Human, demon, whatever—some things are universal, like dumb male hang ups."

His face split into a huge grin. "And what about dumb female hang ups?"

I waved a dismissive hand. "I don't have any of those. I'm a body confident, sweary, sex-loving gal who scorns fashion and embraces fast food. No kale in my fridge."

"That's what you consider self-actualized?"

"Duh! And I'll have you know that Dr. Khatri told me I was remarkably self-actualized."

"No hang ups at all, then?"

"Of course not."

"Keep telling yourself that, Napoleon."

He. Did. Not.

I moved behind him with lightning speed and jumped on his back, wrapping my arms around his neck so I could lightly nip his ear. "That was a low blow!"

"Literally," he said, spinning me around.

It was magic. When was the last time I'd had this much fun? I couldn't remember, but I would grab onto this bit of happiness and enjoy the experience to its fullest. Happiness and I weren't well acquainted, but I hoped we'd get to know each other better with D back in my life.

And not just D. I had friends and teammates who had my back in and out of the field. I had a mother and sister who loved me, and I didn't have to hide what I was from them anymore. What a gift. And I had a cat.

Not just any cat. A mighty demon cat who could morph into a fierce battle cat in the field and return to the shape of an adorable house cat—with wings—while relaxing on my lap at home. Damn, I'd spend so much time worrying about my mission, I'd forgotten the simple joy of being grateful. And I was.

No matter what the future held, I wouldn't be facing it alone.

I wasn't the weird, outcast, lonely girl I used to be. No matter what else came my way, at least I had that going for me.

The night was still young, so we decided to enjoy a stroll downtown before hitting the venue for an up-and-coming rock band. I was admiring the view when a giant eyesore of a billboard stopped me in my tracks. It featured a handsome, confident man in an expensive bespoke suit with a huge subdivision looming in the background, McMansions of all shapes and sizes with tiny yards filling the space. I recognized the guy, presumably the "Beale Bub" behind Bub Reality, from the commercial I'd seen earlier at Lacey's house.

"Changing the face of Nashville with world-class homes. The sky's the limit. Come live the dream and take what's yours!"

Popular opinion held that magic messed with photography. Vampires allegedly couldn't be photographed, and ghosts showed up as floating white mists or other anomalies. I had no idea if those well-known "facts" were true, but I did recognize small sparks of demon light floating in the man's blue eyes, and it wasn't a trick of the camera or Photoshop.

D followed my gaze and swore under his breath.

"You know him?" I asked.

"Oh, yes," D said. "I led his legions on a conquest that wiped out an entire province belonging to a rival demon. And when that didn't satisfy his appetite for colonizing, I led them on two more campaigns. He's more than a gluttony demon. He's Beelzebub, the Master Demon of Glutton, and he's been busy."

"Looks like we found our next target. Something tells me I'm going to enjoy tossing him into a one-way portal back to the hell realm."

My cell pinged followed quickly by the sound of D's phone receiving a text. We took out our phones and stared at the message from HQ.

Cassie stole the Sigillum Dei. Get back to HQ ASAP.

"I'm going to kick that stupid angel's ass!" I yelled.

Hashtag: There ain't no rest for the wicked.

***

Thank you for reading! Did you enjoy? Please add your review because nothing helps an author more and encourages readers to take a chance on a book than a review.

And don't miss book three, HELL BOUND, available now. Turn the page for a sneak peek!

Find all the details about D. B. Sieders including the latest news, giveaways, and more at www.dbsieders.com

You can also sign up for the City Owl Press newsletter to receive notice of all book releases!

SNEAK PEEK OF HELL BOUND

*As I walk through the Valley of the Shadow of Death, I
remind myself that you can't always trust Google Maps—
On a T-shirt worn by Jinx McGee, Demon Hunter*

Something weird was in the air. Literally.

Unlike the last time, there were no exploding buildings or chaos, but the night was still young. There were strange glowing objects flashing to and fro above the downtown skyline before blinking out of existence.

Or to another plane of existence.

I scanned the sky looking for signs of imminent attack. D, my demon boyfriend, ran toward HQ with me in tow.

Then I stopped to get a better look.

The objects weren't flying demons, at least not any species with which I was familiar. The strange beings flitted between tall buildings, over the river and bridges, moving in sync with the music pouring from bars and honky tonks. They glowed with an unearthly light, the creatures. Beneath the glow, there seemed to be an abundance of feathers.

And eyes. So many eyes.

Celestials. Celestials were on the loose. Biblically accurate angels were powerful, hideous, and terrifying.

And they were flying around downtown Nashville in plain sight of modern humans who'd been blissfully unaware of the presence of these interdimensional beings, at least for the past few millennia.

D spotted them, too, and hesitated, tense and ready for battle. He was a handsome devil. Over six feet tall with dark hair, long dark lashes, deep brown eyes that sparked with red demon light when he was angry or aroused, he had a body hardened by training and battle in the depths of hell. Under other circumstances, I'd be admiring that body and making all kinds of delightfully evil plans of what I would do with it later.

It was what I should have been doing and was doing before we were so rudely interrupted by a flock of celestials flying out in the open for everyone to see.

My demon and I had been on a date in downtown Nashville—our first bona fide official date—and about to enjoy some live music, but duty called. When you're a demon hunter, you're always on call, especially when you're in charge of capturing seven deadly master demons and their celestial counterparts who had escaped their realms and come to earth to cause mischief, mayhem, and war.

Make that six.

We'd already dispatched the Master Demon of Sloth back to the hell realm and had her sister, who happened to be the Archangel of Diligence, in custody. We also had the archangel's sidekick imprisoned at HQ. Both had tried to kill me, but Pinstripe the sidekick came closer to bringing about my end with her massive tentacles. Contrary to popular culture, myth, and legend, master demons came in all shapes, sizes, and genders.

All of them were treacherous, vicious, and ruthless. The myths got that part right. And archangels could give their demon counterparts a run for their money in maliciousness.

Now, we had the Master Demon of Gluttony to contend with, not to mention the rogue angel who'd pretended to be our ally so she could steal the Sigillum Dei, an artefact that could open portals to the hell realm and the celestial realm.

Couldn't trust any of these creatures.

Having just received texts from my boss and teammates about the stolen artefact, playtime was over. We needed the Sigillum Dei to send our enemies on a one-way trip away from earth and back to the dimension where they belonged. It was the only way to permanently banish them and stop the coming war that high-ranking demons and angels planned to wage.

We had to get it back pronto.

More flashing from the idiot celestials above us, and the humans were starting to notice. That couldn't be good. They were already rattled. War was brewing between the celestial and hell realms with earth as the battlefield. The combatants were currently confined to Music City, but the barrier wouldn't last long.

And apparently, they'd abandoned the rules of secrecy that kept mundanes blissfully unaware of scary creatures from other dimensions.

The out-in-the-open flying circus of celestials couldn't be a coincidence. The stench of ozone permeated the air, overwhelming the city smells of food, beer, stale urine, and sweaty humans. My ears popped. The people in downtown were covering their ears, noses, and looking up in awe and the beginnings of terror.

When I found Cassiel, the celestial traitor who'd stolen the artefact, I was going to blast her ass into the far reaches of the known universe for pulling this little stunt and for ruining my date night.

I gave my date a look and we took off running.

Demoriel, who I called D for short, was on our demon hunting team, too, and had magic and powers that had helped our mostly human colleagues on demon hunting missions. So far, we'd managed not to run into any pedestrians and weren't garnering too much attention. There were too many other interesting things to see and hear in downtown Nashville, like pedal taverns full of tourists and unidentified flying objects.

HQ would have to wait. We couldn't ignore this.

"Okay," I said, trying to control my breath and focus on endurance running. The demon grafts that had saved my life and enhanced my abilities helped, but they still had to work within the limits of a mostly human body. But I'd trained hard as well. What I lacked in height I made up for with ferocity, tenacity, and an iron will.

My celestial half probably helped, too.

Yup. Part celestial, part demon, part human. That was me. The warrior of three realms or some crap.

"We need to find Cassie first and get the Sigillum Dei before we go after Beelzebubba the Real Estate Tycoon. And I'm thinking Cassie has something to do with this nonsense," I said, gesturing to the night sky above. "How do we track a celestial?"

D shook his head as he kept pace with me. "You'd have better luck than I would. Are you angry enough to tap into your celestial side?"

That shouldn't be a problem in theory. I hadn't fully trusted the angel who'd become my unlikely ally and source of information in my quest to stop the coming war that would destroy earth and all I held dear. But I'd liked her. Even grudgingly respected her. Then she'd stolen the Sigillum Dei. Since I had a real problem with betrayal, I could work up a proper temper flare that would unleash my celestial power, a gift from my deadbeat dad who'd withheld his true identity as a celestial.

Or possibly some kind of ancient deity.

Not that being half celestial, or some sort of demigoddess, was doing me much good right now.

I had power more potent than my borrowed demon powers. But I hadn't figured out how to bend that power to my will. It only seemed to work when I was pissed off or on the verge of death. Try as I might, I was too shocked to muster enough righteous anger at Cassie. And hurt, though I'd never admit it.

But I had another source to tap into, a deep well of rage.

I thought about the people who'd been damaged by the last demon we'd defeated—a demon who'd had help from two powerful celestials. They'd stolen the minds, will, and soul energy of thousands of innocent humans, tortured lesser demons, and had nearly destroyed my mind. The Master Demon of Gluttony would be just as cruel in his pursuit of power, as would any celestial working for or against him.

That made me good and mad. My stomach fluttered with the bubbling sensation I'd come to associate with my celestial mojo. I focused my entire being on Cassie, a.k.a. Cassiel the traitor who'd stolen an artefact that was our only means of permanently banishing the powerful demons and celestials currently on earth. It could also let legions of demons and celestials loose on earth to wreak havoc. My team could never defeat that many.

I grabbed D's hand. A vision of Cassie formed in my mind. She wasn't at HQ, or any place in the city I recognized. She couldn't leave the city. None of the celestials or demons could leave so long as the ward our boss had crafted—or bargained for—held. But the city was big. She could be anywhere.

I focused harder. It was dark. No landmarks, no trees, no familiar skyline. It was a strange, misty landscape.

It was a place I'd been before. Bingo!

"She's in the space between," I said, coming to an abrupt halt. Cassie had transported me there once for a private conversation and to show me a vision. I knew how to get out of that pocket of reality. She'd given me the word—*reditus*—that had brought me back to earth. Some myths and legends were true. Demons and celestials loved Latin. No idea why a dead language held such appeal, but it was their preferred communication tool.

"I'm going to try something," I said. "I think I can take you with me."

D looked at me with an intensity that sent my stomach fluttering for an entirely different reason.

"I trust you," he said.

Invoking whatever higher power might favor me, I gripped D's hand tighter and channeled my power. Then, I spoke another Latin word.

"*Ire.*"

Nothing.

Too easy, I supposed. Or maybe my pronunciation was off? I spoke the word again, growing angrier with each passing second.

"*Deodamnatus! Filius canis!*"

I opened my eyes to find D grinning at me. "That was creative, but swearing won't help, and I don't think *ire* is the magic word. Intent matters when it comes to magic, not language or specific words. Try again."

I took a deep breath, closed my eyes, and focused on Cassie and the space between. The fog and darkness filled my mind's eye. Then, throwing caution and good judgement to the wind, I opened my eyes and said, "Take me to the fucking space between. Now."

Downtown Nashville faded as we entered an entirely different reality.

Don't stop now. Keep reading with your copy of HELL BOUND.

And visit www.dbsieders.com to keep up with the latest news where you can subscribe to the newsletter for contests, giveaways, new releases, and more.

Don't miss more of the *Jinx McGee* series with book three, HELL BOUND, available now, and find more from D.B. Sieders at www.dbsieders.com

---

There ain't no rest for the wicked.

Jinx McGee and her team of demon hunters managed to neutralize the Master Demon of Sloth, relying more on luck than skill. But with six more powerful rogue demons on the loose, she'll need to bring her A-game to the hunt for their next target. The Master of Gluttony and Excess is elusive, clever, and has a knack for anticipating the team's every move. There's likely a mole in their organization, and everyone's a suspect.

As if that weren't enough, her unreliable celestial ally has a lead on her missing deadbeat dad that Jinx can't pass up. He holds the key to the whole demonic endgame, and Jinx has a score to settle.

Daddy issues and demon hunting? It will take cunning, strategy, skill, and a boatload of tequila to get Jinx out of this jam.

Escape Your World. Get Lost in Ours! City Owl Press at www.cityowl-press.com.

ACKNOWLEDGMENTS

I am so grateful to the team at City Owl Press for supporting me as an author, especially Tina Moss and Yelena Casale. Shout out to my amazing editor Tee Tate for polishing the manuscript with her in-depth content edits and making it shine, and to my copy editor Becka Lloyd for the finishing touches. I am so grateful to my beta readers A.J. Scudiere and Victoria Raschke for their super helpful suggestions. And I must give a huge thanks to Jody Wallace for brainstorming sessions that gave me great plot points, including the mind-control video game plotline. Special thanks to SiederTree Studios (a.k.a. my insanely talented daughter) for creating the graphic for chapter headings. And thank you to all my readers. You're the reason I keep writing, and every review inspires me to create bigger and better stories. Finally, I'd like to thank my family for their unwavering support and my three kitties for purrs, cuddles, and for being the inspiration for Jinx's demon cat. I hope you enjoy her!

ABOUT THE AUTHOR

Award-winning author D.B. Sieders was born and raised in East Tennessee and spent her childhood hiking in the Great Smoky Mountains and chasing salamanders, fish, and frogs. She loved to tell stories while sitting around the campfire.

She is a working scientist by day, but never lost her love of telling stories. Now, she's a purveyor of unconventional fantasy romance featuring strong heroines and the heroes who strive to match them. Her heroes and heroines face a healthy dose of angst as they strive for redemption and a happily ever after, which everyone deserves.

www.dbsieders.com

facebook.com/DBSieders
x.com/DBSieders
goodreads.com/dbsieders
amazon.com/D.B.-Sieders/B00D18ZPOY

ABOUT THE PUBLISHER

City Owl Press is a cutting edge indie publishing company, bringing the world of romance and speculative fiction to discerning readers.

Escape Your World. Get Lost in Ours!

www.cityowlpress.com

facebook.com/CityOwlPress

x.com/cityowlpress

instagram.com/cityowlbooks

pinterest.com/cityowlpress

tiktok.com/@cityowlpress

www.ingramcontent.com/pod-product-compliance
Lightning Source LLC
Chambersburg PA
CBHW020825260626

47169CB00003B/834